THE NINJA GAMES
THE WARRIOR WITHIN

THE NINJA GAMES
THE WARRIOR WITHIN

LANCE PEKUS AND JESSE HAYNES

This is a work of fiction. Names, characters, places, and incidents either are the product of the author's imagination or are used fictitiously.

Copyright © 2022, Lance Pekus and Jesse Haynes through CastleBuilders Press

All rights reserved. No part of this book may be reproduced or used in any manner without written permission of the copyright owner except for the use of quotations in a book review. For more information, address: castlebuilderspress@gmail.com.

First paperback edition October 2022.

Book design by Cory Andres

ISBN: 978-1-7344723-4-9

www.castlebuilderspress.com

Lance's Dedication:

To all the smart and athletic people I have known growing up, the people that defy the norm of 'jocks' and 'geeks' and do whatever makes them happy. To all the kids that are not afraid to chase their goals and dreams despite what others might think.

Jesse's Dedication:

To those who aren't defined by brands, followers or camera angles.
To those who are living life.

PROLOGUE:

Even fifty yards away, the blast shook the earth under Grover's feet and rattled his chest. He'd been expecting it to be powerful—that's why he'd plugged his ears and ducked the other way—but he hadn't expected it to be *that* powerful.

Once he uncovered his ears, he heard the patter of rocks and debris falling back toward the earth. The blast site was nearly impossible to see now, shrouded by a cloud of dust, hanging in the still, sticky air of Peru.

The man beside him, a stocky man named Rex, stepped out of the treeline and squinted through the dust to examine the damage that had been done. "Did we get it?"

"Oh, we got it," said a third man, who set off walking toward the blast site.

Except, "man" wasn't quite a fair description.

The voice came from a black suit made of plated metal armor that puzzle-pieced itself together to form an intimidating, form-fitting shell. From what Grover could tell, the only non-metal piece of the entire suit was a thin layer of tinted glass that stretched across the helmet, right where one's eyes should be.

The man's name was O'Brien. At least, that's how he had introduced himself when he'd hired Grover and his partner, Rex, for the job. And O'Brien wasn't alone, either. There was another person in a similar suit, a man who'd been introduced as Cade, and judging by his slightly-distorted voice, he was younger than the rest of the group.

O'Brien paused, looking back over his metal-plated shoulder. "Will you all be joining me?"

Cade was the first to move. Silently, he followed behind Grover.

"Yes…sorry," Grover mumbled. "But after such a detonation, it's usually best to stay back for a minute. I mean, in case there's any more debris. We did just blow a hole in the side of a mountain, after all."

"Are you questioning my judgment?" The words should have been a simple question, yet they sounded more like a threat.

"N-no, I'm sorry." Grover wiped his hands on his pants. *Why were his palms this sweaty? Had they been this way a second ago?* Sure, it was hot, but as a native of Peru, he was used to it.

"Then let's go. And bring your men." With that, O'Brien set forward again, disappearing into the cloud of dust.

Grover sighed. *His men.* Turning back to the treeline behind him, he cupped his hands over his mouth and called back into the trees. The words, spoken in the Quechuan language, meant 'all clear'.

Soon, half a dozen men high-stepped out of the thick trees and into the clearing. As the unofficial guides of this expedition, they wore the unmistakably bright clothing of the Native Incan Peruvians. As soon as Grover, a researcher, had been hired to help on this job, he'd also insisted that these men were hired to lead the way. The money, after all, could be great for them.

As they all looked Grover in the eyes, he suddenly found himself questioning the decision. These men looked worried, and considering that they knew the lay of the dense forest better than anybody, their concern washed over Grover, too. Slowly, he turned and followed behind O'Brien, Cade, and Rex.

As Grover made his way through the dust enough to finally get a close look at the blast site, he discovered that the mountain was…hollow. Instead of more solid rock, they'd uncovered the edge of some sort of ravine. He couldn't tell how deep it went, but it stretched down far enough that not even the midday sun could find the bottom.

His heartbeat quickened in his chest. While he couldn't believe this, it was just as O'Brien had predicted. Behind him, the natives whispered amongst themselves.

"What are they saying?" O'Brien asked.

"Danger," Grover interpreted. "This is dangerous."

Rex let out a huffy snort. "What a surprise."

Grover shot him a look. "Stick to the weaponry. We don't need your snide remarks."

"Boys, please." O'Brien extended a hand toward Rex. "Give me the equipment." Rex shakily handed over a large duffle bag, and O'Brien began distributing headlamps and pulling out repelling equipment.

"Grover, you first. Then your men. Rex, Cade, and I will follow behind."

Grover relayed the message to the locals, and they prepared for the descent. As he began repelling down, his mind wasn't on the technique. It was on something else.

He had a feeling he couldn't suppress—one that he'd only experienced a handful of times throughout his career as an ancient researcher.

He felt like he was onto something. Something big.

This was it. It had to be. The mysterious team of O'Brien and Cade had come out of nowhere and had no apparent backstory, but everything they'd told Grover had all lined up. Everything they'd said had come true, and that was something that never happened in this line of work. That was one reason Grover had agreed to go through with the expedition—well, that and the potential to be the researcher who helped find one of the greatest treasures in human history.

Grover paused. He was about thirty feet down the rope when he noticed something.

"What are you doing?" Rex called from above. "Why'd you stop?"

Grover rolled his eyes. He wasn't sure where O'Brien had picked up Rex, but he wasn't impressed. Rex was a treasure hunter, and while Grover was the same in some ways, Rex preferred firearms and explosives over academia and research.

Finally, Grover responded. "I hear something. Sounds like…water. A stream. There's running water down here."

"Water?" Cade asked. "Why would—"

"That means we're close," interrupted O'Brien's obscured voice. "Keep descending."

"Yes, sir." A bit more enthusiastically, Grover continued the descent. Looking down with his headlamp, he finally made out a welcome sight: ground. Or, perhaps not ground, but water.

Just as he'd said, it was a thin stream. He could see his own light reflected in the gently rippling surface.

"I see the bottom!" he called out.

"How far down?"

"Eighty feet, tops. I got plenty of rope." He quickened his descent, and soon, his military boots splashed into a couple of inches of water.

He relayed his discovery back to the surface, and soon, the natives began descending one after another. The rest of the party followed.

Grover wasn't in the mood to wait around, though. As soon as he reached the bottom, he slowly began following the stream.

And that's when he made yet another discovery. Looking down at the water underneath his feet, he could see shapes glimmering below the water. Perfect squares. Stone bricks.

"What?" He blinked in surprise, but the reality didn't change. This wasn't a natural stream. No. It was a man-made channel. Turning his head, he noticed elevated slabs on both sides of the water, guiding it forward. At most, it was only as wide as his wingspan, but it seemed to trickle forward forever.

And there was something else, too. At first, he'd thought the water's surface was what was glimmering back at him, but that wasn't the case. In between the bricks, stretching out like thick wires running along the channel, was something else. Something that made his heart rate speed up.

Gold.

Thin, wiry coils of the precious metal lined the bottom of the channel in place by the brick around it, and Grover gasped as he saw it. He kneeled, dipping his knee into the slow-flowing water, and traced one of the golden rods with his finger. There was no mistaking what it was.

"What do you have there?"

The words took him by surprise. Grover had become so absorbed with the discovery he hadn't even noticed everybody else splashing down beside him.

"G-gold," he muttered. "I don't believe it."

Rex swore as he confirmed what Grover had said. "That's a helluva find. Look at all of it. There's so much gold! We're all gonna be rich…" Rex took a knee, too, trying to rip some of the gold loose from the channel. He had no such luck.

Grover couldn't help himself. He babbled, "I just don't get it. It…it looks more like…"

"Wiring," Cade answered before turning to O'Brien. "Right?"

O'Brien, after a pause, nodded.

The confirmation was all Grover needed. "I know this sounds crazy," he mused, "but what if…what if these people were using it as a transfer of energy? Gold is a great conductor, you know. And maybe the water is a cooling agent because…" He trailed off. "Never mind, that's just absurd."

With a chuckle, O'Brien replied, "It might not be as absurd as you think. Let's press on. The real treasure should be this way."

He set off down the channel, everybody else following closely behind. As they walked, Grover quietly relayed what was going on to the natives following him, but they seemed eerily unsurprised, only nodding.

They pressed forward. After a bit of silence except for the sloshing of their steps, Rex asked, "So, O'Brien, where did you and Cade get your fancy suits?"

"Made them."

"You...made them?"

Instead of answering, O'Brien pointed and announced, "We're getting close."

Grover followed the gloved finger, and his headlamp locked onto a statue. It was weathered from decades of darkness and solace, and while the features weren't as sharp as they might have once been, it was still...eerie.

"The hell is that?" asked Rex.

The statue appeared to be of a creature, and while the stonework had lost some of the detail over time, the creature seemed to have a slithery tail, long torso, wings, and the head of some sort of cat. It was hauntingly hypnotic, and as much as Grover wanted to look away, he just couldn't.

When he finally did, he noticed the natives. They had taken several steps away from the statue, looking at its distorted form with wide eyes. "What's wrong?" he asked them in Quechuan.

The man who seemed to be the leader, Carlos, answered with one word, "Amaru."

Amaru. Grover thought back to his studies. He'd heard the word before, and after a moment, the answer occurred to him. The Amaru was a serpent creature that, according to the Incans, dwelled underground.

"Come on," O'Brien said, and for the first time, there was emotion in his voice. As opposed to cold and machine-like, he sounded excited. He splashed forward once.

More statues lined the way. Dozens more, maybe even hundreds. They lined both sides of the shallow channel, stretching into the darkness like a ghostly landing strip.

Except there was no light—only dark creatures with faceless forms, widespread wings and scaly tails.

Something about them made Grover so uncomfortable that he didn't want to look, but he also couldn't keep from it. His eyes were drawn to each one, and each one made his stomach tighten a little more. He tried to conceal his fear.

The natives, however, did not. They'd frozen up, forcing him to practically beg them to keep walking and reminding himself that they were just statues. Rex, on the other hand, kept kneeling down and trying to break pieces of gold wiring loose from the bottom of the channel—never with any success.

Thankfully, the walk soon came to an end. As they passed the last statue, the channel of water widened out to a very shallow pool. In the very middle of the pool, cresting out of the dark, rippling water, was what looked like an altar.

"This is it." Moving even faster now, O'Brien began high-stepping through the ankle-deep pool. "This is it! We've found it."

As Rex followed at a safe distance, he hesitantly asked, "This is…El Dorado?"

O'Brien nodded. "Yes. Well, this *whole place* is El Dorado."

"El Dorado," the words echoed from the natives,

whispering back and forth to each other.

Rex looked around in every direction, confused. There had to be more than this, but as far as the headlight could shine in any direction, all he saw was darkness. "I don't understand," he said. "El Dorado is... it's a city. The City of Gold."

A sound came from O'Brien. It was somewhere right between a laugh and a huff. "That's a misinterpretation, I'm afraid," he said. "People like you—treasure hunters—have lost the meaning. It's not a city of gold. It's more like a place full of...opportunity."

"I don't understand," Rex muttered. "You promised us gold. You promised us *all* the gold."

"Look beneath you. Is that not gold?"

Rex's gaze dropped to the golden wiring running under the surface of the water. "I can't get it!"

"It's still gold." Turning away, O'Brien slipped his fingers under the edge of the top of the altar. "Help me, Cade. All of you, come here. Our treasure awaits."

Grover, almost in a trance, relayed the message to the native people. Still looking terrified, they gingerly approached the altar.

"On three," O'Brien said. "One...two...three!"

With a collective heave, they lifted up what turned out to be a thick stone slab over an empty box. It wasn't an altar at all. It was a *sarcophagus.*

At least, that's what it looked like to Grover, but there was nobody inside. As he leaned over to take a closer look, O'Brien explained, "Our work here is complete."

The only thing in the sarcophagus, as far as Grover could tell, was a small box wrapped in a thin cloth. The rest was empty, wasted space.

O'Brien picked up the package and unwrapped it, letting the cloth fall back into the shadows. In his hand was a shiny object. It was six inches long at most, flat and reflective. It appeared to be made of dark metal and laced with gold wiring, much like the floor of the channel.

"What is that?" Grover asked. "That looks like…"

O'Brien held it up for Grover to see. "This is the key to a rich future and better place. One of the keys, at least. We just need to hope…"

Before he could finish the sentence, there was a light coming from the mysterious object, and at first, Grover had thought it was a reflection from his headlight, but no. It was the object itself. It was glowing, as if from electrical light. A faint glow emitted from within, giving the wires a dazzling golden glow.

"That's…that's not possible." He leaned in for a better look. "How…"

"That's our sign," O'Brien answered. "They'll be here soon."

"Wait, what?" This came from Rex, who was kneeling and trying to rip gold wiring from the floor once again. "I've almost got some of this loose."

And that's when Grover saw them. From the distant darkness came red light, a single glow amidst the suffocating black at first, but then came another and another. Five glowing, crimson orbs in total.

And they were moving.

The natives began feverishly whispering, backing away from the orbs. Cade retreated too, moving behind O'Brien for protection.

The lights were not only moving from side to side—they were growing closer. And there was a sound, too—a scraping, like metal on stone. Whatever was responsible for the lights was coming their way, and *fast.*

"O'Brien, what is that?" Grover asked with a quivering voice. "What is that?"

Rex had noticed them too, but he was still busy desperately clawing at the ground. By the time he spotted them, the lights were closing in on him. He froze.

"Rex! Get out of there," Cade yelled.

At the words, something seemed to snap in Rex's brain. He stood, reaching for the pistol strapped to his hip, and fired three shots into the dark.

The sound of a bullet striking metal clattered in the darkness, but the lights kept approaching. Rex's shots had done no good, and realizing this, he turned to run.

He was too late.

There was a scraping sound, much like the sound of a knife being sharpened, and in the light of Grover's headlamp, a blade impaled itself through Rex's chest.

It happened so quickly that Rex didn't have time to process. He didn't have time to scream. The gleaming, bloody blade was pulled back through his chest by a long, spindly metal arm, and he collapsed forward.

He was dead.

"Run!" This came from O'Brien, forcing Grover to peel his eyes away from the gruesome sight. "The exit is this way."

O'Brien was already on the move, Cade right on his heels. The natives were scattering, trying to keep up, but two of them let out gurgled screams as blades whooshed in the darkness behind Grover. He had no doubt they were losing men.

Grover followed, sprinting through the darkness in

the bobbing light of his headlamp while calling out instructions to the men in their native tongue.

O'Brien and Grover continued leading the charge as the scraping metal sound grew closer in the darkness behind them. They were running in the opposite direction they'd entered, but a new set of statues lined the walk. Even in passing, Grover spotted the strange creature with its long tail and strange head, and somehow he knew…

The folklore behind the creature in the stonework—the Amura—had been inspired by these metal creatures. Whatever they were, they had been around for a long, *long* time.

As they ran, the metallic clicks continued behind them, echoing through the chamber. The walls had narrowed in, but in the very faint distance, a light glowed at the end of the tunnel. It was a red light, glowing from atop an elevated, rocky shelf.

"What is that?" Grover yelled.

O'Brien answered, "The Guardian Buzzer. If we can make it past the obstacles and hit the buzzer, it shuts them down."

"Obstacles?" Even as he said the word, Grover had to stop on his heels as the ground basically gave way. He skidded to a desperate stop, his boots ending up against a deep, dark pit.

The sound of the creatures grew even closer. The metal clicking grew louder.

"How do we…" Before Grover could ever get the words out, O'Brien jumped up and grabbed onto a thin stone ridge that ran along one of the rocky walls. "Follow me." He shuffled his gloved hands along the ridge, which was only an inch or two deep.

"Um…ok." As Cade followed right behind O'Brien, Grover relayed the message to the natives, then quickly followed. His breathing was shaky. This was more than he'd signed up for.

And yet, he did it. Following the lead of the two men in suits, he, too, grabbed onto the ridge and shuffled his hands down the wall. The whole time he did it, something nagged at him: the ridge. It was too perfect and too straight to be natural. It had been carved. Somebody *designed* this.

With a *hmph* of effort, O'Brien kicked off the wall and went flying in the opposite direction. Grover followed the dark suit, and turning his head, he found O'Brien now hanging from a ledge behind them. The metal object they'd come here for—whatever it was—was now fastened to the back of his suit.

"Kick over here and grab on, Cade," O'Brien said.

"Yes, sir." Cade did as told. He pushed off the wall, turned a mid-air one-eighty, then grabbed onto a second ledge.

"That's not possible," Grover mumbled.

O'Brien overheard him. "It is if you want to live."

With tired arms, Grover gave a yell of effort and tried to mimic what he'd seen the other two men do. He kicked off the wall, and while in mid-air, he located the second ledge. For just a terrifying moment, he didn't have enough leverage to get there, but he managed to just barely grab onto it as soon as Cade had cleared the way.

He nearly didn't make it. The ledge was so narrow that his hands tried to peel off of it from the weight of his body, but he managed to hold on. It took everything in him, but it was better than plummeting to the bottom of the dark pit.

One of the local men followed him closely, also executing the move, but the last man missed the ledge entirely and, with a scream, fell into the dark pit below. A squishy sound of piercing flesh silenced the scream, but Grover refused to look down.

Gritting his teeth, he shuffled all the way down to O'Brien and Cade, who'd dropped down to the ground on the far side of the pit.

"I've gotta admit, I'm impressed," O'Brien said as he took off down the tunnel once again. "Figured it would be just me and Cade by now."

"Seriously?" Grover couldn't help but shout. "You knew about this? The monsters and the obstacles? How did you not—"

"Guardians," O'Brien interrupted. "They're called Guardians, and they'll tear you in half in a heartbeat unless we keep moving. Come on."

"There are more obstacles," Cade warned.

"Just what I need," Grover spat.

They continued down the tunnel, coming to another pit. Behind them, the Guardians were still following in pursuit, but as far as Grover could tell, the obstacles had slowed them down quite a bit.

The next pit was much like the first, but instead of a ledge to climb, it had a thin, wooden pole running down the center. It was long and narrow, stretching toward the light of the exit.

"Let's hope you have good balance," O'Brien said. With that, he took a step back, then charged forward.

He made it look easy. With three long bounds across the pole, he made it from one side of the pit to the other.

Turning back, O'Brien coached, "Take solid strides and strike the sole of your shoes in the center of the pole. Just like we practiced, Cade."

Cade took a deep breath.

"You can do this," O'Brien called out.

As it turned out, Cade could not do it. He tried to follow O'Brien's advice, but with one bad step, he slipped off the pole.

Cade screamed. It was not the scream of a man in pain, but the scream of a boy in terror. He fell, reaching out and trying to cling to the pole, but it twisted out from underneath him. One second, he was there, the next, he was spiraling into the darkness below.

"No! No!" O'Brien took a step toward the edge of the pit, reaching out in disbelief as the darkness swallowed his companion. "No…" He repeated the word again in disbelief.

Grover was frozen, looking at the pole. He did not have good balance. He knew it. He'd always been strong, but a bit clumsy. This pole, this *obstacle*, was not made for him. If he wasn't careful, he'd meet the same ill fate as Cade.

O'Brien no longer seemed interested in coaching. Instead, the masked man turned away from the pit and began trudging ahead, leaving Grover and the last guide to fend for themselves.

Grover tried to think back on how O'Brien had crossed. He'd taken a step back, bounded forward, and easily made it. He could do that too, right?

With wobbly knees and shaky legs, he took a step back. His heartbeat was about to explode out of his chest. He couldn't catch his breath. He couldn't focus.

But he went for it.

His first step was perfect, striking the very center of the pole and pushing him forward.

His second step was decent, landing on the edge of the pole but carrying him forward.

His third step was the one that cost him.

One bad step—missing his foot placement by only a couple of inches—was all it took. And he did everything in his power not to fall. He desperately reached out, clawing at the darkness all around him for something he could get ahold of, but there was nothing.

Of course, there wasn't.

Much like Cade, Grover's best efforts weren't enough.

With a scream, Grover fell. Further and further he plummeted, slipping deeper into the darkness as the final seconds of his life ticked away.

There was a moment of fear, a moment of anger, and then, all that gave way to a tranquil acceptance.

And then it was over.

ONE

"How do I know I'm doing this right?"

Greyson McEntire looked down with a grin at his best friend Colter. "Well, I haven't heard you face-plant yet, so that means you're at least doing *something* right."

"I'm serious, Grey." An uneasiness ran through Colter's voice. "I'm not trying to break my neck out here."

"Relax. Just remember what we talked about: keep your weight forward, make sure you test your grips, don't overextend, and if you *do* fall, the top rope will catch you."

"Oh, is that all?" With that, Colter trailed off into silence. The only sound was the vibrant hum of the natural world around the two friends.

They were rock climbing, sporting harnesses and all of the necessary gear to make their way up the face of a cliff. For Greyson, this was an everyday adventure—an escape from home, stress, and problems. A place where he could truly thrive. For Colter, this was his first multi-pitch. A *reluctant* first, at that.

Greyson was positioned on the first pitch of the climb, about fifteen feet higher. This gave Colter plenty of rope to operate, but it also allowed Greyson to belay for his friend, or keep Colter's rope tight so that if he were to fall, he wouldn't fall far.

"You're sure this is going to make me better on the football field?" Colter asked as he tried to find his next handhold.

"Yeah. Rock climbing is the most all-around athletic sport," Greyson answered. "Try grabbing that large crimp by your right shoulder."

Colter did as advised, nodding his satisfaction and continuing his climb. "I don't really see a large hold anywhere, but I'm gonna have to trust you on this."

"You'll be thanking me later."

Of the two of them, Colter was the athlete. Or, at least, that's what everybody at Pine High School would have said. He was a tall, muscular All-District quarterback that was dangerous both through the air and on the ground, despite only being a sophomore.

Greyson, on the other hand, didn't play any "real" sports. He'd never put on a Pine Badgers uniform or competed in a school sport in any way. He was quiet, the kind of person that half of his classmates probably wouldn't have been able to name. Rather than score baskets or throw a football, Greyson liked to climb.

And he climbed well.

"Dude, my legs are on *fire,"* Colter said.

"And you're about ten feet in," teased Greyson. "Imagine how you'll feel by the time you get to the top."

"We're going all the way up there? That's gotta be a hundred feet!"

"A hundred and twelve, give or take," Greyson said while looking up the cliff. "And that's how it works. You climb up to the top and hike back down. All part of the process. But I did bring some gear in case you want to repel down instead!"

"I'm thinking that's gonna be a solid no from me," Colter complained with a playful laugh in his voice. "And didn't you say this was an *easy* place to climb?"

"Yeah, it's a route for beginners," Greyson admitted. "But that doesn't mean it's *easy* if you haven't climbed outside much. Just...doable."

"Yeah, yeah. You're just trying to soften the blow."

"Okay, if you can make it to this ledge up here, we'll stop, and you can catch your breath," Greyson offered. "And, while you're catching your breath, you can belay for me?"

"You're a good man, but nothing's free around here, is it?" With a grunt of effort and another laugh, Colter continued to climb.

Greyson's mind spiraled back in time. He'd climbed this cliff once before—a long, long time ago, back when he was first getting into climbing. It had been him and his father on a sunny weekend morning filled with chirping birds and a new adventure. At the time, everything had been perfect.

Perfect.

That might have been the last time *anything* was ever perfect.

"So, how do you know the rope will hold me if I fall?" Colter's question pulled Greyson out of his own head. "I know you're belaying, or whatever you called it, but you realize I'm a lot heavier than you, right?"

"Actually, it's not all about weight," Greyson explained. "Think of it as a tug-of-war between the forces of gravity and friction. The static friction between the rope and the pivot point of the belay compensates a bit."

"Whoa there," Colton cut him off. "I don't need the science. I just need to know that it'll hold me if I fall."

"Trust the science. It's worked for me every single time I've fallen."

The sun glinted off Colter's helmet as he looked up and asked, "You fall out here? I thought you were like a national, regional champ or something."

Greyson shrugged. "You don't get good at anything without scraping your knees in the process. You know that as well as anybody. How did you learn to be alert in the pocket?"

Colter bit his lip in thought. "By taking one too many sacks."

"Exactly. Climbing is the same way for me." Greyson rubbed his hands together as he waited for his friend to reach him. "But to be fair, I do my falling on extreme cliffs. Not the twelve-year-old girl type, like this."

"Hey, you know your sister was way better than this at twelve!"

They both shared a laugh.

"I think I'm getting the hang of this," Colter said. "Seems like I need to learn how to use my feet more."

"Yeah. Climbing isn't about having great upper body strength or using one group of muscles. It's about using your whole body, all at once."

Greyson looked out off the pitch, taking in the world around him. On the horizon, the sun was fully cresting over the forest of pine trees spread out before him. A wet mist hung lazily in the air, encircling the trees and glowing dazzlingly bright under the morning sunshine.

Above him, the sky was painted a swirling mix of orange and blue. Below them, at the base of the cliff, a road wove through the forest, making gentle curves around cliffs and trees.

It was stunning. From up here, removed from the buzz of life and electronic devices, everything was serene. Magical, even. The world stretching out before him was full of opportunity. As his sophomore year of high school came to a close and summer loomed just around the bend, there was so much to do. So much to conquer.

As Colter kept climbing, the faint sound of water tickled Greyson's ear. He turned, searching for the source, and spotted water cascading down the side of the cliff in the distance. The water ran all the way down the cliff. At the bottom, it turned into a stream, and that led to a river rushing beside the road. The river, churning and frothy from a recent round of rain, was the only movement in the otherwise peaceful morning.

Colter was much closer now, looking increasingly more confident as he ascended. Greyson, knowing he was near the crux of the pitch, tightened the rope again as he watched his friend. Perhaps he shouldn't have wanted Colter to succeed—this was, after all, the one thing Greyson truly had over Colter—but he couldn't help but feel pride. Not only had he talked Colter into climbing, but his friend was also doing it *well.*

Or, *mostly* well, at least.

As Colter was nearing the ridge, he made a wrong move, and his foot slipped away. In a flash, he fell, letting out an unexpectedly loud yelp and frantically reaching out to catch himself, only for his body to be caught immediately by his belay.

"You good?" Greyson asked, arching an eyebrow.

"Oh, totally." Colter opened one eye and wheezed.

"Meant to do that."

"Aren't you glad you trusted the science?"

"I'm glad the science kept me from becoming a stain on the rocks down there."

Laughing, Greyson extended a hand to Colter, pulling him up and over the ledge. As both friends sat on the cliff, Colter was panting, desperately trying to catch his breath from the climb and near-fall.

"So, what do you think?" Greyson asked as Colter's breathing returned closer to normal. "I think I'm glad you finally talked me into coming out here and giving it ago."

"You owed me one. Since I tried out for football in sixth grade because *you* asked, this is the least you could do."

Another collective laugh, then Colter added, "I'm just glad you found rock climbing because football, at least back then, was not for you."

"But which one's a more useful life skill?"

"Touché, but I keep telling you we could probably use you somewhere. I bet you're better now." Colter was using his thumb to massage his other hand. "I also think I'm gonna be sore tomorrow."

"This is a lot different from anything you'll ever do in a weight room," Greyson agreed. "Climbing's a free workout plan designed by the one and only Mother Nature."

"You gotta turn me into some sort of pro climber so I can drag the rest of the team out here and get them to do it, too," Colter said. "Imagine if we had the only offensive line in the state that can scale buildings or whatever."

"I don't know that I've ever exactly climbed a *building...*"

"But you could!" Colter insisted. "Drop the Peter Parker thing and just admit that you're Spider-Man."

Greyson grinned. "I mean, I *am* pretty good at this."

Colter nodded. "It's about time I hear some confidence coming out of ya. You're the smartest, most athletic person I know, who refuses to show that to anybody on planet Earth. You gotta flex it a bit, y'know?"

"Don't get too carried away, dude."

"I'm f'real. And for my next act, I'm gonna get you a girlfriend."

"That's a hard pass," Greyson said. "I don't have time for anything like that. Plus, if I really wanted a girlfriend, I'd go get one myself."

"Whoa...there's that confidence again."

Greyson chuckled as he scanned the forest stretching out before them once again. He opened his mouth, paused, hesitated, closed it, then finally asked, "Do you ever just think?"

"Just...*think?*"

"Yeah."

"About?"

"Like...I don't know. Everything."

"I mean...yeah?" Colter couldn't keep the confusion out of his voice. "But, again, what about?"

Greyson searched for the right words, but they evaded him. Finally, he just pointed toward the forest.

"You're thinking about...trees?" Colter asked.

"No...well, kinda." Greyson smirked. "It's just that sometimes when I'm at a place like this, and I can see everything, I realize that there's so much to do, there's so much to explore, and there's so much to…I don't know… *experience*. But we'll never do one percent of it."

For a moment, Colter's eyes stayed fixed on the horizon. Then, after brief contemplation, he offered, "I've never really thought about that, but you're right. Seems like we get pretty busy and end up doing the same things over and over."

Greyson nodded.

"I wouldn't be out here climbing with you if you wouldn't have bugged me about it for *two years*," Colter added."

"I'm the same way, though," admitted Greyson. "Every day, I go to school, study, then *climb rocks*. I need to get out there more."

With a grin, Colter added, "Don't forget to add, 'have deep, philosophical thoughts while climbing rocks' to that list."

Greyson rolled his eyes.

The boys sat silently for a moment, watching the picturesque slice of nature spread out before them as the sun continued rising. Then, just when Greyson was sure they were about to move on, Colter asked, "So, what do we do?"

"To get to the top of the rock?"

"No. About what we were just talking about. About missing out on opportunities and adventure."

"Oh…" Greyson ran his finger along with the straps of his harness while he searched for the right thing to say. Finally, he said, "Let's make a pact."

"A pact?"

"Yeah. This summer, let's make a commitment to ourselves and each other that we'll get out there more.

We'll try new things, go on new adventures, and make sure this summer is the best one yet."

"I'm down," Colter agreed with surprising enthusiasm. "I think you're right, Grey. We don't need to let all this pass us by." He gestured to the surrounding forest.

"Agreed. Plus, you can drive us now. That's gonna make it much easier too..." Greyson dropped the thought mid-sentence, tilting his head to the side.

Colter must have noticed his sudden worried expression. "What's wrong? Grey? Are you—"

"Shh..." Greyson responded, holding his fingers to his lips.

Colter got the message, falling dead silent.

As Greyson listened intently, almost everything he heard belonged. There were the birds, squawking and chirping in the rising sun. The trickling stream burbled in the morning as a gentle breeze tickled the side of the cliff.

But there was another sound, too.

A cracking.

As Greyson heard it again, he quickly climbed to his feet and began trying to locate the source of it. Colter followed suit, still looking more than a bit confused.

Crack. A louder one came, and this time Greyson tracked the source of the noise to somewhere over their head. His stomach tightened even more.

Colter heard the second one and swore before asking, "Was that this *cliff*?"

Greyson nodded. "These cliffs are limestone and granite. That makes them a great climb, but some of the surrounding rock is prone to be a bit unstable after a big rain like we had last night. We should head down—just to be safe."

"Thanks for the geology lesson, Indiana Jones." Colter grabbed at the rope. "But that sounds good to me. So you'll just lower me down like—"

CRACK!

Before he could finish the sentence, there was a mini-explosion from overhead and a rock broke loose from the cliff face. Except, it wasn't a rock at all. It was a *boulder.* A huge, jagged chunk thundered down toward the boys from directly overhead.

"Look out!" Greyson yelled.

Colter was utterly frozen, going deer-in-headlights in the direct path of the incoming boulder, so Greyson shoved his friend toward the only overhang he spotted big enough to protect him.

Colter got the message and slipped to safety as the boulder continued to whoosh down toward them.

Greyson looked up, fixing his eyes on the enormous rock and trying to set up his anchor knot. If the boulder clipped the cliff, it could change direction at a moment's notice, and the tremendous chunk had to easily weigh over a ton. It was enough to crush every bone in his body if he let it.

As it continued to fall, he yelled, "Be ready to catch me, Colt."

"Catch you?"

Greyson didn't have time to explain. He bent his knees, preparing the rope. *How long did he have? When should he make his move*? Thousands of fears exploded in his head in half a second, and then, at the very last moment, Greyson jumped.

He threw himself off the cliff, trusting his climbing gear and friend to do the rest.

It worked.

Just as he felt like he was going to fall, Colter tightened the rope and swung him to the side. As it did, the rock blew past him, narrowly dodging disaster.

It continued falling, busting through a rock guard before it crunched into the road with a tremendous *slam* that sent it splitting into pieces and blasting shards of rock and debris across the road in every direction.

Greyson, still hanging in the air and swaying back and forth under the rope, couldn't tear his eyes off the remains of the boulder. If he'd been a half-second slower, he would have been crushed. Colter, too, for that matter. The shock had clamped onto his body and his muscles had tightened in fear. Even the birds around them had fallen silent.

After the eerie silence, Colter was the first to speak. "That was…that was crazy! You totally saved me."

Greyson, heart still racing, finally looked away from the boulder and into his friend's sheet-white face. "Yeah, well…I knew you wouldn't ever go climbing with me again if I let you get slam-crunched by a boulder the first time. Plus, you returned the favor with the belay."

"I'm serious," Colter insisted. "Dude, I was a goner, except…"

With his feet back on the cliff now, Greyson shook his head. "Don't mention it. I'm the experienced climber, plus you're probably the only person I would ever trust with my life under that amount of pressure."

Colter glanced down at the remains of the boulder and shook his head. "When I said I wanted to do new things this summer, getting nearly killed by a giant rock wasn't what I had in mind."

"Beggars can't be choosy, I guess." Despite the playfulness of his words, Greyson's voice was still shaky. "Let's get down to the ground. I wanna take a picture of the rock that nearly mashed us."

"Honestly, same."

Greyson started lowering Colter once again, but no sooner was he halfway there when yet another sound stopped Greyson.

This time, Colter heard it, too. With widening eyes, he asked, "Is that a *car?"*

Very slowly, Greyson nodded.

The road ran right along the base of the cliff, and judging by the sound of the incoming car, it was headed their way.

Right toward the boulder.

To make matters even worse, from the direction it was coming, the driver wouldn't have any time to slow after curving around the cliff and seeing the rock.

"Should we try to warn them?" Colter asked.

Greyson was already on it. From atop the pitch, he began waving his arms toward the road. "Hey! Hey!" Despite his best efforts, he couldn't spot the incoming vehicle.

Colter joined in, desperately trying to get the driver's attention before it was too late.

It didn't work.

A mid-sized sedan rounded the corner a bit faster than it should have been driving, and the driver—a lady in her mid-thirties—immediately locked up her brakes when she spotted the huge chunk of rock lying in the middle of the road. Despite the sunglasses partially concealing the woman's face, her fear was apparent.

The tires of the car screeched and fought for traction, but it was no use. It didn't have time to stop, and if the driver didn't do something quickly, it would go careening head-first into the boulder.

The tires screeched again even more loudly, and the car veered off the road and away from the cliff.

But the driver's luck didn't get much better there.

The woman managed to avoid both the cliff and the boulder, but she didn't dodge the guard rail. Instead, her car tore through it and began rolling down the slope. Greyson expected the car to slam into a tree, but it never did. Instead, it splashed right into the river running alongside the road.

The engine died at once, and a second later, the entire car started floating backward in the strong current.

Greyson's stomach tightened as he glanced at Colter. A dark thought was in the back of his mind, and he forced himself to put it out in the open air. "Do you know where that river runs?"

"Um…" A moment of silence led to a horrific realization that flashed across Colter's face. "Doesn't that… doesn't that run toward Roaring Falls?"

Greyson nodded. "Yeah. And if we don't do something, her car's gonna take a plunge with her inside it. So hold on!" Knowing the urgency, he let Colter's belay out at almost a full descent.

"Whoa!" Colter called as he dropped toward the ground.

"Change your shoes!" Greyson yelled down to his friend. "You won't be able to run or do *anything* in those climbing shoes."

As Colter reached the ground, Greyson tied the rope

off solid, pulled out his three-bar rappel device, and descended as quickly as he could. By the time he hit the ground, Colter was pulling on his tennis shoes.

A new sound had replaced the breeze, birds, and even the rushing water: desperate shrieks for help.

TWO

"What do we do? What do we do?" Colter repeated over and over as the woman screamed, her car continuing to float down the river.

"I...I have no idea." Greyson's hands were shaking so severely that he struggled to unclip his rope from his harness, but he finally got it free. "C'mon."

He set off in a sprint across the road, not worrying about his climbing shoes thanks to years of calluses built up from wearing them. Halfway across, he stopped and pointed back to Colter. "Grab that gear."

Colter tracked his finger to a dry bag full of climbing supplies: extra ropes, clips, and other necessities. After another couple of seconds, he laced up his shoes, grabbed the bag of supplies and took off after Greyson.

Greyson wasn't waiting around. He made it off the road and began working his way down the soft, muddy slope that slanted towards the river. The best traction he found came in the ruts made by the tire tracks of the car, so he followed them closely.

The water was carrying the car faster than he'd expected, so he had to run just to keep up.

Meanwhile, Colter appeared at the top of the hill, supply bag in hand. "Do you have a plan, Grey?"

"Working on it. Just follow me." Greyson was gaining ground on the car. As he approached, he tried to piece together an idea. He needed *something.* A quick look through the car's windshield didn't help the situation.

The woman looked terrified. She was crying and shouting and desperately pleading for Greyson to save her as she fought to push the airbag out of her face.

In response, he shouted over the rush of the water, "We're gonna help! Just take a deep breath."

The woman continued screaming—apparently, she hadn't heard him from inside the car—so he repeated the phrase, growing both desperate and agitated.

This time, however, it worked. She stopped screaming and flailing, looking to him for guidance.

Now that he had her attention, what was he supposed to do?

He'd caught up to the floating car, so he let up a bit and began trying to talk to the woman. "Can you open the doors?" As he asked the question, he made a gesture to help her understand.

She tried, but shook her head.

Greyson expected as much. "The water pressure," he explained, but then paused after remembering she needed help, not a science lesson. "What about the window?" He yelled, gesturing once again.

The woman tried the window, once again to no avail.

"Didn't figure." Greyson was losing hope. This car was about to become the woman's coffin if he didn't come up with something quickly.

As he looked down the riverside, his gaze locked on

a particularly large Douglas fir tree growing on the river's bank. Its trunk was so thick he couldn't have wrapped his arms around it, and it had strong branches that extended almost all the way across the river. Several boulders were on the side of the river, opposite the tree.

That's when he had an idea.

"Colter, you still have that bag?" He turned to look for his friend, who, to Greyson's surprise, was only a few strides behind him.

"Yeah." Colter hoisted the bag up to show him. "Do you want it?"

"Get out a rope."

"A rope?"

"Yeah." Greyson nodded. "You're gonna throw that to me in a bit. And hook up your belay device. I'm gonna need you to be a counterweight."

"*Counterweight?*" Coulter couldn't mask the concern. "Um...okay."

With that, Greyson was off again, this time sprinting past the car. He ran all the way to the big tree, which was even more impressive now that he was standing right underneath it. He looked over his shoulder, confirming the car was still floating his way, then set to work.

The first limb was so high overhead that he knew it was too high for him to jump. He wasn't tall—especially compared to Colter—so he'd have to improvise. He took two bounds towards the tree, jumped toward the trunk, and kicked off it with both feet, propelling himself toward the branch.

After securing it with a steely grip, he thrust his hips forward, followed by his legs, and began kipping to gain momentum. He swung back and forth twice before giving one more final thrust, and with that, he let go of the limb and flew out over the water.

For a moment, Greyson wondered if this was a terrible idea. As the water rushed below him, chopping and churning, he was sure he was about to take a plunge and get swept away. He'd either drown or be thrown to his death.

But just as he began to fall, plunging down toward the rapids, another limb came into reach. He grabbed it, gritting his teeth as he kept his momentum going.

The car was still floating his way.

"This is *not* what I had in mind for climbing today," Greyson mumbled as he spotted the perfect branch that extended about three-quarters of the way across the river. It was easily more than ten feet away, but he was confident he could cover the distance if he timed the jump just right.

As soon as he had enough momentum, he flung himself forward and soared over the burbling waterway again, latching on to the next branch. After stabilizing himself, he muscled up to a seated position.

"Dude!" Colter yelled from the side of the river. "That was crazy! You just…you…"

"Let's talk about it later," Greyson answered. "Show me that quarterback arm and throw me one end of the rope."

Colter did as told, reeling back and sending a tightly wound bundle of rope spiraling up to Greyson in the tree.

Greyson caught it right over the logo on his shirt. "Good throw. And this is the part where I need you to belay now, got it?"

"Wait, what?"

Greyson didn't have time to explain. The car was getting closer with every passing second. He tied the end of the rope to his harness and took a deep breath.

Estimating the circumference of his swing, he stood up on the branch with the rope pulled tight.

"Okay, now what? Are you gonna go for a swim?"

Greyson shook his head as he tied his end of the rope to his harness. "Not quite. That water's moving so fast that if I did, I'd end up just like the car. I need you to give me about twelve feet of slack. Actually, wait! Fourteen feet."

"What's the plan?" Colter asked again as he adjusted the rope.

Greyson had his gaze fixed on the car, which was closing in on them. "You're gonna hold the rope tight while I swing out over the water and try to turn the car."

"*Turn it?*"

"Yeah. The river is narrower here, so I think we can high-side the car on that big boulder in the middle. Does that make sense?"

"I mean, yeah. But you only have one shot at this or else, well..." Colter pointed downstream, and for the first time, Greyson's eyes ventured that way.

He wished he hadn't looked.

Roaring Falls.

He'd climbed it before. From his best memory, the cliff was about sixty feet tall, with a churning pool at the bottom.

For a nature-lover like himself, a waterfall alongside a cliff made for a great summer rec spot. For a screaming woman trapped behind a steering wheel in the strong current of the icy spring runoff, it would *not* make for a pleasant plunge.

Greyson, suddenly feeling even more anxious, turned his attention to the car. It was close now. This was go-time.

"Hold on!" He yelled once more—both for Colter and for the screaming woman—and then made his move.

As Colter kept good tension on the rope, Greyson jumped up and out, praying his calculations were right as his rope pulled tight over the branch and the angle began to swing him back towards the water.

While cutting through the air, he eyed the incoming car. He had to get this right. One chance was all he'd get. From his timing to his foot placement, everything had to be perfect.

It couldn't have gone any better. As the car floated right into his reach, he tucked his knees to his chest as his back skidded just above the surface of the river. Then, at what felt like the very last second, he kicked toward the side paneling between the trunk and back tire. For just a moment, he worried that his small frame might not have created enough momentum.

As Greyson spiraled away, swinging wildly on the rope, the car rotated. It wasn't much—a 45-degree turn, if that—but it was just enough. With a groan, it caught against the boulder. It had been high-sided, just as he hoped.

"You did it!" Colter called out in disbelief. "Dude… that was…that was great!"

"A bit of luck, I think," Greyson answered as he tried to stabilize his spinning. "I need you to pull me up and lower me down to the car. Got it?"

"Yeah, sure." Colter used his strong legs to step back a few steps, lifting Greyson higher and then lowering him with the belay.

Soon, Greyson had stopped spinning and was suspended directly over the car, which seemed to be holding its place despite the ferocious current. He tried to smash a window with his foot then a rock, but with no luck. He wasn't stable enough to generate the required force.

As he debated his next move, he said, "Can you throw me one more rope?"

"Yeah." Still keeping tension on Greyson, Colter reached out and grabbed the bag. He pulled out a lime-green climbing rope and underhanded it across the river.

Greyson snagged it. "Thanks."

"What are you—"

"We're going to pry this door open," Greyson explained. "First, I'm gonna need you to tie me off to that tree." As he said this, he looped one end of the rope around one of the car door handles, then threw the other end to his friend.

"Oh, I get it." Colter did as told, tying the rope to the thick tree while Greyson urgently tied the other end to the door handle. The car could break loose at any moment, so they needed to be fast.

The woman inside was still wide-eyed. Her cheeks glistened with tears, but she was no longer crying. Instead, she was trying to yell something through the glass.

"I can't hear you over the water!" Greyson shouted back.

He looked at the car again, taking in the entire body of the vehicle and trying to figure out how to get the woman out. Meanwhile, she kept trying to shout something back. It looked like she kept repeating the same words, but that was all he could make out.

"Colter," he yelled. "Remember when I was explaining the gear? I'm gonna need you to tie a piece of webbing around the tree you tied me off to, then clip a carabiner to it as an anchor point."

"Give me a second. I can do that!"

"Good. Then get ready to pull!"

As Colter was setting up, Greyson got into position to help pry the door open. "Ready when you are, Colter!"

Colter's labored grunts came as a response, and very slowly, the door began to open. Through the cracked door, he could finally make out the phrase the woman was repeating over and over: "I have a baby!"

Greyson's stomach dropped. "In the car?" he answered his own question as his eyes locked onto a car seat in the back. His stomach tightened even more. Turning to his friend, he said, "Colter, there's a baby in the car, too."

Colter groaned from effort. "You gotta do something, man. I can't hold much longer."

Greyson knew his friend was right. No matter how strong Colter was, friction would always win.

Friction. Another idea popped into his head.

Spotting a softball-sized rock beside him, he scooped it up and wedged it in the cracked door. "You can relax for a minute, Colter."

Colter did as told, letting out a big sigh of relief.

Greyson said, "We need to tie another piece of webbing to the large boulder about eight feet in front of the tree. That'll create a second anchor point, which should increase both your friction and pull force. Make sense?"

"Um...no. But are you sure it will help?" Once again,

Colter set to work.

"Yeah, it's called a Z-drag. Rafters use it to turn over wrapped boats."

As Colter set up the Z-drag, Greyson wedged some more rocks in the door and worked to pry it open a bit further. "Can you reach your baby?"

She responded with a frantic nod. "Should I get him?"

"Yes. I think we can get him first, and then I'll come back for you. I promise. But move very slowly. It won't take much to rock the car and send it floating toward the falls again."

She nodded. Pale and sweaty, the woman freed her baby and, very carefully, slipped her crying son through the crack in the door.

Greyson took him, holding him tight to his chest as he began to build up his swing on the rope. With every swing, he kicked off the nearby boulder for more momentum, moving closer to the bank.

By that point, Colter had finished the Z-drag. "If you can swing to that rock, I'll come get the baby."

Greyson nodded. "Good plan." As he kept swinging, Colter hopped across the surface of a few rocks that were barely poking out from under the river. He made it to the rock he'd pointed out, and Greyson swung his way.

"Ready!"

"You better not fumble this handoff," Greyson quipped. "Think you can make it back to the shore?"

"Yeah."

As he swung past, Greyson handed the screaming baby to Colter. "Nice one."

Colter nodded, then adjusting his grip, he returned

to the river's bank "I'm not really sure how babies work. Can I just, like… lay it on the rocks here?"

Greyson rolled his eyes as he redirected, swung back to the car, and started pulling on the door. "Lay it down gently and somewhere safe… *away* from the river!"

Colter did as told as Greyson turned his attention back to the car. With the Z-drag in place, he should have enough force to open it—at least enough for the woman to squeeze out.

It didn't work. The river was still too strong.

"Colt, toss me the dry bag if you can! Maybe there's something in there I can use to pry the door open."

Colter tossed it over and Greyson began sifting through the bag as he hung above the river. He spotted an old collapsible walking stick, the same one he used to make fun of his dad for using on their climbing adventures, which he wedged in the door.. If he could just get the door to open enough, the Z-drag should take effect.

The door began to open, and once it did, it happened much faster than he ever expected. All of a sudden, the current caught the inside of the door and snapped it open with so much force that it pulled the car off the large boulder. The rope ripped the door handle from the car, and the vehicle—with the screaming mother inside—began to float down the river once again.

As the car continued floating away, Greyson knew what he had to do. At the bottom of his climbing bag, he found his knife. "Colter, listen *very carefully*. I need you to let all the slack out on the Z-drag and be ready to pull me in."

"Greyson! Don't do something crazy!"

Greyson flung the rest of the contents of his dry bag

to the shore, puffed some air into the bag, then tied it off with the air inside. "I've heard it's only crazy if it doesn't work." With that, he sliced through the rope suspending him in the air, and plunged into the river.

In no time, he noticed two things. First of all, the water was cold. Perhaps he should have expected it, especially given the recent rain, but it still stung at first. Second, the water moved *fast.* So fast, even, that he had no pretense of control. He was at the complete mercy of the river, but thankfully the dry bag was helping him stay afloat.

Greyson pushed the chilling temps and fear out of his mind as he focused on keeping his feet in front of him, a technique he learned while white-water rafting. And, even more importantly, he had to find the rope that Colter had loosened from the z-drag. It had to be floating in the water somewhere.

He needed to find it. His life depended on it.

And that's when he spotted it, floating atop the murky surface of the running water. He grabbed it and managed to secure it onto his harness. "Gotcha!"

Meanwhile, the woman was trying to climb out of the car, which was permanently bent open from the force of the river.

Greyson swam toward her, propelled by the river, as she fought the water and worked her way to the edge of her seat.

In a matter of seconds, the woman's head emerged through the car's door, and with terror in her eyes, she yelled to Greyson, "There's a waterfall!"

Greyson answered, "Don't worry! We're gonna get you out of there, but..." He paused and coughed as water blasted him in the face. "...But I need you to jump toward me. Climb onto the car."

The woman looked even more scared. "Then we'll go flying off the cliff!"

"Just trust me!" Greyson had to shout to be heard.

With that, he put his head down and began to swim even faster. By this point, the water seemed to be speeding up, too, like it was preparing to take the plunge, but he was close to the car. He could feel it.

And once he looked up, he found the car only a few feet away. The woman had climbed onto its hood, as the trunk slowly started to turn towards the waterfall.

"Hurry!" He yelled as his eyes focused on the waterfall behind them—*right* behind him. It was so close by this point that the back tires of the car were beginning to dip.

The woman clambered to her feet, fighting to keep her balance. As the trunk began to fall over the edge of the drop, she took two steps before throwing herself toward Greyson.

He met her with open arms, grabbing her as tightly as he could and shouting, "Hold on!"

She clenched onto him as, just feet away, the car gave one last lurch before tipping over the waterfall and falling out of sight.

Greyson could feel the woman quaking as they, too, floated to the edge of the drop off. Below them, a loud *boom* echoed through the trees as the car crashed into the bottom of the falls.

Gravity started to pull at Greyson as he and the woman began to follow the car over the falls. The water churned more aggressively and he was falling faster and faster.

But then, just as the woman began to scream, it was over.

Greyson hit the end of his rope.

The sudden jolt was jarring enough that his head jerked forward, as did the woman's, but instead of pushing them *over* the waterfall, the water suddenly began carrying them to the side of the river.

The woman looked around in astonishment, but Greyson didn't have the energy to explain. He just held on for the ride.

And seconds later, the shore was within reach. Greyson's shoes pressed down against the solid ground and he stood up. First, he helped the woman to the bank, and then, soaked and water-beaten, he crawled out right behind her.

With his heart pounding in his chest, Greyson laid down on his back and stared at the morning sky. Behind him, the woman climbed to her feet and ran to Colter, who had her baby. She took the baby and held him close. They both cried.

Colter came and kneeled down beside Greyson. "Are you okay? How did you…" He didn't have the words to even finish the thought.

Almost reluctantly, Greyson sat up. At his feet, the waterfall spewed gallons of the murky water over the edge of the cliff and out of sight, blowing the spray in his face.

"All good," Greyson said. "Thanks for the rope."

"No prob. You're the one who did all the work."

"Not true. Without your help, three people might have died. Guess you gotta start climbing with me more often." He gave a coy grin.

"Guess so."

As Greyson staggered to his feet, the woman wrapped him in a hug with her non-baby-carrying arm. "Thank you." It was all she could seem to say, and she repeated it over and over.

"No worries. But hey, what's your name?"

"Krystal," she answered.

He nodded, still wrapped in her hug. "So, um, Krystal…I've got to ask you something."

"Anything. Anything at all."

"Does your car insurance package include waterfall damage, by chance?"

She stared back in confusion, apparently still too in shock to realize he was joking, when a movement caught his eye.

A person.

A man in his late twenties came climbing down the slope from the road above. He wore a bucket hat and a wide-eyed, open-mouthed expression. Clutched chest-level was his cell phone. Everybody else seemed to notice the man at the same time. Krystal finally let go of Greyson, turning to their new visitor as he stammered, "That was…that was *amazing!*"

Nobody spoke, either too exhausted or emotional from what had just happened.

He added, "I…I parked because of the commotion and came down here. I caught the end of that and…wow, I can't believe what I saw." Then, after a pause, he held up his phone and said, "Oh, I also called the police!"

As the words left his mouth, Greyson heard them. Sirens. They were distant, but growing louder with every passing second.

Something told Greyson it was going to be a very long day.

THREE

Buzz! Greyson picked up his phone. He was lying on the couch in his living room with Max, his old dog, on his lap, anxiously watching the TV and awaiting the evening news.

He'd received a short text from Colter: *Did u see this one?* A link followed.

Greyson clicked on the link and a news story filled his screen. His eyes brushed over the title, which read, *Local Heroes! Two Pine High School Students Save Mother and Infant Son.*

Right under the header was a picture that he'd already seen *way* too many times. It was a picture that had been taken by James, the man who'd first arrived on the scene, and had gone viral in local news. It showed Colter handing the crying baby back to his mother …and Greyson laying on his back.

As far as the picture was concerned, Colter had saved the day. And it was Colter who was getting all the attention from their classmates, too. It wasn't Colter's fault by any means, but Greyson still felt a small twinge of jealousy.

The story accompanying the picture, however, made up for it. It treated both boys like heroes, focusing in particular on Greyson's efforts.

And this was the fourth story just like it.

After the events of the climb had unfolded, Greyson had felt like a celebrity at first. For the first time in his life, his name was floating around the news. He'd been called "clever," "quick-witted," and even a "savior."

This was new for Greyson. Colter might have always been Mister Popular, but Greyson was the quiet, reserved shadow who was only Colter's best friend because they had grown up right across the street from each other.

While the attention was nice—at least for the day—he didn't like talking to cameras and had never enjoyed being around large groups of people. That was more of a Colter thing. Greyson preferred to be left alone with a book, his laptop, an outdoor adventure, or a cliff to climb.

And despite this, a well of excitement stirred inside him as he heard the nightly news report tease, "Tune in for our lead story tonight about two high school heroes."

He texted Colter back. *Hadn't seen that story. About to watch the news tho.*

The reply came almost immediately: *Same. I'm at Jen's. She doesn't know what to do now that I'm basically famous haha.*

Greyson, at first, hadn't cared for Jen, Colter's on-again, off-again "girlfriend." Perhaps he didn't like anything that came between him and his best friend. Perhaps he didn't think Jen was in Colter's best interest. But he came around after being forced to spend a little time with her. He didn't *like* Jen, but he didn't *mind* her, either.

Footsteps drew Greyson's attention away from the TV. He turned to see his mother walking in from the garage with a stack full of reports, and he asked, "Hey, do you wanna watch the news report with me? It's about to be on."

His mother paused, taking just long enough to turn toward him that it seemed like she'd had to think about what she was doing. With a glance down at her pile of work, then back up, she said, "I'm really, really proud of you, honey. But I need to get started on some of these reports, then I'll come watch with you."

"All right, Mom."

Slowly, his mother walked to her office, closing the door behind her. Despite what she said, Greyson knew he would not see her for the rest of the night. He never did.

But that's how it had been for the last six years, ever since his parents split. Apparently, losing your high school sweetheart to your best friend was enough to mess with a person—it had certainly caused Greyson's mother to become hyper-focused on her job. She used to be very family-oriented, but now she barely left her home office, even *after* coming home from her job as an associate law clerk.

Work, for her, was a crutch and an escape from the pains of the real world.

Greyson was ready to be gone. He was jealous of Gabby, his older sister, because she was off at college. She never came back to visit, either, and he couldn't blame her. Besides an occasional check-in via text, Gabby was yet another missing piece of his life.

He wasn't angry. He was just…sad. He'd spent several years hoping his family would come back together to resemble something he'd grown up with, but eventually, that hope had faded. Now he was ready to move on. Colter's mother, Debbie, acted more like a mom to him than his own. And she'd embraced the role, frequently joking that she had three boys instead of two.

The news broadcast began to play, and he leaned forward in anticipation.

It opened with a blonde woman and dark-haired man talking in a studio, going back and forth about the rising temperatures and making bad jokes with great smiles. Then, as promised, the report kicked off with Greyson's story.

The woman's lead-in encapsulated the day. "What started as a fun rock climb for two local high school students turned into a life-saving effort today. Here's an unbelievable recount of how Greyson McEntire and Colter Rickman—Pine High School's quarterback—saved a mother and child in need."

With that, they dove in. To Greyson, the next five minutes were a seesaw of emotions, from seeing himself on TV, which was surprisingly fulfilling, to seeing the poorly-timed picture. Worse still, he was watching it all alone.

Not even his own mom would join him.

He looked down at Max and patted him on the head. It seemed like he was the only one who enjoyed Greyson'scompany nowadays.

That didn't stop him from enjoying the broadcast though. He particularly appreciated a segment of Colter's interview, in which he said, "It was unbelievable. I've never seen anything like what Greyson did, really."

Hearing the words brought a smile to his face. He was thankful to have a friend who'd so readily share the spotlight with him.

However, the most surprising part of the broadcast happened *after* all the footage from the scene was aired. The broadcast cut back to the studio, where the smiling blonde woman said, "While this story has been a local sensation today, it's also getting national attention. Nathaniel Coffman, technology icon and native of Pine, even weighed in on the events while at a press conference in Silicon Valley."

Greyson's eyebrows raised. "Wow, did you hear that, Max? *Nathaniel Coffman* talked about me!" Coffman was, without a doubt, the most famous person to ever come out of Pine. He was a technology giant and CEO of Kloud Inc, a multi-billion dollar tech company.

The news cut to a short clip of Coffman, who was standing on a stage while wearing an all-black suit. The blue background behind him had the Kloud logo—a swirling line that sort of looked like a mashed "3"—and a sign behind him read, *Kloud's Upcoming Releases.*

Instead of talking about pending tech, however, the question from the press was completely unrelated. An off-screen voice asked, "Since you're from the little town of Pine, I was wondering if you had any comments concerning the amazing story that came out of there this morning."

Coffman flashed a smile. "You did your homework. Yeah, I saw that story when it broke this morning, and all I can say is 'wow.' There's something in the water in Pine. It's a special place, and it's nice to see the next generation of leaders are already stepping up and doing incredible things. Those boys—Greyson and Colton, I think—I'm so thankful they were able to step up and help the family in need. They're heroes, and something tells me they have bright futures ahead of them."

With that, the video clip ended, and the news transitioned to a warning against leaving pets in hot vehicles.

Greyson's mind, however, kept playing the interview over and over in his head. Nathaniel Coffman, one of the men Greyson had always admired most, had called him a hero. *A hero!* His heart was racing just as much now as it had been during the incident, but this was a different kind of racing. A good kind.

And, with shaky hands, he texted, *Hey Colton, Nathaniel Coffman thinks we're heroes.*

Colter's response came within thirty seconds. *Lolol @ him for messing up my name but dude I know!! Just saw that.*

We've officially made it, Greyson replied.

He briefly debated tapping on his mom's closed office door to tell her what had happened, but ultimately decided against it. She was busy and probably wouldn't care. Not enough to matter, anyway.

Max lumbered over to him, giving him a look, and Greyson smiled. "Don't give me that look. I'll feed you too, buddy."

He cooked dinner instead, and he even fixed a plate for his mother as well, slipping into her office just long enough to set it on her desk while she was on the phone. She looked up briefly to mouth "*thank you*" but didn't miss a beat in her conversation.

Greyson checked his phone again and found several new messages. Two were from guys at his school, distant friends who he'd forgotten even had his number. Another was from Gabby, saying how proud she was and that they needed to call each other once her semester slowed down and she got past finals. And yet another that was the most surprising of all: a text from his dad saying that he was proud of him. It felt hollow and forced, like his new girlfriend had written it, not him.

The final text was from Debbie, Colter's mom. *Quite a news segment,* it read. *I'm still amazed at what you did. So proud of you, Grey. Love you!*

Thanks a lot, he texted back. *Love you too.* With a sigh, he put his phone back down and looked at Max. "Why is this my life?"

It was an innocent question, but one tied to so many darker questions, too. Why had his father moved on to a different life, why had everybody close to him had abandoned him, and why did his best friend's mother act like more of a mother to him than his own?

These were questions neither he nor his dog could answer. Or, rather, were questions he didn't *want* to answer.

Greyson stood, put his plate in the dishwasher, fed his dog, and went to his bedroom, Max following closely behind.

His room was small, containing just his bed, Max's dog bed, a bookshelf, and a desk, but it was all he needed. He walked to the desk, sat down, and turned on his laptop. It was a mindless-TV kind of night.

He was just about to look for something to watch when an email notification popped up on the bottom corner of his screen: *New Message. No Preview Available.*

"What?" Arching an eyebrow, he opened the email, reading it under his breath. "*The opportunity of a lifetime.*"

He'd never seen that one before.

But the email that opened was also something he'd never seen before. Except, it didn't exactly *open.* His screen went black, with a fresh new message floating at the very top.

His very first reaction was to close it as soon as possible. Greyson was reasonably tech-savvy, and every single thing about this message told him that it was a virus, but there was no exit button. Heart racing, he frantically mashed the power button.

But that didn't stop him from reading the pop-up: *Greyson McEntire, this is a protected message for official viewing only. Click to continue identity verification.*

He rubbed his eyes, making sure he was truly seeing this.

He looked down at Max. "The warning looks legit. Or, at least, not like any virus I've ever seen or read about."

Reluctant but curious, he clicked *continue.*

Immediately, his screen flashed all-white for a moment, then black, and then something happened.

The first thing that flashed on the screen was some sort of shape—a seal or crest of some sort. It was a silvery thing with ornate curves and edges. If Greyson had to describe its shape, he'd say it had the body of a sea turtle. The head, however, was a circle, and in the circle was a twisting ladder or loops and geometric patterns.

And then it was gone.

There was no music. No animation. Just the white fading into a black screen.

Then came the voice. "Greyson McEntire," it said. It was a friendly voice. Not an old voice, but not a young one, either. Not deep, but also not *not* deep. "You're an impressive young man."

The darkness transitioned into a shot of a man sitting behind a desk in an office. The man had short, dark hair and a friendly smile, and was dressed in a polo. If Greyson had to guess, he'd have placed the man in his early-to-mid-thirties.

"My name is Jon," the man continued, "and I'm calling on behalf of the National Interdisciplinary Notable Juveniles Association. I wanted to get in touch after hearing about what happened today, Greyson. Do you have a couple of minutes?"

Greyson glanced around his room and then responded with a hesitant nod. "Yeah, for sure. But what was your group called again?"

"The National Interdisciplinary Notable Juveniles Association," Jon repeated. "I know it's a mouthful, so you can just call it the *NINJA* program."

"Oh, I like that," Greyson approved.

"Good." Jon checked his watch, then said, "I am a member of an organization for very special, very talented people, Greyson. And as we grow and expand, we're looking for young, talented individuals to take part in a once-in-a-lifetime internship program."

Greyson couldn't believe what he was hearing: was he being recruited to…*a cult?*

Jon must have sensed his skepticism because he laughed. "It's not what you think, I promise. But to be frank, I can't give all the details at the moment. What I can say is that I'd be honored to meet you in person and give you a glimpse of the bigger picture."

"Bigger picture?" The words tumbled out of

Greyson's mouth as he tried to unpack everything Jon was telling him.

Jon smiled in a friendly but incredibly unhelpful way. "Yeah, I'd like to show you a bit more of what our NINJA program offers outstanding young men and women like you."

Greyson had another thought. Maybe this was the government. Some sort of secret government branch. The CIA?

He didn't have long to ponder, however, as Jon wasted no time in continuing his vague message. "I can tell that this is a lot to take in at the moment, but I'm personally inviting you to take part in our eight-week internship program. Please get a pen and paper and write down what I'm about to say."

Greyson scrambled to find his writing stationery. *Everything was digital now, right?* Thankfully, Jon paused just long enough for him to get what he needed.

After he'd found both on his somewhat messy desk, Jon explained, "You will learn from the best minds in every major field of study. This program will expose you to major tech companies, non-profits, and government entities, pushing you both physically and mentally. Be assured that if it is too intense, you will be allowed to disenroll at any time, but keep in mind that completing our program will set you up as one of the most sought-after high school graduates in the country."

"Really? I've never heard of the NINJA program."

"It's not a name everybody knows," Jon said with a shrug. "But the *right* people know it. I assure you that. Our past graduates have gone on to graduate from Ivy League schools and intern at the largest companies in the world. Also, top-performing cadets will be receiving full-ride scholarships to the university of their choice."

"That's... crazy." Greyson wasn't one to normally have poor handwriting, but between the speed he was writing and his confusion about the entire situation, his frantic notes were barely legible.

Jon nodded and flashed another friendly smile. "It's our way to incentivize the program and say thanks for your time and effort. Only the brightest young men and women are selected for this opportunity, and we want to reward recruits for being as such."

"I...wow." Greyson didn't know what to say.

Fortunately, Jon seemed content to do all the talking. "The program has two sections. Recruits will first work with NINJA mentors, then they'll be partnered up for an internship with industry-leading companies who sponsor the program. As I mentioned, in total, this lasts eight weeks."

Greyson scribbled the information down, nodding as he did so. "What kind of companies did you say? Like can you give me an example?"

Jon nodded. "They're all Fortune 500 companies, with most being high-growth technology companies."

"Gotcha," Greyson said. "I'm really interested in big-tech."

Jon turned off screen for a moment, clearly listening to something, then looked back. His face was darker, more serious. "I apologize, but I better run, Greyson. I want to reassure you that even though this seems like a strange way to contact you, this program is very real, and this video call is a way for our mentors to gauge interest and screen recruits before official invites go out."

"Wait...that's it?" Greyson raised an eyebrow. This couldn't be it.

Jon nodded. "For now. I understand if you can't leave on such short notice for such a long time during the summer, but I hope I get the chance to meet you and tell you more about the NINJA program very soon."

Putting down his pen and pad, Greyson pushed his hair back and out of his face. "Yeah...yeah, I'll see," he said, trying to process everything. "I'll let you know. How do I..."

The video of Jon flashed with a brush of static, then he offered a wave at the camera and added, "Thanks for your time, Greyson, and thanks for being a standout young man. From our records, it appears that you're not only saving families from peril, but also working very hard in school as well. People always notice, trust me. Please watch for an official follow-up email with more specific details on the program, and we encourage you to share the info with your parents and guidance counselors as you make your decision."

"Okay...yeah, thanks." Greyson had a hundred other questions but didn't manage to ask any of them. With a flash, the video went to black, and his laptop fell silent.

"What on earth..." Greyson leaned back in his chair, staring up at the ceiling and trying to determine if any of this was real or if he'd just been imagining everything.

As he rubbed his eyes, he muttered, "This feels completely ridiculous. Is this a joke?" It seemed like something too absurd for real life. More like a movie.

And yet, he was intrigued.

Everything about the interaction made him think that there was even more to the picture than what he could see.

But that was also part of the appeal. He couldn't get the idea of working for a high-level government agency out of his mind. *Was he being recruited to work as a spy? Covert ops?* It was far-fetched, but he couldn't shake the thought.

He wanted to learn more.

He *needed* to.

But he couldn't do it alone.

Letting out a sigh, he looked down at Max. "Can you believe this?"

Max blinked back at him.

"Me neither." After a moment of contemplative silence, Greyson added, "Should I tell Colter? I honestly don't know if he'd be jealous, or like...excited for me. And I have no idea what to do. This would be so much easier if we both got to do it, y'know?"

Max continued staring back with his best listening face.

Greyson took his phone out of his pocket, opened his contacts, and selected Colter's number. His thumb hovered over the call button.

Then, his phone rang.

It was Colter.

Greyson's heart raced. He had to play it cool. "Hey man," he greeted as he answered the phone. "Pretty cool news report, right?"

"Yeah..." Colter replied, but from the single word, Greyson could tell that his mind was elsewhere. "But something really weird just happened."

"Weird in what way?" Greyson's nerves turned into recognition.

"I...well...I just got a really strange video call."

FOUR

"That wasn't even the weirdest thing about it," Colter explained. "I wish I would've screen recorded it just so I don't sound crazy, but I didn't think of that when it was happening. It was all so fast." He'd been at it non-stop for at least five minutes.

Greyson grinned. At least he wasn't the only one who had been confused.

Finally, Colter asked, "So...what do you think?"

Eyeing the pad of paper and scribbled notes in his hand, Greyson answered, "I think I wouldn't have believed you...except I got one, too."

"Wait...really?" Surprise flooded Colter's voice. "Are you serious? Why didn't you say something?"

"You were talking a thousand-words-per minute. It's not like you really gave me much of a chance!"

"Okay, fair," Colter admitted, but then he continued. "So like...this is nuts! I felt so weird telling you because I knew I would sound crazy, but I also know you're a nerd so I wanted to see if it was possible that a program like this existed—"

"You're doing it again," Greyson interrupted. "How about this: tell Jen goodbye and I'll meet you at your house so we can talk about it. I want to use your scanner for something, anyway."

"Okay, deal. I can be there in half an hour."

"Sounds good." Then, one more thought struck Greyson. "Hey, did Jen see the video?"

"Nah. She was in the backyard with Rufus. Should I tell her about it?"

Greyson bit his lip, deep in thought. "I mean, that's up to you, but I probably wouldn't. I think…well, I think we need to keep this between us until we know more. It seems like a legit thing, yeah, but do you know how stupid we'll look if we tell everybody about this and it turns out to be just an internet scam?"

"Yeah, man. That makes sense. Gotta save face." Colter laughed.

"Ha, yeah. Talk soon."

"See ya."

Greyson hung up, closed his laptop, and took a bit to unpack everything that had happened in the last ten minutes. There was too much to sort out by himself.

"Well, Max…" he said, "...shall we go try to figure things out?" He went downstairs, tapping on his mom's office door. "Hey, I'm going to Colter's."

He could hear her on another important phone call, and she paused just long enough to offer a soft, "You two have fun. Proud of you."

"Thanks."

Outside, the evening breeze was cool and the sun was dipping below the tree line. So much had happened since Greyson had seen it appearing over the pine trees just this morning.

With his mind still spinning, he made his way across

the street, Max trailing slowly behind him. He knocked on the front door of Colter's house as Max plopped down at his feet.

Colter's father opened the door, a big smile on his face. "Greyson! It's not every day a local hero shows up at my house."

Greyson laughed. "Hey, Mr. Rickman. I don't know about that...according to the news report, I heard one of those big-shot local heroes lives here."

Mr. Rickman shook his hand and led him and Max inside. "When Colter was telling me about everything that happened, I couldn't believe it. Sounds like you were really thinking quickly out there."

"Or being really stupid and really lucky," Greyson countered. "But I couldn't have done it without Colter. If he hadn't come with me this morning, the news would have been featuring a very different story tonight—a sad one."

Two arms wrapped around Greyson from behind. "There he is! We're so proud of you, Grey."

"Hey, Mrs. Rickman. Thank you." Greyson awkwardly reached around to hug her back. "I was just doing what made sense."

"That's why you're Colter's best friend," Mr. Rickman joked.

Mrs. Rickman finally released him. "When Will and I were watching the news, that's when it got real. We'd read the articles and heard the stories, but like...seeing you and Colt on the news report—my boys really are heroes!"

"Even got a shout-out from a billionaire," Mr. Rickman added. "That was neat, too."

Greyson didn't know what to say. It was all too much.

"What do you want for dinner, hon?" Mrs. Rickman asked. "I was gonna cook something for Ty when he gets home from soccer practice, and I'll just double it."

Ty was Colter's 12-year-old brother who, as far as Greyson was concerned, was pretty cool...at least, for a baby brother.

"I already ate, but thanks," Greyson said. "I doubt toaster-oven chicken nuggets hold up to whatever you'd fix, though. Ty gets a better deal, here."

Mrs. Rickman headed toward the kitchen. "How about a bowl of ice cream then? I think you deserve something sweet after today."

"I definitely wouldn't say no to that."

The front door opened, and Colter popped in. "Sorry, am I breaking up the autograph session?"

In front of Colter's parents, they talked about everything except the one thing that was most on the friends' minds as they ate their ice cream. Then, once both had found the bottom of their bowls, Colter said, "Well, we're gonna go up to my room and, uh, play some PlayStation."

"You guys have fun," Mrs. Rickman replied. "If you need anything, just let me know."

Greyson and Max followed Colter up the stairs. As soon as they were in Colter's room and out of earshot, Greyson said, "I can't stop thinking about the message."

Colter nodded. "I'm the same way. I've never been offered an opportunity like this."

Max plopped down in the corner of the room while Greyson sat down on the bed and Colter took his office chair.

"So what did he tell you?" Greyson asked.

Colter thought hard. "Um...I'd imagine it was about

the same as yours, right?"

"I mean, probably. But we don't know for sure."

"Okay, point taken." Colter turned back in fourth in the chair and recounted. "So, the guy in the video said that he was from a NINJA organization that was offering an internship of a lifetime, but he was vague about the companies or organizations involved. Does that sound right?"

"Yeah. Spot on. I got the exact same thing."

"Figures. He also said it was an intense, eight-week program that would end in a full-ride scholarship for the top recruits and that we would be sought after by major universities."

Greyson nodded. "Ditto."

Colter paused, shoving his hands in his pocket and pulling out a wadded-up piece of paper, which he unwrinkled and began to read aloud. Again, it was exactly the same. Every detail—including the part where you could leave at any point—was almost word-for-word what Greyson had been told.

When Colter finished, Greyson said, "We both got the same message. Maybe even the same script."

"So, what do you think?"

"About which part?"

"I don't know…all of it, really."

It was a big question and one that, truthfully, Greyson couldn't answer.

"What do you think this organization even is?" Colter asked.

"The NINJA organization. I can't even remember what that stands for, though."

"Oh no, me either." Colter looked back down at his

notes. "But, I mean, beyond that. Who are they?"

"You want my honest thoughts?"

"That's what I asked for."

"I'm getting government agency vibes. It seems dumb to even say, but my gut instinct was some type of secretive government operation."

"Reaching out to *us*? Two boys from Small Town, U.S.A., just because we made the news?"

"Listen, I'm all ears if you have better ideas."

"That's just the thing." Colter dropped his gaze. "I don't. I was…um, I was actually kind of thinking the same thing. It's just weird to hear somebody else say it."

Greyson laid back on the bed and stared up at the ceiling. "So, does that mean you trust them?"

"It means…" Colter trailed off for a moment. "Well, for one, I want to say that it's obviously pretty weird, but if we could get a full-ride scholarship to any university, it's probably at least worth investigating, right?"

"Yeah. But there was something about how he was talking that made me feel like—I don't know—like it was something I could believe in. I didn't feel threatened or anything at all. Sure, you can't trust anybody you meet online, but he did at least *seem* like a good guy. Am I crazy?"

After a moment, Colter gave the most straightforward answer he could. "No. You're not."

Greyson sat up again, locking eyes with his friend. "Okay, good. The message was very weird, but there was just something about it that also made me feel…I don't know…Like Jon was somebody I could trust."

"Wait…Jon?" For the first time, Colter looked confused. "Who's Jon?"

Greyson scrunched his eyebrows together. "Um, the

guy from the video? Short, dark hair? Kinda looked like he'd be a good fit to help with my math homework?"

Colter was already shaking his head. "Dude, I talked to a *way* different person. I talked to a really buff black guy named N.J.. He was probably in his late-twenties."

"That's definitely not the person I was talking about." Greyson's mind was racing. "But you know what's kind of funny about that?"

"Please, enlighten me."

"Well, we listened to two different people talk, but we both came away with the same impression about the video…*and* that these guys weren't a threat."

Colter asked, "So you're saying we should believe these internet strangers?"

"Um…yeah. Basically. It sounds better in my head, though." Greyson turned away, gazing out the window. In the evening light, his house was visible. It was dark. It looked nearly vacant, with only a glimmer of life inside.

In many ways, his mom was the same way.

"What about my scanner?" Colter's words snapped Greyson out of his thoughts.

"Hmm?"

"You said you wanted to use my scanner."

"Oh! Right. Can you gimme that pad?" Greyson pointed at a pad of paper sitting on Colter's desk. After Colter handed it to him, he scribbled out a quick drawing. He bit his lip as he looked at it and decided it wasn't what he wanted, so he scratched it out and tried again.

Colter leaned over as he was finishing with the second attempt. "Is that…what is that?" He then answered his own question. "Wait! That's the emblem thing! From the beginning of the video call. I knew I'd seen it somewhere."

Greyson nodded as he shaded in the shape he'd drawn, then he tore the sheet out of the binder and held it up. "Does that look right? The emblem only flashed on the screen for just a second at the very beginning."

"I don't know, Grey. It just flashed on there, and I was so surprised by everything that I didn't even give it a great look."

"Fair enough."

"...But, I think that looks as close as we're gonna get."

"Good. Now, will you turn on your scanner?"

Colter reached over to the device beside his computer and pressed a button. It came to life with a quiet, mechanical whir. "There, but what for?"

Greyson stood. "I'm just gonna scan this in, convert it to a digital file, then cross-index an image search and—"

"Whoa, whoa, whoa. Forget I asked. Just do whatever you want to do and explain to me what you're trying to accomplish."

As Greyson laid his sketch on the surface of the scanner, he said, "I'm going to search the internet for this image."

"See, you definitely could have just said that." Colter stood, offering his chair. "You can sit here while you're doing your internet sleuthing."

"Thanks." Greyson set to work. As soon as he'd scanned the image and rendered a digital version of it, he began to run a search.

Click. The sound coming from over his shoulder sent him spinning around. Colter was holding up his phone, pointing it straight at Greyson.

Turning the screen to show the picture to Greyson, he explained, "This is for my socials. I was thinking of using 'Grey: on the way to save more babies' as the caption, but is that too on-the-nose?"

Greyson playfully rolled his eyes. "Don't let the fame get to you." Despite his words, he couldn't help but feel a twinge of pride that he was even making Colter's social media.

Colter had two distinct friend groups. One consisted of athletes and the more popular students at Pine High School. The other group was just Greyson. There was rarely any overlap between the two, and as far as Greyson was concerned, that was okay. But, especially considering that most of the high school didn't seem to understand how Colter and Greyson could even *be* such good friends, it was still nice to feel like Colter was bragging about their friendship.

Greyson turned his focus back to the task at hand. He pulled up the image-searching site, uploaded the file he'd created, and clicked *Search*.

"What do you think?" he asked Colter.

"I think the caption was too much. I changed it to—"

"No, about this. Are we gonna find…" Greyson trailed off as the results loaded onto his screen.

One matching result, read the search bar. There was a link underneath to QuickChat, a popular online discussion forum.

Reading the title of the post made Greyson's heart beat a bit faster: *Has anybody ever seen this shape? Seen in weird vid.* The author was @SKYguyWrestler. And then, accompanying the message, was an image. It was hand-drawn, with pencil on lined notebook paper.

It was just like his.

"Whoa..." Colter had noticed it too. "That's...wow. You're not the only one who's ever done this, apparently."

"Apparently not," Greyson answered, but his words were barely above a whisper. He was focusing on the images, leaning forward to get a good look at the one on the screen and comparing it against the one in his hand.

While the overall shape was about the same, there were a few differences in the detailing. Greyson's emblem was a little more precise, with sharper corners than the one from the internet. Greyson's also looked more like a turtle, which he suspected might not be in his best interest.

"Click on it, Grey," Colter coached. "Let's see the discussion."

The discussion. Greyson had grown so excited by the teaser that he'd almost forgotten to look if there even *was* a discussion thread, but he then read something that stirred his excitement even more.

Four Comments.

But, as soon as he clicked on the image, his stomach dropped. His computer opened to a blank screen plagued by a single message: *Sorry, that post is no longer available. For reasons why posts could be removed, click here.*

"Oh..." Colter sounded just as disappointed as Greyson felt. "I mean, at least we know somebody else has tried to learn more too, right?"

"Yeah," Greyson mumbled back, unable to mask his disappointment. His fingers began to fly across the keys again as he typed out a new search: "*John NINJA*"

As soon as he pressed the search button, he was rerouted to the page of a famous wrestler. Another suggestion pointed him to an attorney. Neither of them looked anything like the man in the video.

Refusing to give up, Greyson tried the search again, but this time with a different spelling of the name. He'd never seen it in writing, after all, so maybe he just needed to adjust.

Nothing. Absolutely nothing. No matter how he spelled the name and no matter how many keywords he included in the search, not a single useful result came up.

Finally, Greyson accepted defeat. "I just don't know, man. I figured we could find something. Can you name one thing you can't find online?"

"I…I don't know. No, honestly."

"Me either." Greyson stood, moving back to the bed and giving Colter his office chair back. Head in his hands, he sat on the edge of the bed and thought about everything. It was frustrating.

"Whatcha thinking?" Colter asked.

"That this is annoying."

"What's annoying? Our heroics getting noticed by a lot of people and attracting the attention of a mysterious organization?"

Greyson rolled his eyes at the sarcasm and pushed his hair out of his eyes again. "When you put it that way, it does sound pretty cool, actually. But not knowing is what is annoying."

"I think you're overthinking everything," Colter argued. "This is starting to sound like the opportunity of a lifetime. I say we go for it."

The familiar feeling was back—the rush in Greyson's chest. "You really want to do it? What about your mom?

What about…your football camp? I don't think your dad would let you miss that."

Colter shrugged. "My mom will understand—especially if we can learn more about this program. But my dad and Coach? Eh…we'll see." He laughed.

Greyson lowered his voice. "Yeah, but think about what your mom would think if she knew how mysterious everything has been. She's already overprotective, so I can't see her going for this."

"That's why we gotta learn more," Colter insisted. "Let's wait for the official invite and just see what happens, okay? My mom wouldn't say no to a full-ride scholarship opportunity, and think about how stoked my dad would be if I could go to college and walk-on at Iowa. Keep it in the family, you know?"

Greyson wasn't giving in quite that easy. As he spotted the furry lump sleeping in the corner of the room, he asked, "What about Max? I doubt my mom would remember to feed him."

Colter shook his head. "Eh, Max is at my house half the time, anyways. I bet Ty would love to feed him."

Silence hung in the air until Greyson finally asked, "You're serious, aren't you?"

"Dead serious. And didn't we just make a pact about this kind of thing yesterday? C'mon. What do you say?"

Greyson let out a long, nervous breath. "...Fine, let's do it."

Almost as soon as he said that, both of their phones vibrated. The boys looked at each other, holding their breaths.

Slowly, they picked up their phones.

Greyson couldn't believe what he was seeing. A new

email notification was at the top of his screen with an unmistakable message: *IMPORTANT: National Interdisciplinary Notable Juveniles Association application.*

Looking between his phone and his friend, he asked Colter, "Was yours…was yours from them?"

"Yeah. Yeah, it was."

"So, we're really doing this?"

"We're doing this."

FIVE

"So, sir, can you confirm whether or not you are recruiting us to join a top-secret government organization?" Colter broke the silence by cracking jokes with the courtesy driver who'd picked them up outside his house.

The driver was a muscular man wearing a cowboy hat. He turned and smiled from the front seat, a twinkle in his eye, before saying, "Just enjoy the ride. It could be quite a busy couple of months for you boys."

Colter leaned back, apparently unsure whether the driver was joking or not.

Greyson was leaning against the window, watching the trees whiz by and breathe a bit of personality into the otherwise flat, mundane roadside. This all felt like a dream.

About an hour earlier, he and Colter had been picked up in a slick, black truck driven by a very nice man who'd provided them with drinks from a minifridge built into the back of the truck.

It was a truck unlike any he'd ever seen, too. There were two bench seats in the back facing each other—almost like a limousine. Greyson and Colter were sitting opposite each other, and both of them were struggling not to look impressed.

When they'd agreed to participate, the follow-up email they'd received had made it easier to convince their parents it was a good opportunity. As Jon had mentioned, many companies affiliated with the NINJA program, including Kloud Technologies, were big-name companies and were all listed as references on a legit-looking website.

As soon as Colter and Greyson had shown the email and instructions to their parents, they were met with excitement. Mrs. Rickman had initially asked a few questions and had a call with somconc from the NINJA program, but she quickly came around and encouraged the boys to go. Greyson's mom was excited, too, but her excitement seemed to be for other reasons—having one less responsibility for the summer.

That was how they'd ended up here, being chauffeured toward what promised to be the summer adventure they'd been chasing.

From the front seat of the truck, the driver said, "I'm going to give you guys some privacy. Just let me know if you need anything. Press the red button."

"Gotcha, thanks," Colter answered.

"Also, make sure you're buckled up," the driver added. "We're about to go through some construction, so you might feel a little movement back there."

With that, a tinted pane of glass lifted between the seats, walling off the boys from the driver. As that happened, the windows of the truck began tinting as well. Soon the entire back seat section was shadowy and secluded. Greyson felt like a celebrity.

Immediately, Colter said, "This is freaking insane. We're in, like…the coolest truck of all time. A NINJA-mobile. I can't believe this is happening."

True to the driver's words, the truck jostled, bouncing both the boys around a bit more violently than Greyson had expected. He turned to the window behind him, only to see construction equipment and people hard at work.

As he watched, Greyson couldn't help but wonder if this was a very, very bad idea. He had felt that way all along—at least to an extent—but it hadn't really sunk in until now, as the plan was actually going into motion. According to the itinerary, this truck was en route to the airport, where he and Colter would catch a flight toward the small college that would be hosting them for the summer.

In some ways, everything seemed too good to be true. They would get hands-on experience with top companies, which would majorly bolster his resume even if there wasn't a scholarship at play. Greyson took a deep breath, filling his lungs with some sweet aroma that filled the air. He couldn't place the scent, but he liked it. It was…relaxing.

Again it felt like they were going through some turbulence, but a quick look out the window didn't show construction this time—just a normal road. Greyson leaned in for a closer look, and this time, under very careful inspection, he noticed something that made his stomach turn.

Pixels.

They were on the very outside edge of the windows: tiny dots of colored light just like what Greyson would see if he were to study a computer monitor up close.

He blinked, and they were gone.

He looked at the front seat, but the tinted glass was so dark he could only see the faint outline of the driver and nothing more.

Confused and alarmed, he turned to Colter, but just as he began to say something, Greyson's phone started vibrating in his pocket. He took it out to see a number he didn't recognize. *California*, according to the caller ID.

He let it ring.

"Who was that?" Colter asked.

"No idea. Unknown number. But hey, I noticed something that's kind of…I don't know. Look at you—"

Before he could finish, Colter's phone started ringing. He took it out of his pocket, studied it, and said, "California?"

"Hmm. I think that's who called me?" It was a half-question.

Colter asked, "Did they leave a voicemail?" The phone continued to ring.

"No."

"Then should I answer?"

"At this point, we might as well. Apparently, somebody wants to talk to us."

"Okay. I'll put it on speaker." Colter answered as professionally as he could. "Hello, this is Colter Rickman speaking."

There was a brief delay, then a second voice said, "Colter, very nice to meet you. Thanks for taking my call."

Greyson and Colter shared a glance. To Greyson, this voice sounded somewhat familiar, but he couldn't place who it was or where he'd heard it.

Colter answered, "Thanks, but can I ask who you are?"

"Oh, my apologies." This was accompanied by a good-spirited laugh. "I guess I don't make non-scheduled phone calls anymore. My form is slipping! My name is Nathaniel Coffman."

Greyson's eyes widened. He knew the voice sounded familiar, and with good reason.

Colter seemed equally surprised, but he didn't lose his tongue quite as badly as Greyson knew he would've. Instead, he said, "Mr. Coffman! Wow, um, it's incredibly nice to speak to you. You're a local legend, you know? Well, just a legend in general, by this point."

More good-spirited laughter filtered through the phone. "I appreciate that a lot, but we're just living in a time that favors tech-preneurs, you know what I mean?"

"I mean…honestly, no."

A door closed in the background of the call. "There were a lot of brilliant, disruptive innovators that came before me," Coffman continued, "but it wasn't until the dawn of the internet and social media that people like Musk, Bezos, Dorsey and others like myself have been 'celebrated.' When I was growing up, the media didn't give tech pioneers the same attention as, say, athletes, but that's really changed over the last decade or so."

"Oh, gotcha." Colter nodded, clearly lost in the conversation. "You definitely do make a lot of headlines, but here's my hot take: inventing things to make our lives easier is more important than scoring touchdowns, and that's coming from a life-long football player."

"You have a good head on your shoulders, my friend." Coffman replied. "So I've got to ask, do you know where your friend Greyson is, by any chance? I tried to call him a moment ago and I'd love to talk to you boys together, if possible. But if not—"

"He's right here," Colter interrupted. "Funny timing, we're actually headed toward a summer internship program that your company sponsors. Do you know about the NINJA program?"

"Oh yes, I know all about that. It's a very elite program that's kept pretty quiet and quite an honor to be selected, so congrats on that."

"We noticed," Colter said. "Good to know we're not the only ones who think that."

"Not at all," replied Coffman. "The NINJAs put a lot of effort into keeping their recruitment and training program pretty quiet. With good reason, of course, one being that they produce the most talented and sought-after individuals out of all of the programs we endorse, but that's neither here nor there. For now, would you mind putting me on speaker? I'd like to talk to you and Greyson, if possible."

"Yeah, hold on." Colter paused just long enough to pretend he didn't already have the call on speaker, then said, "Greyson, it's Nathaniel Coffman."

Greyson, suddenly thrust head-first into the conversation with one of his most-revered celebrities, stammered, "Hey…hey there. It's so nice to meet you, Mr. Coffman."

"Right back atcha, Greyson. Congrats on being selected for the NINJA program. That's quite an accomplishment."

"Thanks a lot," Greyson answered, trying to control his breathing. "We were excited when we found out your company was involved."

"Funny how that works out, no?" A chuckle came,

then he added, "I guess it's just an odd coincidence."

"Must be, but a fortunate one," Greyson replied.

There was just a moment of silence. "It's my honor to get to meet both of you," Coffman said. "I've been reading your names a lot and I appreciate you taking the time to connect."

Greyson, feeling a bit more confident, replied, "That's how I feel about meeting you, Mr. Coffman. I'm very tech-focused, and your work is inspirational." *Did that sound lame? How many times did Coffman hear that on a daily basis?*

"Please, call me Nathaniel. And really? That's great. You're a climber *and* an innovator. Can I ask what field you're interested in?"

"I'm trying to learn to code. I know Python, HTML and Javascript, but I'm more interested in coding at a macro level and all aspects of engineering. How I can use what I know to create disruptive technology, not build dashboards for a corporation, you know?"

"You don't say?" There was no mistaking the excitement in Coffman's voice. "You sound like a young version of myself…except for the part where you and your friend save civilians in need. When I was younger, I basically played on my computer all day." Another laugh.

"I'm nowhere near a Nathaniel Coffman, I promise. I'm just a self-taught dabbler who has watched more than his fair share of YouTube videos."

"That's how all the greats start these days, though." Coffman changed direction a bit, asking, "Since I've got you both together, I'd like to run an idea by you. Is that okay? Do you have a couple minutes?"

"We've got plenty of time," Colter answered, rejoining the conversation. "Fire away."

"Perfect. For starters, I want to say just how impressed I am by all the news I see coming out of Pine. When I first read the report, I couldn't believe it. But all the news outlets have basically told the same story."

"It's definitely hard to believe," Greyson said. "We're really fortunate. It all happened so fast. Things are finally settling back to normal."

"That's why I was calling, actually," Coffman interjected. "I wanted to ask what exactly is normal for you two?"

"What do you mean?" Colter asked.

"I mean...what do you usually do with your time during the summer. I know a bit about you now, Greyson. What about Colter?"

Colter bit his lip, and Greyson could tell his friend was struggling to think of something he did in his free time that wasn't football-related. Finally, he answered, "I...I'm an All-American on my football team—the first in my school's history, actually." Then, as a sort of second thought, he added, "I also like to study film, and Greyson's teaching me more about rock climbing."

Study film? Greyson held back a chuckle when he realized Colter had to be talking about binge-watching Netflix.

Coffman, however, seemed impressed. "Film, you say? There's a lot of high-growth opportunities for a man who's good with a camera, from ads to production."

"Oh, I know," Colter riffed off the comment. "Lots of money in advertising these days." It sounded exactly like something his father would say.

Coffman didn't seem to notice the inauthenticity.

Instead, he only grew more interested. "Advertising is booming." There was a crackle of static, then he continued. "First, let me back up a bit. I am beyond excited you're taking part in the NINJA program. I'm not sure how much you've heard about the program's structure thus far—"

"Not much, except what was in the official emails and website," Greyson said.

"I'm not surprised, but I know the recruits work with the NINJA mentors for a few weeks, and then the program ends by pairing the recruits with a high-growth company for the hands-on work portion."

"That sounds great," Colter said. "We got some paperwork that said something like that, but it was all very vague."

"That seems to be how the NINJAs operate," Coffman answered matter-of-factly. "I know there are a lot of details to be ironed out, but I wanted to reach out early and get to know you two boys, then ask if you'd consider requesting Kloud as your high-growth partner for the second phase of the program."

Greyson and Colter exchanged a look of excitement.

Coffman went on. "I would actually think of it more as an apprenticeship where you would do some work with me personally along with the other leadership teams at Kloud. That's what I wanted to call and tell you guys about. And I can't guarantee that you'd be the two recruits chosen, but let's just say I could call you two 'preferred applicants'."

Colter wasn't one to beat around the bush. "So you're basically saying it's ours if we want it?"

Coffman chuckled again. "Let's just say this…Pine

made me who I am, and I'd love to give back to my town by investing some time and knowledge in the leaders—and heroes—of tomorrow."

The increasingly more familiar feeling of *this can't be real life* crept over Greyson as he fumbled for words. "That's…wow. That's amazing. Thank you so much, Mr…*um,* Nathaniel."

"Don't thank me," Coffman dismissed. "Seriously, it's the least I can do after what you boys have done. And, to be honest, you already sound like the perfect applicants. Greyson, you'd be interested in learning from our development team, and I think Colter might find a home in the advertising sector of the internship."

"That sounds amazing," Colter said.

"When would all this take place?" Greyson asked. "Like I said, we really don't have a feel for the timeline yet. We just know we'll be away from home for eight weeks." His head was spinning. It felt like each moment brought new surprises.

"I think it will be about a month from now, but just focus on this NINJA program to start," Coffman replied. "I'll poke around, so be on the lookout for more details coming soon. More than anything, I just wanted to reach out, make your acquaintance and give my thanks for helping keep Pine safe."

"That means a lot," Greyson answered.

"You bet. Now I have a meeting coming up, so I better jet, but I hope to meet you in person soon. You have my number now—call if you need anything. Goodbye, for now!"

"Bye-bye," Colter answered. The line clicked off.

Greyson's mouth hung agape. "Did you…did you

hear that? Nathaniel Coffman just told us we could call him. Like *anytime*. Us."

"I know! Can you imagine what it would be like to spend weeks as his apprentice at Kloud headquarters? Everybody would be so jealous. I've heard they have a zero-gravity tank and nap-pods." Colter had quickly pivoted from playing it cool to speaking rapid-fire.

"And think about everything we could learn."

"I mean, yeah, there's that, too."

They both laughed.

Still jittery with excitement, Greyson took out his phone and opened his GPS. The screen loaded, but it was wrong. He refreshed it.

It loaded again, and he knew it was wrong…but it showed the same thing.

Colter must have seen the look on his face because he asked, "Grey, what's the matter?"

"We're…we're entering Minnesota."

"What? No way. That's…" Colter took his phone back out.. "That's not possible. We've only been driving for about an hour. Maybe 90 minutes, at most—not *four* hours."

"Check your phone."

As he did, Colter looked confused. "Mine says 'signal not available'?"

Greyson glanced back at his phone to see 'signal lost' as well.

There was a beep, and over the intercom, the driver's voice calmly instructed, "You boys should relax a bit. You can play some video games on the console under the rear seat. Orientation will be here before you know it."

SIX

"You boys gonna sleep all day?"

Greyson's eyes cracked open. "Huh?" he mumbled groggily.

The voice of the courtesy driver swam up through the foggy lake of coherence. "We're here."

Greyson sat up and blinked against the bright light flooding into the truck as Colter stirred beside him. "Wow, I was out. I must have slept hard."

"You both did," the driver responded with a light chuckle. "One minute, y'all were playing video games, and the next, you were passed out. But I can't blame you. I love to sleep on car rides, too."

As Colter unbuckled, he asked, "What next? Where do we go?"

The driver pointed out the window. "We'll get your belongings out of the back, and then you'll head to that hangar."

"Hangar?" Greyson also unbuckled, peering out the window to take in his surroundings.

It was nothing like he expected. They were in a large parking lot with hundreds of spaces, currently occupied by only a few shuttle trucks, similar to the one they were in.

Casting a shadow over the lot was the largest building Greyson had ever seen. Its exterior was a sad gray that had probably been a pearly white when it was first built. The hangar looked old with lots of brick and large steel beams, and it couldn't have been simpler in design, either. While it definitely didn't have any bells or whistles to make it visually eye-catching, it was gigantic, seeming larger than any football stadium Greyson had ever seen.

"What…what is that?" he asked.

"An old aircraft hangar used last during World War II," their driver explained.

"I thought we were flying to, like…a campus? Dorms? Something?"

The driver let out another chuckle. It was the 'if only you knew' sort of laugh, but good-natured. "I won't be the one to explain, but you'll figure everything out soon, I promise. So let's get your bags out and I'll send you on your way."

After they got out of the truck and the driver unloaded their suitcases, they were left standing in the middle of the giant parking lot, which was filling up with more confused teenagers as their shuttles drove away.

Greyson couldn't silence the thousands of questions pinballing around in his head. *Was he making a mistake? Had he bitten off more than he could chew?*

"Have you ever seen those TV shows with a ghost plane?" Colter suddenly said. "Like the lost planes that are always in crappy shape?"

Greyson nodded. "Yeah."

"This has to be where they park. I mean, look at this

place. The building seriously looks like it's tired of being a building."

Greyson was too deep in thought to get heavily involved in the conversation. "That's actually a really good way to put it."

"Let's go check it out." Colter began wheeling his bag across the cracked parking lot. "Everybody else is."

He was right. While none of them looked confident, all of the teenagers around them were taking their bags toward the hangar.

Before they ever made it ten paces, a third voice called from behind them, "Hi there!"

Greyson and Colter stopped and turned around.

That's when Greyson saw her.

The girl approaching them was one of the most beautiful creatures that he had ever seen. Her bright, blue eyes and her friendly smile made his heart beat double-time, and the way her curly red hair bobbed at her shoulders as she walked with a confident-but-cute stride made his brain screech to a halt.

Colter was somehow unfazed by the girl's magic spell. "Hey, what's up?" he greeted her.

"Just carrying my luggage toward a mysterious hangar," the girl answered as she approached. "So I've got to ask...are you two just as confused as me?"

Colter laughed. "Yeah, we have no idea what's going on either."

Greyson finally found his tongue. "I thought we were headed to campus. The NINJA camp, you know?"

"Same here!" The girl's voice bubbled with enthusiasm. "I definitely wasn't picturing an ax-murderer hangar."

Greyson grinned.

"What's your name?" Colter asked. "I'm Colter, and this is Grey."

"Grey, did you say?"

"Yeah, Greyson," Greyson affirmed. "He's the only one that really calls me Grey."

"Can I call you Grey, too? I really like that." She flashed a slightly-nervous smile. "I'm Macie."

Was this girl–Macie–flirting with him? What was happening?

Colter had apparently picked up on the same thing, because he stepped up to play wingman. "Grey and Mace. Sounds good together—you two could be friends. What about you, Grey? Whatcha think?"

"Um…" Why was this so hard? Why couldn't Greyson figure out what to say?

Macie looked at him, expectantly.

And when Greyson finally managed to speak, he immediately regretted it. "Yeah. It sounds good together because of assonance. That's what they call it when words sound the same based on vowel sounds."

As the words spilled out of his mouth, he hated himself with a burning passion. With everything he could have possibly said, *that's* what he'd said? Why couldn't he play it cool? Why couldn't he be more like Colter around a cute girl? Why was he better geared for *Jeopardy!* than a date?

Despite all of this, somehow, Macie laughed again. And it wasn't a sympathetic or fake type of laugh, either. It was a legitimate, cute laugh. "Are we *all* like this?"

"Like…what?"

"Nerds," she said. "No offense, but like…*assonance*?

You're clearly book-smart."

"Wait, you're a nerd, too?" Colter asked with obvious surprise.

"I mean, I might be a different kind of a nerd, but yeah. I love science."

"Science?" This caught Greyson's attention. "I'm actually more into science myself. What do you like to focus on?"

"A little bit of everything. I actually just won the Great Lakes Ecology for a Difference contest for my water-purification project."

Colter offered the slightest of smirks."Yeah, you guys really need to get to know each other. Honestly, I would have guessed you're more likely to be a star athlete than a scientist. No offense."

Macie arched an eyebrow and shot him a look. "Who says I can't be both? All-district volleyball *and* led the state in kills…as a sophomore."

"Okay, I see you." Colter was obviously impressed now, too, and that usually took quite a lot. "If the NINJAs are looking to build a team of super-nerds, I'll be the first one out. I just play football."

"You get straight A's, too," Greyson objected.

"Only because you teach me all that stuff!"

"Point is, don't sell yourself short. You can be smart *and* a good football player."

"Yeah, yeah," Colter dismissed. "Like I've never heard you say that before."

Greyson looked around, noticing that most of the teenagers had passed them by while they were talking in the parking lot. On top of that, the stream of trucks had finally run dry. He looked around, trying to estimate the number of teenagers. There were probably fifty to sixty. Seventy, tops.

A distant rumbling coming from the hangar caught Greyson's attention. As he fixed his eyes on the tremendous building, he spotted a small gap between the two giant hangar doors and quickly realized that the space was growing wider.

The doors were opening—moving so slowly that it was almost imperceptible, but they were opening nonetheless.

The rest of the group was nervously filtering toward the doors.

"I think…I think that's our cue." Greyson looked at Colter. "Do we just…walk in?"

"Let's do it. Are you going with us, Macie?"

Macie nodded. "Definitely."

And with that, they began making their way across the parking lot.

As Greyson walked, he couldn't help but feel grateful that Colter was with him. As far as he could tell, everybody else had arrived on their own.

They reached the hangar door at about the same time it finished opening. The rumble died down, and an eerie silence overtook them as Greyson scanned the scene before him, trying to make sense of everything.

A line was forming in front of a scanner—the airport security kind. But, unlike at an airport, the teenagers were carrying their bags right through it. As each one passed through the gate, a bright blue light flashed overhead.

Most of the rest of the hangar was hidden from view. A thick, dark curtain draped down from the ceiling just a short ways behind the scanner. Between the curtain and the scanner was a terminal, which looked sort of like an ATM, but smaller.

One man was sitting behind a table beside the scanner, directing traffic. Colter pointed and leaned over to Greyson, asking, "Hey, that's N.J.."

Greyson spotted the man. "Gotcha." As they stood in line, he turned towards Macie. "See the guy at the table? Do you recognize him?"

Macie leaned over to look, then shook her head. "Should I?"

"Not really. I just wondered if he was the guy who made your invitation call."

"No. Definitely not."

He nodded. "Mine was with a guy named Jon, but N.J.—the dude behind the table—he's the one who called Colter."

Again, she shook her head. "Mine wasn't with a 'guy' at all. I talked to this very athletic-looking black woman. Super pretty, and had a voice where you can tell she'd be a great singer, y'know? Her name was Meg."

They shuffled a few steps forward as the line continued slipping through the scanner terminal.

"Did you hear that, Colter?" Greyson asked.

"Yeah," Colter replied. "I wonder how many people made the calls."

"No telling."

Before much longer, they were at the table. Colter was up first, and N.J. checked a box off a list as he greeted them. "Colter Rickman, so glad you could join us. Step right through here."

"Do you want my phone or bag or—"

"No, sir." N.J. shook his head. "You can keep all your

belongings on you. Stop at the terminal before going through the curtain."

Colter shrugged and slipped forward. Greyson was next up.

"Greyson McEntire," N.J. greeted, once again checking a box on his list. "Welcome to the NINJA course. Step right through, please."

"Course?" Greyson asked as he passed through the security gate. A blue light flashed once again. For just a moment, it dazed him. It was brighter than he expected, but he couldn't spot its source. In addition to the flash, a two-toned sound buzzed in his ear. It was a high-frequency, sort of like a dog whistle, and it knifed right through his skull.

Taken by surprise, he rubbed one of his ears as he asked, "What are you scanning us for?"

N.J. smiled cooly. "Just taking attendance. I'm sure all your questions will be answered right through there." He pointed toward a dark curtain a bit beside them. "But before you go in, please be sure to stop at the terminal. You'll answer a simple question—no pressure either way."

That was even more confusing. Greyson was the kind of person always seeking answers…not more questions. Nevertheless, he felt the pressure to move on and reluctantly exited the line.

Colter was already at the terminal, and as he read the screen, he ran his hand through his hair. Even from behind him, Greyson could tell he was confused.

"What's it say?" Greyson asked as Colter tapped a button on the screen.

"Um… something that doesn't make much sense."

Greyson stepped up, facing the terminal. There was

a screen about the same size as a standard tablet, and one word flashed across it: *Detecting.*

Then, after a few seconds, another message: *Welcome, Greyson McEntire.* The text went away after a moment, only to be replaced by a short question: *If you are dismissed or choose to leave, would you like to: A) go home or B) continue on to the internship program.* Each of the options had a button to press on the screen.

"Wait, what?" Greyson asked the question aloud.

"That doesn't make any sense to me," Colter said.

"I get the going home part, but the other part is what gets me. If we get dismissed, how would we continue with the internship program?"

"That's what I'm saying, too… that seems…contradictory. Right?"

"Yes. But what did you answer?"

"I said I wanted to continue. Maybe it's a typo or something."

Greyson hesitantly pressed the same button as his friend just as Macie reached the kiosk. While she was busy looking at the screen, he told Colter, "Something's off, here."

"What do you mean?"

"Well, this is nothing like I was expecting. Like… why the hangar? And like…the car ride. Something was off with that—"

Macie's voice interrupted them. "Did you guys read the terminal? I'm confused. How could we continue with the internship if we are dismissed?"

"That's what we were just talking about," Greyson answered as she pressed a button and joined them. "And hey, did you notice anything strange about the ride here?"

"The ride? No. I just started watching some TV on the fancy screen in the truck and fell right asleep. The driver woke me up when we arrived."

"That's...uh...that's what happened to us, too," Colter said, sounding at least slightly uneasy. "How about we head to the back and see if we can figure out what's going on here."

Greyson nodded. "That sounds like a very good idea. We need some answers."

Together, they slipped around the curtain, entering a slightly larger room than the first. Except, this wasn't a "room" either. It was an open area of floor surrounded on all sides by more of the black curtain. In the middle of the floor were about a hundred foldable chairs, all facing a very small podium that was elevated by a short stage.

Hardly anybody was sitting down. Instead, most of the teenagers were standing on the open floor behind the chairs. Some were on their phones, but others were mingling. As Greyson and his friends made their way toward the chairs, he heard snippets of various conversations.

"I don't understand why we're here..."

"Did the question on the screen out there make any sense?"

"You recognized him? I haven't even seen the lady from my video."

One particular comment caught Greyson's attention: "I tried to reverse image search the emblem from the video, but my post was taken down almost immediately."

Greyson spun around to find the boy who'd said this and he spotted a small, African-American boy with wire-framed glasses matching his slight frame. The boy was talking to a Latino girl who was at least six inches taller than him—and maybe even a couple of inches taller than Greyson.

Greyson said, "Hey guys, sorry to butt in, but I overheard what you were saying, and...well, I tried the same thing as you."

The boy raised his eyebrows. "You did?"

"Yeah, are you..." Greyson thought back for a moment, "...are you SKYguywrestler? I saw your post."

The boy's face flickered with recognition. "Yeah, that's me. Skylar." He extended his hand, which Greyson shook.

Colter asked, "You're a wrestler?" Despite his best efforts, he couldn't keep the obvious doubt out of his voice as he took in the boy's small stature.

"State champ, believe it or not," Skylar said. "There are weight classes, you know?"

"Fair enough," Colter said. "And congrats. I'm Colter. This is Greyson and Macie."

The friends waved, and the tall Latino girl said, "I'm Kenzi."

As the introductions wrapped up, Greyson was anxious to get back to his conversation with Skylar. "So you posted the picture of the emblem online?"

Skylar nodded.

"How long was it on there?"

"Gee, I don't know." Skylar shrugged. "Couldn't have been more than six hours. It was reported and pulled down fast."

"Did you get an email? What was the reason for pulling it?"

Skylar made the "one second" gesture as he took out his phone and began to scroll through it. After a moment, he read, "Your post has been removed from the QuickChat platform. We're sorry for any inconvenience. Thanks for chatting!"

The words sank in, and Macie jumped in. "That's a terrible explanation. That didn't even...explain."

"Exactly," Skylar agreed. "I pulled up the terms and policies to see what I could have violated, and it's all things you'd expect...no racism, inappropriate images, or violence. The sort of things that I don't even want to see. But this...I don't know. This doesn't violate any of the rules."

Greyson nodded. "I looked at the policy statement too. It doesn't make sense why the image was flagged and beyond that, why it was pulled after review. You know what it makes me think?"

"That somebody is working really hard to keep their business off a chat forum," Colter said.

"But you all saw the NINJA website, right?" Kenzi asked. "My parents went over it before agreeing I could come."

Greyson nodded. "Yeah, same here. But it looked way different. I never even saw the emblem, logo-thing on that site. It felt more like...I don't know. A college? Kinda like a cover."

Everybody else nodded in agreement.

"So what does that mean for us?" Kenzi asked. "If these people are actively trying to discourage online discussion, isn't that...um, worrisome?"

She said the exact thing Greyson was thinking, but instead of affirming her question, he tried to be optimistic. "It could, or it could mean they're doing something so important that they want to control what's said."

"How will we know?" Colter asked.

As if on cue, a voice crackled through a loudspeaker from the direction of the stage. "Ladies and gentlemen, would you mind taking a seat? There's a lot to discuss before we begin, so we better start now."

Greyson peered through the crowd, and there, standing behind the podium, was a face he recognized.

Jon.

The man looked just as friendly in person, with a warm smile and intelligent eyes. Greyson leaned over to Colter, whispering, "This is how."

SEVEN

Greyson, Colter, and their new friends took a seat in the middle of the audience. They were close enough to the stage to seem interested, but far enough away to not seem like a teacher's pet. Jon didn't appear to be too worried about where everybody sat, though. He was more engaged with the people joining him on stage.

They came from behind the curtain, one after another, until there were six people total. Of them, Greyson knew both Jon and N.J., and he also spotted an African-American woman, who he guessed had been the person who'd invited Macie. There was also a dark-haired woman who was an eye-catching mixture of thin and muscular, and a man with tattoo sleeves on both arms and neon-green hair.

However, the sixth and final man caught Greyson's attention perhaps the most. While most of the people on the stage were dressed in athletic clothes, he wore blue jeans and a cowboy hat. And shadowed under the brim of the hat was a face that Greyson recognized after a puzzled moment.

"Hey, Colt, is that our driver?"

"Who?" Colter leaned over and whispered back, "Oh! The cowboy up there standing by The Joker? Yeah, I think it is. Who *are* all these people?"

"Hopefully, they'll tell us."

They didn't have to wait long. As a confused silence befell the crowd, Jon leaned into the microphone and began to speak. "Thank you all for joining us. We promise this is going to be a fun, beneficial summer where you'll learn a lot of valuable things. I hope you're all excited!"

No response came from the audience. No heads nodded. Nothing. Just a lot of confused stares directed right at the six people on the stage.

Jon was unfazed. He went on, "My name is Jon, and I'm going to be one of the coaches working with you. There are more NINJAs back at headquarters, but today I'm joined by quite an impressive lineup. From left to right, this is N.J., Jamee, Lane, Meg, and Jess."

Greyson tracked the line of people with his eyes as Jon introduced them. Jamee was the green-haired man with tattoos, Lenny was the cowboy, and Jess was the dark-haired woman. And, as he watched them, another thought came to him: if he wouldn't have known better, everybody on the stage could've been a professional athlete.

They all looked incredibly athletic. While Lenny and Jamee looked more like they could be linebackers than the more thin, wiry people standing alongside them on stage, they were all muscular and fit in their own, unique ways.

Greyson pointed this out, whispering to Macie and Colter, "Why do they all look like CrossFit champs?"

His friends shrugged.

Jon went on. "We have a lot of ground to cover, and I'll do everything I can to answer your questions this morning, but the ones I don't answer, we'll cover later. Does that sound fair?"

Finally, a few heads nodded in the audience.

"Good. So…where to begin?" He shifted his weight, and for half a second, Jon looked concerned, like he was a doctor about to deliver bad news. "You all are aware that you have been selected as participants in our NINJA program, which recognizes students who achieve excellence in both sports and academics. Is that correct?"

Everyone nodded, but for Greyson, this was the first time he'd ever heard the word "sports" used in regard to the applicants. As far as he knew, he was here because he was smart. But being smart *and* athletic? For some reason, that made him feel even better— especially after meeting everybody else in the room, who all seemed to be a state champion at a much more 'traditional' sport than his own.

These NINJA people recognized rock climbing as a sport. In their eyes, he fit in.

"All the communication we've sent out—to you, to your parents, and to the companies we work with—is all very true," Jon added. "But, as you're aware, it's also been pretty vague thus far regarding the nature of our program. You'll be on a four-week-long retreat with the NINJAS, and then you'll be assigned to a tech partner for another four-week program that will better prepare you for the future and will connect you to some of the most innovative companies in the world. But…"

The same pensive look came across his face again. He glanced down the line of people beside him—the ones he'd called mentors—and Meg nodded at him with an encouraging smile.

"...But that's not where this story ends," he finally said. He spoke like he was trying very hard to select the right words as he went on. "My organization is a secretive group that uses advanced technology and physical skills to help protect people. Kind of like..." He trailed off again.

From the stage, Jamee offered, "The FBI?"

N.J., only a half-second later, said, "The Avengers?"

Jon couldn't help but laugh. "Let's just say we're somewhere between the two. We only recruit the brightest and most gifted people in the world, and in fact, you are the first group of teenagers to ever be invited. If you pass our trials, you'll earn your membership to our organization. A membership that can be revoked at any time, mind you, if you fail to meet any requirement or violate the policies."

This sent a buzz through the crowd of teenagers. They were all looking around, whispering to one another. From all around him, Greyson picked up bits of concern.

"Is he serious?"

"A membership?"

"Is this a cult? What's going on?"

Jon put an end to it as quickly as he could. "Please don't be worried. I assure you that we *are* the 'good guys' in this story, despite any doubts you may have. I know we haven't been entirely transparent to this point, but only because of the importance and nature of our group."

There was something in Jon's voice—the way his words seemed like a desperate, honest plea—that spread comfort through the room. Greyson was typically very good at reading people, and Jon seemed like a very good, very honest guy who was telling the truth, no matter how crazy it sounded.

At least, that's how he felt until Jon carried on. After adjusting the microphone a bit, he said, "Here's how this is going to work. Today is what we call 'trial one.' Basically, while we've gone to great lengths to make sure we've recruited a collection of both athletic and academic applicants, the athleticism is hard to prove. That's why we've designed a skill-based competition in this hangar, which all of you will participate in."

Colter and Greyson exchanged a look.

Jon didn't give them time to gossip. "This is the part that will be slightly upsetting to hear, but it's something we couldn't explain until you arrived. If you pass the test, you'll be taken to our training grounds, where you'll take part in the most advanced mentorship program on the planet, learning new skills and more about our organization. If you do not pass, you'll be taken to an amazing STEM summer camp that you'll study at for four weeks before transitioning to a four-week internship at a high-growth company with which we're partnered. You'll be given a list."

As the words sank in, Jon added, "Either way, you'll learn for four weeks and then partner with a company for four. The nature of the partnership, however, will be a bit different."

Some concerned chatter rippled across the room.

Jon held up a hand, silencing everybody. "Don't worry," he said. "Even if you fail to qualify on our course today, you'll be getting the STEM camp experience that is technically what you signed up for in the first place. And, of course, you can choose to go home at any time, which we will arrange to happen."

Once again, no response. The teenagers didn't seem as upset, just...confused. Greyson was feeling the exact same way. A thousand questions were churning around in his brain.

Jon continued on. "We will get started with the testing very soon, but first, you need to learn about the rules. To explain that, I'm going to ask N.J. to take the mic."

With that, Jon and N.J. switched places. N.J. had a serious face, but when he offered a faint smile to the room, Greyson felt a bit better about the situation.

N.J. started with a forced laugh. "You probably are all wondering why we asked you to wear athletic clothes, right?"

That triggered a series of heads nodding from all around the room.

"That's the fun part. You're all going to take part in a trial. We've set up an obstacle course in this hangar just on the other side of this curtain. One by one, you'll be invited to go behind the curtain and take on the obstacle course, which consists of a blend of strength, speed, and balance obstacles. If you can complete the obstacle course in under five minutes without falling into the water, you'll automatically move on to the next phase of training, and eventually, the next trial."

Deep inside Greyson's chest, he felt his heartbeat quicken. He could feel something stirring...

Excitement.

It was the nervous kind, but exciting nonetheless. And he wasn't the only one feeling it either. Colter leaned close to him and said, "An obstacle course? That sounds awesome."

Greyson nodded, locked in on N.J.'s words as he explained. "The rules are very simple: *do not fall into the water.* While you are all athletes, I'd imagine none of you have experience on an obstacle course of this nature. You're going to have to adjust and learn on the fly. It will take some creativity."

Looking around the room, Greyson could tell the mood had changed once again. Any confusion or worry had been replaced by competitive fire. N.J. had said this himself: all these teenagers were athletes. They all wanted to win—it was in their nature.

And for Greyson, this competition represented something else. At his school in Pine, rock climbing was not celebrated. He might be the most decorated athlete in the entire school, but most of Greyson's classmates had no idea he even climbed. They only cared about "real sports."

Today, according to N.J., he'd compete against all the "real" athletes and show them what he could do. A level playing field. No excuses.

Just how he liked it.

N.J. went on. "There are seventy-two of you in attendance, and to be honest, we have no idea how many will automatically advance through the trials. It might be seventy-two. It might be zero. But we will be taking the top thirty recruits, so even if you fail, if you make it far enough fast enough your life will be forever changed. That's something you can count on."

Macie was sitting to Greyson's left, and for the first time since they'd sat down, she spoke, "This…this is insane."

He didn't respond. This time, it wasn't because his brain had iced over in her presence. No, this was even worse.

He had no idea what to say.

All he could think was how correct she was. Just half an hour ago, he'd been expecting to be going to a camp with his best friend where he'd learn about technology and science. Now, at least from the sounds of it, he was doing nothing of the sort.

And yet, he was totally on board with it.

"To echo something Jon mentioned earlier…" N.J. continued, "...remember that if you do not pass the course, you'll be headed to a prestigious STEM camp, just as advertised, and then partnered with a major tech company for your internship. I say that because I want to emphasize that you should not feel pressured—this is truly a win-win situation."

Going from serious to smiling again, N.J. leaned into the mic, looked over at the teenagers, and said, "one question left to ask…shall we begin?"

EIGHT

"We have a lot to get through, so let's not kill any more time," Jon said. "We'll go one by one. When we read your name, just head through there." He pointed to a space in the curtains. "Jamee will get things started."

Jamee unfolded a piece of paper. "First up, Mr. Colter Rickman. Marren Littlefield is on deck. Tyler Edwards in the hole."

Colter gave Greyson a look, eyebrows raised and clearly not ready. He voiced his displeasure, asking, "So, like…do I get to stretch or something? Get a sweat going?"

Jamee nodded. "Yeah, you'll have time for that. I'd advise all of you guys to get some sort of warm-up going, honestly, if that's your style. I'll announce the next three up at all times, so you should have a solid twenty minutes to prepare."

Greyson saw something on Colter's face he hadn't seen in a long time: nerves. Colter was usually level-headed and cool, especially during a competition, but he looked much different this time. His normal confidence was absent.

Greyson couldn't blame him. The whole thing had all happened so fast. One moment he was expecting one thing, and the next, he'd been thrust into something else.

"Wish me luck, brother," Colter whispered. "I guess I'll see you on the other side?"

"Yeah," Greyson nodded. "You got this. There's no obstacle course that can stop you."

Colter grinned, and somewhere behind the forced smile, Greyson spied just a flash of the confidence he was used to seeing. "Thanks, Grey."

"See you on the other side."

Colter walked toward the back, and most of the coaches from the stage joined him. Soon, Jess and Jamee were the only two left.

Once Colter and the rest of the coaches were gone, Macie asked, "Okay, what are you thinking?"

"About?"

"Everything."

"I'm thinking I wish I was watching Colter right now. Will I even know how well he does?"

Macie shrugged apologetically. "Honestly, I don't know."

"I'm also thinking this has to make more sense soon…" Greyson added, "...or I'm *really* gonna regret my new summer plans."

To that, Macie nodded emphatically. "That's the most accurate thing I've heard all day. I don't know *what's* going on, but I need some answers."

"Let's go get some, then."

"What do you mean?"

Greyson stood. "Let's go talk to the guy in charge."

Macie followed him to the front of the room, where Jamee was sitting on the edge of the stage and making small talk with Jess.

Greyson felt all eyes on him, but he didn't let that slow him down. "Hey, can you guys tell me what's going on?"

Both Jess and Jamee greeted him with friendly expressions, but neither of them immediately replied. Then, after a moment, Jamee said, "Well, all of you teens are gonna give our obstacle course a run, and based on how that goes, you're going to one of two locations for summer camp." He spoke the words like Greyson hadn't been in the room when it had first been explained.

Greyson shook his head. "Not what I meant. I heard all that, but like, what is going on? What's *really* going on here?"

Now, Jamee and Jess shared a look. It wasn't an annoyed look, and it wasn't an uncertain look, either. It was…deliberation.

Finally, Jess said, "There's only so much we can really say for now, but I'll be happy to answer any specific questions you may have to the best of my—"

Boop, boop, beep! She was cut off by a series of loud beeping noises coming from behind the curtain. Each one was a bit higher-pitched than the last.

"Sorry," she apologized. "I'll answer any question you have to the best of my ability. Sound fair?"

"We're not trying to keep you in the dark," Jamee added. "We'll be as straight-shooting as we can as soon as we can. Promise."

Greyson reluctantly nodded. "First, why can't you say much? If this is a STEM camp, why the secrecy?"

Jamee fielded his question. "That's the nature of high-level STEM, is it not? You're a computer wizard, correct, Greyson?"

"I know a thing or two."

"I thought so. So consider this: when it comes to science, tech, engineering, and mathematics, the companies doing it at the highest level don't publicly share what's going on within the company, so the competitors can't learn. That's why they have press conferences: to make big sweeping announcements of all the internal secrets. We're producing the most highly wanted recruits, so why would we want others to know our process?"

As much as Greyson wanted to rebut, he didn't. It was a good answer—as good of one as he could have possibly hoped. Even Macie, who'd matched his skepticism, was nodding slightly.

"Okay, fair," he said. "But next up: why the obstacle course? If this is a STEM camp, like you're saying, physical skills seem irrelevant, don't they? Something tells me Steve Jobs didn't require his engineers to do ten pull-ups before they checked into work."

With this question, neither Jess nor Jamee offered an immediate response, but after a moment of deliberation, Jess answered, "Your physical skills will determine the role you play. *Everybody* here is getting an awesome opportunity this summer. Those who are best equipped for a more physically demanding role, however, will be seeing a slightly different opportunity than those who aren't."

"I don't think you really answered the question."

"Just put it this way: the ones who do the best on the course will be ambassadors for the NINJA program, basically," Jamee said. "That's about as much as we can say for now."

"Okay, fine. Who do you work for?"

Jess huffed out a laugh., "You ask the big questions."

"And you said you'd try to answer them, right?"

"We work for the NINJA organization," Jamee said.

"I mean, I get that. But who is that? Are you with the government? Are you a tech group?"

"Yeah, we're a tech group," Jess agreed, but the way she said it made Greyson regret giving her the options—like they were a tech group, but they weren't really.

"No government ties?" he asked. "Because you're really giving some pretty strong secret-agent spy group vibes."

At this, both Jamee and Jess laughed. It was a real laugh too, not the forced type. "We are not a government agency," Jamee answered, and the definitiveness of his statement actually surprised Greyson.

"You're not? I thought—"

Before he could finish, a radio crackled to life. "Jamee, you there?" Jamee reached into his pocket and pulled out the radio.

"I'm here."

"Perfect," N.J.'s voice said from the other end of the line. "Next up."

"One sec." Jamee turned off the radio, gestured for Greyson to wait, then called out, "Marren Littlefield, please proceed back. Tyler Edwards on deck. Macie Adkins in the hole."

"Me?" Macie asked.

"You're Macie Adkins?"

She nodded.

"Then yes, ma'am. If you want to start warming up,

this would be a great time."

"First, answer Grey's question." Macie wasn't playing around. Greyson liked her even more.

Jess stepped in and said, "What Jamee was saying is that we're not a government agency, but we have a lot in common with them, at least in goals. We protect people using advanced technology and communication. That's really all we can say right now, but you'll learn more soon enough. I promise."

Greyson could tell that that was as much as he was going to get, but it was also enough. "Thanks," he said. He meant it, but he was also frustrated. Colter was already gone, and now Macie would be soon too. More and more, he was feeling alone—and that was coming from somebody who spent a large portion of his life by himself.

He missed Max. If only he could have brought his dog.

Greyson and Macie walked back to their seats, but Macie didn't sit down. Instead, she said, "I guess if I'm about to do this course or whatever, I better get ready."

Greyson nodded. "Yeah, warm up. It's just hard to prepare for what we can't expect."

"Exactly my thoughts."

And yet, Macie prepared. Or, at least, she seemed to do everything she could. She jogged, she stretched, she did high-knees and even a few pushups, and as soon as she'd finished the routine, she was being paged to the back.

Soon, Greyson was on his own. He thought about trying to make some friends, but he wasn't up for it. He had too many questions to sort out in his own head.

And it stayed that way, too. Greyson sat in his chair, bent forward with his chin in his hands, and he remained deep in thought as one by one, person after person, was called back. Names were read off the list, and as he listened, he recognized a couple, but there was one name, in particular, he never heard.

His own.

He watched the minutes tick by on his watch. A quarter-hour turned to a half, which turned into a full hour, and eventually, three of them.

Where was Colter? Where was Macie? By this point, Greyson was interested in continuing his conversation with Skylar, but the wrestler had been called backstage nearly ninety minutes ago.

The beeping was driving him crazy, too. Beeping and honks. Every ten minutes or so, he'd hear the familiar *boop, boop, beep* from just on the other side of the curtain ahead of him, and breaking the monotony of that sound was another one, an irritating honk: *Bwwaa!*

The noises were about the only thing left breaking up the deafening silence, and that alone made them maddening.

At one point, Greyson had looked for his bags. He wanted his headphones—a podcast sure would have been a nice escape from all this—but his belongings were nowhere to be found. He'd checked them at the front, and had regretted it ever since.

He took out his phone, too, tempted to text Mrs. Rickmanand update her about how things were going, but he didn't. He didn't want her to worry about him or Colter—she did enough of that without any encouragement. And he couldn't have texted her even if he wanted to since his phone had no signal.

The wait carried on, a miserable blend of boredom, anxiety, and confusion.

Finally, there were just three people left—a red-haired girl wearing high-top sneakers that didn't look ideal for doing any sort of athletics and a very, very tall boy who nervously paced around behind the chairs in the back. Even watching the boy made Greyson feel for him. He moved so awkwardly, like he wasn't used to or trusting of his giant frame.

By this point, Jess was the one with the list. From a seated position on the edge of the stage, she read, "Robert, you're next, Annie on deck, Greyson in the hole."

Robert walked to the exit, ducking underneath it and following Jamee backstage. Greyson couldn't help but think of a baby giraffe as he watched the poor, tall boy go.

Boop, boop, beep!

The sound came just a bit later. By that point, Greyson had stretched down the row of chairs, lying on his back and staring up at the ceiling.

"You want to warm up a bit or anything, Greyson?" Jess asked. "You're up next."

He sat up and looked her dead in the face. "Feels pretty pointless to warm up if I have no idea what I'm warming up for."

"You'll see pretty soon. Trust me, it could be worth the wait."

"I'm sure." Begrudgingly, he stood and began to jog in place, feeling a bit silly given how few people were left in the room.

Annie, the redhead, was called to the back a short

while later, and then, after another five minutes or so, it was Greyson's turn.

"You ready, Greyson?" Jamee asked. This was it. There was no more "on deck" or "in the hole." Just Greyson. Dead last.

"I guess I better be," he answered, and while he knew he was a bit snappy, he also didn't feel bad in the slightest. "You sure there's nobody else left?"

Jess gave an apologetic smile. "We randomized the names beforehand. I guess you just had really bad luck. Or, perhaps, really good luck if you can look at it that way. You've had time to process and prepare."

Greyson didn't argue, although he was tempted to. Instead, he followed Jess and Jamee through the exit. As they pointed out, he'd had nearly three hours to prepare, but as he walked down the narrow hallway with the muscular woman and green-haired man, the nerves began to creep back in.

What was he getting himself into?

Soon, his questions were answered. Or, at least, *some* of them. Jess led him into an enormous room. As far as he could tell, it was the rest of the hangar—stretching back at least the length of a football field, if not more. Bright lights shone down from above, illuminating every square inch of the hangar.

"Whoa..." He couldn't keep his surprise to himself as he observed not only the enormity of the room, but the thing standing in the middle of it.

An obstacle course. It was just as Jon and the coaches had promised, but seeing it in person was more than Greyson could have ever expected. It was at least fifty yards long, with obstacles of all sorts built over tanks of water. The obstacles, from a sweeping glance, were made out of a combination of metal, protective foam padding, and wood.

As he looked at the course, Greyson's heart began to pump a little faster. He'd never done anything like this, but it was…incredible.

Jon wasted no time with the introduction. "Greyson, I'm sorry you had to wait until the very end," he said. "Don't worry, though. The course is prepped and ready for you."

"I…I see that."

"I'll give a quick rundown of how this works," Lenny said, stepping forward and gesturing to the course behind him. "You'll start from that platform down there, and there are six obstacles to conquer in under five minutes. Understand?"

Greyson nodded, not taking his eyes away from the course.

Lenny started to explain the layout. "First up, you'll bound across the Detached Steps. That leads you to the Soaring Eagle, where you'll jump from the mini-tramp to the pivoting bars overhead. Using your momentum, you'll swing from one to the next. Conquer all three, and you're through the obstacle."

Greyson moved to the side a bit, trying to get a better look at the course so he could keep up with the explanation.

Lenny pointed to the next obstacle. "That's the Rolling Stones. It's a series of three spheres fixed to a long pipe. You'll need to keep your balance as you jump from one to the next, but be warned, they rotate and will try to throw you off!"

"Gotcha," Greyson nodded.

"Obstacles four and five are upper-body tests. First is the Hangman's Alley. Another mini-tramp, and this one leads to the peg board overhead. You'll grab onto the pegs, and while hanging underneath, you'll have to repeatedly relocate them into new slots while making your way down the narrow alley. Then, if you get through there, you'll reach Pole Position. In that one, you'll grab onto the loose pole and leap it into progressively smaller cradles."

Greyson arched his eyebrows as he took in obstacles four and five. They looked brutal. "What next?" He asked.

Lenny pointed toward a very steep ramp leading up to an elevated platform. "If you stay out of the water through the first obstacles, all that's left is the Wall Run. Run up the curved wall, grab the fourteen-foot high ledge, then pull yourself up. If you hit the buzzer at the top, you finish."

"And under five minutes?" Greyson reaffirmed.

"Yes, sir."

N.J. pointed to a large clock posted on top of the final platform. "There's a clock right there, but call for time at any point, and I'll let you know."

"Okay, cool. Thanks."

"How do you feel?" Meg asked him. "Does everything make sense?"

Greyson gave the most honest answer possible. "As far as the course goes, yeah. Everything else? Far from it."

"Understandable," Jon replied. "We get it. And we don't mean to leave you in the dark. Everything will make sense very soon, I promise, and I hope you can forgive us for the reasonably vague introductions."

Greyson nodded, but not as much in acknowledgment more so than in agreement. "So, where's everybody else?"

"Through that door." Jon pointed across the hangar. "There's a lobby out there, and your suitcase will be there too. You'll be able to change clothes if you end up getting wet on the course."

"I don't plan on getting wet." The words tumbled out of Greyson's mouth before he could rein them in.

Fortunately, none of the coaches seemed put off by his unrestrained confidence. If anything, they seemed to like it.

"So, are you ready to get going on the course then?" Jon asked.

"Oh yes." Greyson nodded. "I'm ready."

NINE

Boop, boop, beep!

The now all-too-familiar sound counted down Greyson's run, and as soon as the final beep sounded, he sprinted ahead.

A feeling washed over Greyson. Or, perhaps more so the *absence* of feeling. No longer was he thinking about the organization, his doubts, his friends, or anything else. He only had one concern.

He had to run.

And that's just what he did.

The first obstacle was the Detached Steps, which were exactly what the name implied. They were like stairs, climbing marginally higher with every passing one, but instead of being connected, they were each several feet apart and elevated above the water by a pole.

Greyson calculated his steps as he approached them. They were far out enough that he needed to cross in one move, but any *wrong* move could send him splashing down.

Left. Right. Left.

He jumped off his left leg, planting the sole of his

right foot in the middle of the first step. At most, it was only a bit wider than his shoe—there wasn't much room for margin of error.

He jumped again, this time off his right foot. Once again, his landing was as square and solid as he could have hoped.

Jump, jump, jump. With five moves, he cleanly made his way over the water and landed on the padded platform on the far side.

One obstacle down, five to go. The thought ran through his head as he dried his palms on his shorts. Did he need to? Probably not. They weren't even sweaty. But as he sized up the next obstacle, it felt natural.

The Soaring Eagle. That's what Lenny had called it. Greyson was only seconds into the timer, so he took a moment to evaluate the task at hand.

The Eagle was made up of three T-shaped pieces that were upside down, with a fulcrum in the base of each T to allow it to pivot. They were all parallel to each other but perpendicular to the platform, and each of them was about eight feet apart. To complete this obstacle, Greyson would have to generate enough momentum to swing from one to the next, and a lot of that would come from his lower body.

Completely focused, he bounced off the mini-tramp and grabbed onto the first T. It was solid—a bit sturdier than he'd expected—but he wasted no time rocking side to side with his legs and hips. In an obstacle like this, every second he spent hanging was more time for his arms to tire, and he'd be needing them later.

With just a few swings, Greyson had enough momentum going to make the first leap. He practiced the timing in his head, swung back, and then made the move. For just a moment, he was flying—so high, even, that his head nearly scraped the metal scaffolding above. When he came back down, he latched onto the second T.

This time, he already had momentum on his side. With a couple more swings, he launched himself to the third and final T, then down to the platform. As his shoes slammed into the pad, he heard a mild whoop from one of the coaches and a bit of applause.

The nerves he'd been feeling were completely gone. Now, Greyson was caught up in the thrill of the competition. He had no fear—only a desire to succeed.

The Rolling Stones came next, and he approached them with a bit of hesitation so he could plan his approach. Eyeing the three large orbs fixed to the pole, he planned his steps. On an obstacle that was as balanced-based as this one, his margin for error was impossibly thin. He had one shot.

That's all he needed. Greyson took a running start, chopped his feet a bit on the pad to establish a solid positioning, and then darted across the boulder. He moved so fast that he felt like he was never bearing his entire weight on any of them, stepping lightly and precisely as he made his way to the other side.

With so much forward momentum, he struggled to stop, but when he did, he let out a long exhalation. *Had he been holding his breath during the Rolling Stones?* Apparently so.

"You got this, Greyson!" He recognized Meg's voice from the sideline.

"Doing great, kid," approved Jon.

Greyson couldn't help but grin. He had the coaches, and perhaps even more importantly, *time,* on his side. As he looked up to the clock, he discovered he was just under a minute.

The next obstacles would take longer—there was no doubt about that. Lenny had described them as an upper body challenge, and it seemed there was no other way to put it. A brutal upper body gauntlet awaited Greyson, and despite that, he couldn't help but smile.

This part seemed made for him.

The first of those obstacles was Hangman's Alley. It had two pegs with balls attached to the end, and they were slotted in a board that was at least fifteen feet long. The board had many similar slots so that the pegs could be removed from one section, positioned correctly, then reslotted. Each slot had a round end for inserting the ball, then it had to be slid to a thinner section to lock it in.

For probably the first time in his life as an athlete, Greyson was thankful he was skinny and light. That, combined with his grip strength, could be a tremendous advantage.

He jumped up to the pegs, grabbing onto them and eyeing the board above him. It was impossible to move both at the same time, so he picked a side and went with it. He pulled his body up and used his right arm to slip the peg out of the slot. Then he reached forward, putting the ball-end of it into the next slot, sliding it down until it bit, and then coming to rest.

Now, hanging primarily from his right arm, he did the same with the left peg: unslot, move to the next position, slot, advance.

It was a slow process, but it wasn't difficult. An obstacle of that nature required what was known as lock-off strength, or being able to hang from one arm without becoming fully extended. Thanks to his rock climbing experience, he had more than enough to spare.

Still, it was tiring. But by the time he'd moved each of the pegs three or four times, his shoulders were beginning to burn. He looked down, spotting the platform just a few feet away, and with a big kip of his hips, he swung forward and dropped down on the platform.

By this point, his hands *were* actually sweaty. He dried them on his shorts again, rubbed his palms together, then shook out his arms to get the blood flowing through them while looking at the next obstacle.

Lenny had called it Pole Position, and Greyson could see why. The obstacle couldn't be more straightforward. He had to grab onto a four-foot-long metal pole that was held above the water by two cradles—one on each side. Then, he'd swing forward and, in theory, carry the pole with him to another set of cradles, then another, then another. Every time, the cradles grew a bit smaller.

Greyson glanced at the clock. He was just over two minutes in with two obstacles left. His pace was great if he could keep it up. And, more importantly, if he could stay dry.

His arms feeling recovered, he jumped up and latched onto the pole. From underneath it, he debated how to make the move. If he looked at one arm, would he misjudge the other? *How could he land both in cradles if he couldn't watch both hands?*

He was overthinking, so he forced the question out of his mind and stared forward. The second cradle was four or five feet away. He tried to get a feel for the distance, then as precisely as possible, he swung back, kipped forward, and flew through the air.

Clang. The pole slammed down into the second set of cradles with surprising force. Greyson was jarred, but managed to hold on. He assessed both ends of his pole, noticing that he was a bit heavier on the right side than the left, so he shifted the pole back to his left and readjusted.

"Easy..." somebody called from the sideline, but Greyson was too preoccupied to figure out which coach was talking to him.

He planned his next move. With the pole back where he wanted it, he started to rock back and forth underneath it. Then, once he had good momentum going, he leaped forward and landed the pole in the third cradle.

He almost lost it.

One instant, Greyson was making contact with the cradle with both hands on the pole, and the next, his right hand had peeled off and he was gripping on with his left out of desperation. For just a moment, he had nothing but his fingertips holding him up, and then, with a groan of effort, he lifted his other arm back up and latched onto the pole with both hands.

It was too close for comfort, and as Greyson eyed the fourth and final cradle, he decided he would *not* be going through that again. Instead, he'd try something perhaps equally as crazy: he'd dismount from here.

The landing pad was a long way away, but as he looked down at it, Greyson convinced himself that if he were going to beat this obstacle, this would be his best chance. He had to go for it right *now.*

And he did. Clutching onto the pole, he began to swing. Back and forth, back and forth. Each thrust of his hips generated more momentum, but he also had to keep the pole sitting in the cradle while building up enough force to make the jump. On top of that, he had to calculate the right trajectory to release at to combine distance and height. If he was wrong, he'd come splashing down short of the pad.

Finally, he let go of the pole, and with a cry of effort, went soaring through the air.

For a brief moment, everything slowed down. Greyson looked at the landing pad ahead of him, trying to estimate his landing position and adjust the best he could. As he started coming down, there was a half-second of fear that he was going to be short of the pad, but that quickly washed away when his feet slammed down onto the rubber below.

There was an energetic cheer from the room of coaches and a couple shouts as Greyson scrambled forward, heading to the Wall Run without checking the clock. *What good would looking at the clock do at this point, anyway?* he thought. He had to go for it regardless.

As he charged toward the wall, Greyson tried his best to keep his weight backward, pushing *into* the wall just like when he usually climbed.

Compared to the last few obstacles, the wall felt like a piece of cake. Using his on-the-fly form, he easily made it to the top, grabbing on with his hands and pulling himself to his feet on the top of the elevated platform.

"Hit the buzzer!" Jamee called to him.

Greyson looked around. A pole was against the back rail, and a buzzer was on top of the pole. He brought both hands down on it, triggering a steam whistle-like honk and a big round of applause from all the coaches.

Greyson wasn't sure what had come over him, but

he couldn't contain his excitement. He flexed his arms together and shouted as the buzzer sound ended, smiling down at the coaches.

"That was amazing!" Lenny called up to him. "You really tore that course apart, Greyson!"

Jon was writing something down on a clipboard, but looked up to add, "Greyson, you were our fastest finisher by over a minute and a half. That was an amazing run."

"Climb down from there," Jess advised. "There's a ladder on the back."

Greyson did as told, and once his feet were back on the hard cement floor of the hangar, the coaches were already coming up to join him.

There was a circle of congratulations: some verbal, some fist bumps, and even an enthusiastic high-five from Jamee that turned into a jarring bro-hug.

All the skepticism he'd been feeling earlier had now watched away. Greyson couldn't describe why, but he also had a feeling that this is where he belonged. The support that these people, these *strangers,* showed him was something that gave him a sense of belonging he hadn't experienced in a long time.

"I was the fastest?" Greyson asked after everybody had paid him their respects. He'd heard Jon say it, but he still couldn't bring himself to process the words.

"Easily," N.J. said. "We had seventy-two runners today, and nobody came close to putting together as solid of a run as you, Greyson. You clearly know your way around an obstacle course."

Shaking his head, Greyson said, "That's the first time I've ever done anything like that."

N.J. raised his eyebrows. "A natural, I see!"

"Yeah. But it felt a lot like rock climbing, and that's something I do every single day."

"Your rock climbing skills definitely translated well to that course. We had quite a few runners that made it to obstacles four and five, but only seventeen got through Hangman's Alley and only four made it through Pole Position."

"Four?" Now it was Greyson's turn to be astonished. "Only four made it to the wall?"

"Yeah," Meg confirmed. "They all made it up the wall, too, but our list of finishers is a short one."

The words took a bit of time to sink in, and as they did, a new feeling bubbled up inside of Greyson—*pride.* Every athlete, no matter what sport they played, played on a level playing field here—this crazy obstacle game—and somehow, he'd beaten all of them. The boy who spent his time climbing rocks had also climbed to the top of the leaderboard.

Then another thought struck Greyson. "Wait, how did Colter do? Did he do well enough to make it through?"

"Colter…Colter…" Jon looked through the list, whispering the name under his breath. "Ah, Colter Rickman?"

"Yeah."

"I forgot you had a friend with you. You and Colter are the only set of friends we invited," Jon said. "That said something about you guys in itself." As the words left his mouth, an odd look fell over his face.

"What's wrong?" Greyson asked.

"Colter." Jon spun around the clipboard. "Looks like he placed thirty-first."

Greyson's heart sank. "And the top thirty advance?"

A slow nod.

Suddenly, the wind had been sucked out of Greyson's sails. This couldn't be. By doing so well, he'd essentially cost Colter his spot. Even worse, he knew just how much it would mean to his friend. Of the two, Colter was the competitive one.

"I can't do this," he muttered. "I don't want to be the reason Colter misses out. That would crush him. Please, give him my spot. Tell them I fell really early or something…"

As the words spilled out of Greyson's mouth, a silence beset the coaches. They looked at each other, clearly not sure how to handle the situation. Then, with the slightest of smirks, Jon said, "I like you, Greyson. I like you a lot. But we have specific rules that we are required to follow. Like I said from the very beginning, this whole program is completely voluntary. If you choose to leave, your spot will be given to Colter. But you have a gift. We all can see it, so I highly encourage you to continue."

All the coaches nodded in agreement.

"No need to decide right now," Jamee added. "You'll have a bit to think about it. But I encourage you not to waste your opportunity."

With that, Greyson followed the coaches across the hangar. Head down, he grappled with everything going on in his head: how could he do this without Colter? How could he do this *to* Colter?

A hand reached for his shoulder. It was Jess. With a faint smile, she offered, "I know this is a lot, and you have a kind soul. I can see the thought of hurting your friend is taking its toll, but sometimes you need to care about your own well-being and future as much as you care about others. My good friend always told me, 'Sometimes you need to be your own hero'."

Greyson didn't say anything, just nodded.

They passed through a door where a slew of tired, confused-looking teenagers greeted them. They'd almost all been sitting around tables but stood up when Jon led Greyson and the coaches into the room.

The first thing Greyson noticed was his suitcase leaning against the wall, and he grabbed it at once. It was so nice to finally have his belongings back.

Jon went to the front of the room, thanking them all for their participation. From there, he explained that he would read the list of top recruits, in no particular order. He told each recruit he named to grab their stuff and head through some double doors on the far side of the room, where they would then make their final decision of the day.

Greyson arched an eyebrow at the explanation, scanning the room for Colter.

Then the names started. Jon started to read off a list of names, congratulating those who had qualified. He recognized some of them, including Skylar, Nikki, and Macie.

Shortly thereafter, Greyson's own name was called, and he followed the instructions, heading toward the double doors.

Colter was near the front of the room. His head was down, and he looked quite depressed, but as Greyson walked by, he squeezed out, "Congrats, Grey."

Greyson didn't know what to say, so he gave an awkward, sympathetic nod. "Thanks. I'll see you really soon." With that, he turned toward the double doors, knowing the decision he had to make.

Lenny was leaning against the wall beside the doors and he offered a tip of his hat and a wink as Greyson entered a small room with two paths to take.

"What am I doing?" Greyson asked the friendly cowboy.

"It's easy," Lenny explained. "Go left, and you'll find your way back to the rest of the recruits and carry on with the traditional program. Go right, and you'll participate in our advanced program."

Greyson eyed the two paths. The left path wound back to the front of the building, passing through the strange blue flashing light he'd seen when he entered. The other wound to a dark hall with more doors on the far side.

He froze, staring down the two paths. One was safe, traditional, and would help his best friend. The other was mysterious, exciting, and adventurous, but would be a selfish decision. *Or...would it?* Greyson's hands started to sweat even more than when he was on the course.

After staring at each choice for what seemed like an eternity, finally, the double doors opened behind him, and Lenny peeked his head in. "Not to put any extra pressure on you, kid, but you do need to decide."

Greyson reluctantly shook his head. "I know. I'm sorry. But I don't know. What would you do? Can you help?"

Lenny shook his head. "This needs to be your own decision, but listen to your heart and your surroundings, and I know you will make the right choice." As the door slowly closed behind him, he heard something in the distance that made his heart race.

It was the faint voice of Jon, saying, "Colter Rickman, congratulations..." just as the door closed and the room fell silent again.

Greyson's eyes widened: somebody else must have declined the advanced program. That meant Colter had gotten a spot, after all, and Greyson wouldn't have to give up his own to help his best friend.

Excited now, Greyson headed down the path on his right. If he hadn't heard them calling out Colter's name, he might have made a choice he'd always regret.

But that's when another idea struck him. The way Lenny had opened the door *just* when Colter's name was about to be called…had he done that on purpose?

Greyson didn't have time to stew on it. Soon he reached the end of the hall and exited the building out to a parking lot. As his eyes adjusted to the bright sun, he spied a bus on the far side of the lot.

The doors opened behind him, and three other teenagers made their way outside. One was Colter, who grinned as he ran up to Greyson and gave him a big hug, picking him off the ground. "Dude, I'm so happy we made it through! If you and I weren't going together, I was gonna quit. I'm not even kidding."

Greyson smiled. "I wouldn't have gone without you."

"How did it go?" Colter asked. "Where did you fall? I made it to the thing with the pole where you had to swing."

"I…" Suddenly, Greyson felt sheepish. "I actually finished."

"Wait, *what?*" Colter seemed enthusiastic.

"Yeah. I think I got lucky on a couple good breaks, but I made it through."

"I…I guess that makes sense," Colter said. "You're dry. Most of us had to change clothes immediately. Well, congrats, man."

"Thanks. This is the one sport where it pays to be a climber, I guess."

"Totally." Colter looked around. "Whoa, fancy bus."

He was right. Unlike the yellow antiques at Pine High School, this bus was sleek with a reflective metal body, much more like a high-end car than a transportation wagon.

N.J. opened the storage hatch underneath the bus. "All your luggage can go in here, ladies and gents. Once you've got it stashed inside, board up, and we'll get this show on the road."

Greyson turned to Colter. "Any idea where we're going? Did you hear anything while you were waiting for everybody to finish?"

"Not a word," Colter admitted, but then he shrugged. "But hey, who cares? We're going on an adventure, Greyson. Just like we promised."

"I guess you're right about that."

TEN

"Please be sure to fasten your seatbelts," N.J. said as the final teenager took a seat. "I'll explain in a moment."

Colter, who was sitting beside Greyson, mumbled, "Going seatbeltless is half the fun of a bus ride. What gives?"

"Extra liability? I have no idea." Either way, Greyson did as told, fastening his seatbelt along with the rest of the passengers. It was the heavy-duty kind of seatbelt, too—the five-point harness type, not the loose-fitting solo-strap he'd been expecting.

N.J. stood in the middle of the aisle as the bus engine started, rumbling the floor underneath their feet. "I'll lead by putting this very bluntly, what you're about to see will be hard to believe, but please don't be alarmed. We do this all the time."

"What's he talking about?" Colter whispered.

Greyson shrugged.

Suddenly, there was another rumble, but this one was more than the bus engine coming to life. It was a whole shudder that vibrated the seats pretty aggressively.

"Whoa," somebody said from the front of the bus. "What is that?"

More murmurs swirled around the cabin, and Greyson looked around to figure out what was causing the excitement.

As it turned out, it wasn't anything inside the bus at all, but rather what was happening on the *outside*. As he looked out the window to his right, Greyson's eyes latched onto metal blades that had emerged from the side of the bus.

"Colt, look at this."

Colter practically climbed into his lap to look out the window. "What is that? Are we…is this a Transformer?"

Greyson shook his head, unable to keep a smile off his face. "I mean, basically. I think… I think those are wings."

"You mean—"

"Yeah." He nodded. "I think this is a bus-jet."

"No way. No freakin' way."

"It sure looks that way," Greyson insisted. "And I'm pretty sure the trucks we arrived in were the exact same way. I was gonna ask you what you thought, but I never had the chance."

N.J. spoke up over the excited buzz. "Over the next few weeks, you'll learn about the technology used by the NINJA organization. In short, we are significantly more advanced than anything you've ever seen or dealt with at this point in life, and this will be the first example. As you've probably noticed, our Model 327 Bus actually converts into a jet…complete with a cloaking device. Pretty secretive stuff—that's why we keep her parked in this old hangar."

Colter muttered, "There's no chance. He's not serious, right? This has got to be some sort of joke."

The engine's sound suddenly grew from a rumble to a high-pitch hum. "Um…" Greyson replied. "I think he's dead serious."

"Everybody needs to stay in their seat for the next few minutes while we get off the ground," N.J. continued, "and then once we've reached altitude and have entered our ley line, I'll explain a bit more about what's going on."

Colter went white as a sheet. "I've never flown before," he muttered. "And there's been a very good reason why. I'm not tryin' to die in a plane crash. Or…bus crash?"

Greyson wanted to offer some sort of consolation, but he didn't know what to say. What *was* there to say, anyway? He'd flown several times, but never like this.

Finally, he said, "I'm sure we'll be okay. They're probably expert bus drivers."

"They better be, because there isn't much of a runway to take off on!"

Suddenly, there was a jostle within the buzz. Greyson gasped as he looked through the window and watched as four blades of blue light formed, one on each side of the wings. The blades of energy looked similar to propellers on a drone, glowing with a powerful light source.

Colter tensed and grabbed onto his knees with so much force that his knuckles went white.

"Breathe," Greyson prompted, and Colter reluctantly took a breath in.

With a lurch, the bus suddenly started to rise off the ground, rising higher and higher as the engine continued to whirl.

Greyson peered out the window. The driveway and hangar grew smaller and smaller, and as far as Greyson could tell, they were rising to a height similar to a commercial flight.

Colter's eyes were closed, so Greyson nudged him and whisper-sang, "The wheels on the bus go off the ground, off the ground, off the ground…"

Colter's eyes snapped back open and he shot Greyson a look.

"Sorry, bad time for a joke." Greyson turned back to the window, peering past the wings and staring at the ground below in complete astonishment. "This has to be the craziest thing I've ever seen in my life."

"Oh, I agree with that," Colter said through gritted teeth, but while Greyson had said it in admiration, Colter's tone was not quite as favorable.

Greyson chuckled. "Try to relax. Clearly these people know what they're doing."

Colter's eyes reluctantly opened once again, and after looking around a bit, he started to panic even more. "How high are we?" he murmured.

Greyson peered out the window at the layer of clouds far, far below him. "I'm not sure, but this has to be a higher altitude than planes fly."

N.J. stood up and said, "We're at the point of entry, so make sure your seatbelts are secured now. This might seem a bit scary, but I promise we'll all be fine."

Colter started frantically securing his harness. "What does that mean—point of entry?"

Greyson looked out the window, noticing the drone blades of energy were slowing down and starting to fade. "Not sure, but I think we're about to find out what the wings are for."

And with that, the plane rocketed forward and began to plummet.

All the teenagers screamed, including Greyson. But it was more like a rollercoaster hitting the bottom of the track than a freefall.

Greyson's stomach lurched as the bus started to plummet, but the terror of the drop only lasted a few seconds until the nose of the bus pulled up, and the ride began to level out.

"I'm *definitely* gonna be sick," Colter mumbled.

N.J. popped back to his feet. Looking around the cabin, he said, "What do you guys think? Pretty cool, right?"

There were a few whoops and cheers from the kids.

N.J. smiled. "Glad you guys are impressed. There's a lot more where this came from. You'll see everything once we reach the grounds."

Very slowly, Colter reached for his seatbelt and unbuckled it, letting it retract against the seat. Shakily, he exhaled.

"We have about an hour flight," N.J. continued, "so while we're in the air I wanted to give you a bit of a debriefing on what's really going on here. As you can tell from the bus, there are some things we have going on that, quite frankly, we need to keep secret from the rest of the world. I'll try to answer any of your questions, too."

Heads nodded all around the bus.

"Good. So, let's start with an overview. I'll try to answer all the big questions at once. Sound fair?"

A relieved "yes," echoed throughout the bus.

N.J. rubbed his hands together. "Okay, for starters, the NINJAs are an elite group of thinkers and athletes working together to ensure the protection of the human race." N.J. delivered the message the same way Greyson would ask somebody to pass the salt at the dinner table.

He went on. "We've been a secret for a very long time. In fact, the roots of the organization date back to ancient times. Of course, the NINJAs have changed over time, but the premise is the same: work together to do good and fight evil."

"Evil?" Colter whispered, apparently able to speak once again. "Isn't that a bit extreme?"

It was almost like N.J. had heard him, because he added, "You're probably wondering what I mean by 'evil'. In short, evil can come in a lot of forms: corruption, greed, and conquest. We've seen lots of it over the course of the NINJA Order, and that's why we keep agents deployed in the field at all times. These agents have assisted in many significant historical events."

"Like what?" somebody asked from near the front.

"Many different cases of innovation," N.J. answered without missing a beat. "Particularly, times when lives are at stake. The most notable in recent memory was the Manhattan Project, which helped end World War II. Using secret field agents, we've also contributed to the Space Race, and even lower-stakes events like the construction of the Hoover Dam."

"He can't be serious," a girl whispered from behind Greyson.

Greyson, however, knew that N.J. was *very* serious. He didn't know how, but he could tell.

N.J. continued his explanation. "We actively recruit

every year, but this is the first year we've led a recruiting campaign of this magnitude. In short, we hosted four different regional events, including the one you just participated in, and the qualifiers from each will be coming together on our main campus to learn and train some more. Then, at the end of training, we'll have another qualifying event, and those who qualify during it will be offered a position within the NINJA Order."

"What about those who don't?" This came from the very tall boy who had moved like a baby giraffe. Upon seeing him, Greyson was surprised that he'd wound up in the top thirty of the qualifiers. *Guess anybody can be good at obstacles,* he thought to himself.

N.J. answered the question as politely and professionally as possible. "Great question, Joey. Those who don't qualify will be dismissed and asked to join the rest of the recruits in the traditional program."

"But like…you're a *secret* organization."

"We are," N.J. nodded. "But we'll discuss all of that at a later date. I'll say this: nobody we've ever dismissed has ever done anything to harm us or our secrecy in any way. There are never any hard feelings."

The explanation was enough for the tall boy, who nodded.

"Let's talk about our schedule, yes?" N.J. asked. "During the original invitation, you were probably all told that you'd be attending a STEM camp for four weeks and then partnered with a large organization for a valuable internship at the end, correct?"

More nods from the teenagers.

"That's largely true. Except the STEM camp is more of a….*NINJA* camp. But you'll still be learning valuable science, tech, engineering and math skills the whole time, so it's basically STEM, right?" He smiled at this, as did a few of the teenagers.

"Equally importantly, though, we'll work on physical training. A large part of the recruitment process is finding individuals who can succeed both academically and physically, and obstacle courses are the core of what we do because they best capture all-around athleticism: from leaping to balance, strength, and even split-second decision-making. In other words, you'll spend a *lot* of time with obstacles over the next four weeks."

Greyson couldn't fight back a grin. As much as he loved rock climbing, his time on the obstacle course had been even better.

There was a momentary jolt in the bus-jet, and N.J. grabbed onto a seat beside him for a moment before apologizing, "Sorry...bit of turbulence from switching lines." It passed, and he stood up tall and continued his explanation. "You met some of the coaches today in the training, but there will be more at the grounds."

"What are the grounds, and what are ley lines?" This came from a voice Greyson recognized: Macie.

"Great question." N.J. cleared his throat, then explained, "The grounds are our headquarters. It's a small campus where you and a partner will be assigned a room, and each day, you'll attend classes, train, and learn more about the NINJA Order. This is also where you will learn about the technology and the energy sources we utilize, like ley lines."

"So...kinda like a summer camp?"

He smiled. "Exactly like that. When we said you were invited to a STEM camp, we meant it."

"I don't believe this," Colter said. "There's no way that this is true. It can't be."

Greyson leaned in close to his friend before saying, "I don't know that I need to be reminding you of this… but we're in a flying *bus*. At this point, it would be crazy not to believe what they're saying."

"Okay, fair enough."

N.J. looked toward the ceiling, squinting his eyes, obviously deep in thought. As he mumbled something, he counted something off his fingers, then announced, "I think I've covered everything—at least for now. But does anybody have any questions?"

With this, at least a dozen hands shot up from all around the bus.

"Guess I should have seen that coming," he joked. "How about you…Skylar?"

Greyson turned to spot Skylar, the wrestler he'd chatted with earlier. Skylar asked, "So what about the people who didn't qualify? Are they…are they on a flying bus, too?"

N.J. laughed at this. "No. Definitely not. They're on a very normal bus headed to a very normal summer camp."

"Oh, gotcha."

"What's your question, Bryce?" N.J. nodded to a boy in the very back.

"You said other kids were coming. Where are they coming *from*? Are they already there?"

N.J. answered, "Not yet. We have four qualifiers in total. Two were today, and two will be tomorrow. So, over the next forty-eight hours, you'll be joined by three more groups that did well at their training."

N.J. then moved on. "Do you have a question, Reeza?"

Reeza, an Indian girl with glasses, asked, "What are we supposed to tell our parents?"

"The truth," N.J. answered matter-of-factly. "Well, most of the truth. You'll tell them you're learning from many smart people at a camp and learning life skills that will benefit you for a very long time. Simple, right? Unfortunately, any mention of our top-secret tech will lead to your immediate dismissal, but again, that has never been an issue in the past."

In a mix of acceptance and compliance, heads nodded from all around the bus.

N.J. pointed toward a sandy haired boy with a thin build and confident smile. "How about you, Shafer?"

The boy, Shafer, asked, "No offense, but how do we know we can trust you? Like, how do we know this isn't some crazy scheme to kidnap us?"

"You don't, really," N.J. said, again very bluntly. "I can assure you that we're the good guys and you *might* believe us, or I can *show* you that we're the good guys, and you *will* believe us. That's our policy."

Shafer's only response was to lower his hand.

The questions kept coming. "How has nobody ever posted about you? Why aren't the NINJAs all over social media? Surely something would leak."

N.J. let out a little huff, but a good-natured one. "Do you think we could figure out how to make a bus fly but not be able to minimize our search engine presence?"

"You got me there."

Other questions flew around, but none of them really mattered, at least to Greyson. He didn't care what food they'd be eating or if the beds already had sheets—he was on a flying bus that belonged to a secret organization! The details didn't really matter.

But there was one question that was on his mind, and after a long wave of mundane questions sloshed by, he decided to ask it himself.

"Greyson, what's going on?" N.J. asked.

Greyson searched for the right words before asking, "You said you're trying to stop evil. Can you be more specific? That's so…I don't know. Sci-fi? No offense."

N.J. slowly nodded. "None taken. That, Greyson, is a very, very good question."

Suddenly, all the noise in the bus died down. Nobody spoke. Everybody was solely focused on what N.J. had to say.

He seemed to sense the weight of the situation and handled it as smoothly as possible. "There is no immediate threat—I can say that—but we've caught word of a potential problem that might arise down the line unless we actively work to stop it. That's why we've heightened our recruiting efforts. I don't want to say too much, however. Jon will explain further."

"So Jon's the shot-caller?"

"No one person, in particular, is in charge," N.J. said. "There's no CEO or president, but rather an interdisciplinary team that specializes in a particular field of study, votes on decisions, makes sure rules are being followed, things like that. Jon leads communications between departments, and that's why he's better equipped to explain."

"Gotcha."

Suddenly, Jamee's voice called out, "Yo N.J., we're getting ready to exit our energy current and start our descent. Better wind it down for now." Greyson didn't even realize Jamee had been flying the bus-jet, but he was impressed nonetheless.

N.J. nodded. "That's all for now. Buckle up. We'll be landing soon. You'll see the grounds, and we'll probably have a welcome party come say hi."

With that, he sat down.

Greyson turned his eye to the window, trying to figure out where they were located, but all he could see as the bus started decreasing in altitude was a thick layer of clouds and that the drone blades of energy were back.

Colter's phone buzzed. With a chuckle, he said, "Mom wants to know how things are going. She also says Ty is having fun with Max."

Greyson smiled, knowing his dog was in good hands. "You tell her we're in a flying bus?"

"You heard what they said! I can't—"

"Joking. I'm totally joking." Lowering his voice, Greyson added, "And I wouldn't be surprised if they're monitoring the messages we send out, just to be safe. Like N.J. said, if they're capable of inventing a flying bus, they can do a lot more than that."

"I don't doubt it." Colter sent a message back, reading out loud, "Things are going well. Grey and I are having lots of fun." He pressed *send*, and after a bit of a delay, it went through.

At that point, the shift in gravity became evident as the plane began to descend. Quickly, Colter shoved his phone in his pocket and went back to the scared stiff, hands-on-knees look.

"Relax," Greyson told him again. "This is the cool part."

He pressed his forehead against the window, peering

through the glass as the bus dipped through the thick layer of clouds. Suddenly, the ground became visible below. They were headed down to a forest—thick and lush as far as he could see. But, weirdly enough, no matter where he looked, Greyson couldn't see any buildings or signs of life.

"Where's the campus?" he asked as they continued to drop. For all he could tell, they were heading straight for the trees.

Until they weren't.

Suddenly, as the bus continued downward, the campus just appeared. It was missing one moment, then was there the next. Many of the kids, including Greyson, gasped.

The speaker crackled overhead. Jamee said, "Using atmospheric mist and a high-tech projection system, we reflect the image of the surrounding trees back into the sky. Basically, it creates a camouflage bubble over the whole campus."

"That's the coolest thing I've ever seen," Greyson said. *"Ever."* He looked at Colter, hoping his friend had seen it too, but Colter's eyes were still tightly shut.

The campus itself wasn't huge, but it wasn't small, either. As far as Greyson could tell from above, it looked like it had about four buildings—all pretty large in size—and some outdoor tracks. The buildings formed an interesting pattern, but Greyson couldn't quite pinpoint where he had seen it before.

As they descended even closer, he spotted another obstacle course and in the center of the campus was a fifth building, which Greyson could only describe as a pyramid.

But the aerial sight-seeing didn't last for long. After a few seconds, the bus came in contact with the ground, lowering so smoothly that you couldn't even tell the exact moment that contact had happened. Greyson almost lost it when he looked at Colter, who still had his eyes shut tightly. "You can relax, Colter. We're safely on the ground."

Almost playfully, Jamee's voice chimed over the intercom, "You may now unbuckle your seatbelts and move about the cabin."

N.J. was already on his feet. With a newfound enthusiasm, he said, "Everybody, welcome to Headquarters!"

ELEVEN

From the moment Greyson stepped out of the bus and onto the grounds, everything became a blur. He was struggling to learn the names of all the coaches and teenagers in his group, and on top of that, there would be plenty more to meet.

A man in a red athletic shirt came up to greet the group. He had short dark hair, and greeted everyone with a standing back tuck. "Hello, everybody," he said as he flashed a brilliant smile. "It's so nice to see all of you. If you've made it this far, you must be pretty special."

Greyson, along with most of the other teens, offered a wave, but he was too distracted by all the vibrant action around him to be too focused on any one person.

"Everybody, this is Elliot," N.J. introduced. "He's one of the greats, and when it comes to courses, you'll be able to learn a thing or two from this guy."

Elliot cupped his fingers around his mouth and half-whispered, "Don't let him play the humble card. N.J. can fly on an obstacle course himself."

N.J. acted like he hadn't heard him, saying instead, "I've gotta go submit some information about who qualified and reserved your rooms. In the meantime, Elliot will give you a tour of the campus."

Elliot nodded, clapping his hands together. "Sweet! It's gonna be fun, I promise. N.J., do I meet you at the Great Hall when we're finished?"

"That works perfectly for me. I'll have assigned everybody a room by then."

"Great."

With that, N.J. slipped away, heading toward the largest of all the buildings, which was behind the bus. From inside the bus, Jamee waved goodbye and then slowly drove away.

"Let's go for a walk, shall we?" Elliot said. "The Grounds are basically a big square, so we can walk it all, and you'll see everything in one pass. Right, this way."

He led them down a sidewalk, and just as he'd said, the shape of the square began to stand out to Greyson. Long sidewalks connected and created the four sides, with a large building on the outside of each. In the middle was the pyramid-shaped building surrounded by fields that held several training grounds, a few tents, and the landing pad on which they currently stood.

"Are you all excited to be here?" Elliot asked as they walked. "Or, and you can be honest...are you all a little weirded out?"

This brought a few laughs from around the group, but it was also nice to hear somebody acknowledge just how absurd everything felt to this point. As they walked, Greyson found his way toward the front half of the group so he could better hear, with Colter staying by his side.

Coincidentally—or at least that's what Greyson was telling himself—Macie ended up on his right. When she saw him, she leaned over to him and whispered, "I'm so glad you qualified on the course, Grey. Can you believe any of this?"

He shook his head and lamely parroted back, "I'm glad you're here, too."

The group made it to one side of the square, and behind it was a short, square building made out of a light-colored stone. As Elliot gestured to it, he said, "This is Nuaki Hall, or basically the school hall. We have six different rooms in total. Number one is on that end, and they go all the way down to number six." He made a sweeping gesture to show direction.

Reeza asked, "Are we going inside?"

"Not right now, but you're not missing much if you've ever set foot in a high school classroom. You can expect about the same setup. Don't worry. We have all the school supplies you'll ever need." While his words dripped with a playfulness, Elliot answered something Greyson had been wondering but too sheepish to ask.

"Come on this way," Elliot said, leading them alongside the building. "If you look to your left, you'll see some of the training grounds. The building on the far side of them is the indoor training facility, and that's where you'll get a lot of your gear for training. We'll get there after the Tech Labs."

Greyson had not only locked his eyes on one of the training grounds, but he had also spotted a small group in the process of actually training. There were three people total, two boys and a girl, and they were only a few years older than them.

As he watched, one of the boys swung from ring to ring over a large protective pad. After the third and final swing, he thrust his hips forward, let go of the ring, and flew through the air, only to latch onto a bar with both hands.

The bar looked like a pull-up bar, except it wasn't fixed in place. Instead, it was cradled at both ends within a frame, and as Greyson watched, the boy thrust the bar up from one cradle to the next, climbing higher and higher.

"Did you see that, Colter?" he asked.

"Yeah, man. I think I could do that."

"Really?"

"Yeah. What about you?"

"Um, I'm not sure. But I bet we're going to find out."

Onward they walked, but Greyson had a difficult time looking away from the intense training session on the grounds. He couldn't wait to join them and take on more obstacles. The combination of skill and problem-solving that the course offered had grabbed ahold of him, and now he couldn't let go. He was addicted to it.

After a couple more minutes of small talk, they reached the end of the sidewalk and turned left. The building Elliot had referred to as the Tech Labs was right beside them now, and Greyson ran his eyes over it. This was one of the most interesting buildings for a variety of reasons. It was made out of the same light-colored stone as the school—all the buildings were, for that matter—but it looked more high-tech and guarded.

For one, it was shaped like a pyramid. Security cameras were posted above the main door and under the awning, and it had very few windows, which were blacked out, unlike the rest of the buildings. On top of that, the building was located in the center of the campus, and the large double doors in the front were metal. As Greyson watched, a woman in a white coat walked up to the door, pulled her wrist to her chest before the doors opened, and slipped inside.

"These are the labs. As you can tell, this is the most highly-guarded building on campus," Elliot said, gesturing toward the building as the door sealed tight behind the woman. "Given the amount of advanced technology that goes on inside, we have to be sure to keep it protected at all costs."

"I noticed the top of the building is made of the same materials as some of the vehicles we arrived in," Skylar noted.

Greyson liked Skylar. He was curious, inquisitive, and never afraid to say what was on his mind. They had a lot in common.

"Very observant! It's Skylar, right?" Elliot replied.

"Yes, sir," Skyler responded.

"They are, in fact, composed of the same element, which you all will learn more about in future classes."

Greyson was intrigued. He had never noticed that the cap on the pyramid-shaped building was, in fact, an interesting blue color that almost seemed to be shining with energy, very similar to the bus-jet.

"Wait, what are you afraid of?" a voice asked from the back of the group. "One of the recruits getting inside?"

Elliot didn't flinch. "It's a combination of several things, really," he said. "We're not worried about the recruits leaking anything to the rest of the world. But we *are* worried about safety. There's a lot of dangerous technology in there, at least for those who don't know how to use it. And well…this building provides a lot of protection… actually, no. That's really it."

The sudden change in direction caught Greyson off guard. He glanced at Colter, trying to see if his best friend also found the answer a bit unusual, but Colter was only nodding in agreement.

As Greyson looked back at the building—all its safety precautions glaring back—he couldn't help but wonder if there was as much effort spent keeping something locked *inside* as there was keeping everybody else *out*. Staring at his own reflection in a blacked-out window, he felt a bit uneasy.

"Are we gonna take a tour?" The words spilled out of his mouth before he ever realized he'd asked them.

"Yes," Elliot answered immediately. "You most definitely will get the full guided tour. But not today. That will be later into training."

"Okay, cool," Greyson answered, still not peeling his eyes away from the menacing dark glass.

"You're…are you Greyson?"

Elliot's question finally pulled Greyson's attention away from the ominous building. "Yeah," he confirmed. "How'd you guess?"

"N.J. mentioned you." Elliot gave him a knowing look. "He said you had a pretty good run on the course."

"I see," Greyson said. He couldn't explain why, but for some reason he desperately hoped Elliot didn't reveal just *how* successful Greyson had been. He didn't want the whole group to know.

He didn't want a target on his back.

"I'm looking forward to training together," Elliot said, and just like that, they were back on their way, heading down the sidewalk and away from the labs.

As they walked, Colter whispered, "Dude, what happened on the course?"

Greyson shrugged. "I mean, I finished it. I guess that's what he's talking about."

The answer seemed to be good enough for Colter. "Must be," he said.

They continued forward, Elliot narrating a bit as they went, but somehow Greyson's concentration shifted to his right, where Macie was walking. He didn't want to get caught watching her, but he also couldn't help but occasionally sneak a look her way.

"And this is the indoor training facility," Elliot said, dragging Greyson's attention back to the tour. "We have more course training, individual obstacle training, and even sparring training. You'll learn more about all of it very soon."

"Can we take a look?" Colter asked.

Elliot nodded. "I don't see what it could hurt. You wanna see the training grounds?"

A lot of enthusiastic affirmations came from the group.

"Let's check it out, then."

Elliot led them inside. The double doors slid open as they approached and a cool blast of air hit Greyson square in the face as he headed inside.

Both the floor and walls were white, giving the interior a very modern look. The group didn't have long to sightsee, however, as Elliot kept walking deeper into the building.

As they followed, he explained, "The room on your right is the course training room. There are all sorts of obstacles that can be taken apart, reconfigured, and made into new courses with new challenges, and they are all easily changed through our applications. The course on the left is how you get good at individual obstacles. In that room, you can practice any obstacle that is giving you problems."

Impressed whispers came from all around. "Whoa," a boy whispered.

"Look at that!" said another.

They were right—there really *was* a lot to take in. So much, even, that Greyson wasn't sure where to look. Nobody was training in either room, so his eyes drifted first to the individual obstacles room. It was the smaller of the two, but was still packed full with different personal challenges.

He recognized a couple from the course he'd run in the hangar, including Pole Position and the curved wall. But, unlike the obstacles in the hangar, these seemed even more difficult: the pole's cradles were farther apart, and the wall was taller than the one he'd run. It was mega, to say the least.

On the very far side of the room, tucked behind all the individual obstacles, was something that Greyson recognized immediately—one obstacle he was sure he could conquer. A rock wall. He'd learned to climb on an indoor training wall just like this, and even seeing it made him feel at home.

The other room was much larger, but also much more spread out. As Greyson scanned it, he could see at least two different courses that had been assembled. They both started with the Detached Steps and ended with a Wall Run, but the obstacles sandwiched between them were much different than what he'd done at the hangar.

Even seeing the courses made his heart race a bit.

Macie raised her hand.

"Go ahead, Macie," Elliot said. "And no need to raise your hand. We'll keep it a bit more fun than school."

"Okay, cool." She blushed, then asked, "So why the obstacle courses? They seem so central to everything you do, and N.J. even said we'd be spending a lot of time on them."

Elliot nodded. "They are, really. It's the sport of NINJAs, and that's because we truly believe there is no better way to demonstrate all-around athletic and mental ability than to master an obstacle course. If you can conquer our most advanced courses, you can do *anything.*"

A silence fell over the teenagers, and Elliot added, "The sparring room is through those doors, but that will not be a focus for you, yet. For the summer, our attention will primarily be obstacle course training."

Greyson tried to peer past Elliot, looking into the room he'd described as the sparring room, but the light was off, and there was nothing to see.

"Let's continue the tour, shall we?" Elliot was backed down the hall, trapped behind a crowd of teenagers, so he pointed and added, "If you all will head out the building, we'll go to the dormitories and see if N.J. has the rooms prepared yet."

Once thc group entered the front doors of the enormous building called the Great Hall, they were greeted with a list of names and numbers read aloud.

"Kerkins and Guirt, you're in 2A," N.J. began after asking the group if they enjoyed the tour. "Jones and Rundy, you're in 2B."

To Greyson's left, Skylar was looking around. "Who's Rundy?" he half-whispered.

N.J. continued like this, pairing two boys in a room and two girls into a room until all thirty teenagers had been assigned a dorm. There were a total of twenty-two boys and eight girls, and most of the girls ended up on the third floor.

Finally, N.J. read out, "Rickman and McEntire, you're in room 3F. And I believe that's everybody. If your bags aren't already sitting outside your room, they will probably arrive very soon. And, of course, I have keycards, too."

As the appropriate keycards were distributed, Elliot bid the group farewell, slipping out the door and heading toward the training grounds.

Greyson was itching to go check out his room, as were most of the rest of the teenagers, it seemed, but N.J. held them up a bit. "Before you go, a few more announcements."

The excited whispering from within the group died down.

First, he pointed to the right down a hall, one with a swooping high ceiling and decorative tiling that, much like the rest of the lobby, reminded Greyson of a high-class hotel. "The dinner hall is down that way. We'll eat at 8 AM, Noon, and 5 PM every day. Please try to make the meals, as those are the only times the room will be open."

Some nods came from around the lobby.

"Thanks. Next up, since we're working on limited time, we're going to dive into class first thing tomorrow. Following breakfast, you'll have a 9:30 class in room 5 of Nuaki Hall. Elliot showed you the building, right?"

More nods.

"Did he show you where the classes were?"

The teenagers collectively shook their heads.

"No worries either way. In each of your rooms will be a package with class descriptions and syllabuses, along with campus maps. Everyone got it?"

"Yes sir," Colter answered for the group.

"Good." N.J. counted with his fingers again, just like he had on the bus. Then, apparently remembering something else, he added, "Last thing, I promise. The coaches are in the bottom and top rooms. That's the first floor and sixth floor. If you need anything at all, you can always come knock on any of our doors, day or night. I'm in 1B if you want to start there."

Greyson looked at Colter, still trying to wrap his mind around if this was really happening. As much as he wanted to believe, it still felt like a dream he could wake up from at any moment.

Except, it wasn't.

As soon as N.J. had shared all the PSAs, he dismissed the group and sent them to their rooms for an evening of getting situated.

Although N.J. had told them to get a good night's sleep, Greyson knew that was very unlikely for him. He was far too excited.

Tomorrow, he'd have his first NINJA class.

Tomorrow, his adventure would officially begin.

TWELVE

The first evening on campus was a blur of exploration, socializing, and trying to fall into something of a routine.

First, Colter and Greyson went to their room, where they found their bags waiting on them outside the door, just as N.J. had told them. The room was like what one could expect in a nice hotel: two queen-sized beds, a TV, a comfortably-sized bathroom, and a couch. That said, it had a few unique features that weren't to be found in most hotel rooms: elastic stretch bands, a pull-up bar, and two foam rollers.

On top of that, both nightstands housed a tablet. One had Greyson's name on it and the other had Colter's. After swiping through his tablet, Greyson found that it had a campus map and listed his first class of the morning. Apart from that, there was nothing. The tablet didn't even have an option to download apps.

After unpacking, they made their way downstairs to the cafeteria, which was a large room with shiny tile, and lots of windows with maroon curtains framing them. They sat by one of the windows and ate a meal of smoked turkey, mashed potatoes, green beans, and a side salad while overlooking the training grounds outside.

Before they'd finished, Macie joined them, as did a girl she introduced as Sydney, who was a competitive cheerleader from Florida. Skylar also took a seat at the table shortly thereafter.

The dinner was good, the conversation was better, and the day left Greyson with a lot of questions. When he and Colter finally made it back to their room, he asked, "What do you think about this?"

"About…everything?"

Greyson nodded. "Everything."

"It's a lot," Colter admitted. "And some of the stuff still doesn't make sense to me, or at least seem believable. But I know you gotta be feeling the same way, right?"

Again, Greyson confirmed.

"But I think something special is going to happen," Colter went on. "Everything about this place seems magical, and that might sound dumb to say, but like…I mean it. Something cool is going on here."

"No, I totally agree." Colter said. "Something tells me tomorrow will be a *big* day."

It was.

After a restless night of excitement fighting off sleep, breakfast the next day was the same style of meal, the same table, and the same cast of friends. Only this time, the small group was also joined by the incredibly tall boy, who took the last seat at the table. He introduced himself as Joey, and throughout the breakfast discussion, he proved to fit in very well.

As the meal was winding down, suddenly everyone's tablets chimed at the same time.

"Looks like we're getting a fifteen-minute reminder for our first class," Greyson said as he turned it off. "Guess they don't want us to be late. Ready to go?"

The rest of the friends agreed, so they cleaned up their table and slipped into the stream of teenagers that were trickling out of the cafeteria.

As far as Greyson could tell, one of the three other regional groups had arrived so far. There had been about sixty teenagers in the cafeteria that morning, half of whom he didn't recognize from his qualifying course.

But as he led Colter and the rest of their new friends across the campus toward the classrooms, Greyson noticed that the rest of the teens on the same route were all familiar faces. Since N.J. had told his group that they had class at 9:30 during the orientation, he'd been expecting that the class would be composed entirely of his counterparts from regionals, but he couldn't tell if the second regional group was heading to class as well.

He pointed this out to Colter, who said, "I think they're over there."

Greyson followed Colter's finger to the training grounds. Sure enough, a group of fifteen or so teenagers were standing around the outside course while a few more trickled out from the cafeteria.

"Wow, wish we had the outdoor class," Joey said.

"Yeah, but my guess is we'll be doing it pretty soon, too," Greyson replied.

They slipped into Nuaki Hall and found classroom five upstairs. As promised, it was everything Greyson expected, thanks to his high school experience: desks, a podium for lecturing, and even a smart board at the head of the class.

About half the desks were full, so Greyson took a seat in a cluster of open desks. His friends settled in beside him, patiently waiting for class to start.

9:30 came, but nothing happened. Greyson checked his watch a couple times, but he did it discreetly, trying to play it cool.

"What class is this?" Colter whispered from beside him.

"What do you mean? Like, the subject?"

"Yeah. I just realized that I have absolutely no idea. It's like first-day-of-school nerves, but also with a blindfold."

Greyson couldn't help but laugh. The description was almost too perfect.

And with that, the sound of footsteps came clicking down the hall. Upon hearing them, the students all fell silent and sat upright. Greyson's stomach twisted with surprising nerves as the footsteps grew louder.

And then Jamee walked through the door. He looked as jovial and energetic as always. Colorful tattoos—nearly as bright and eye-catching as his hair—peeked out from underneath the sleeves of the white v-neck t-shirt he wore. Unlike every teacher Greyson had ever had, Jamee was also wearing black joggers. He looked more like he was ready to run a marathon than teach a class.

But, as professionally as possible, he walked to the front of the class and greeted, "Hello! How are you all today?"

There were a few weak-but-favorable responses from the audience of teenagers, who all seemed a bit taken aback by his informal attire.

Jamee didn't seem to notice. Instead, he clapped his hands together and said, "I'm super excited for this class! You can probably tell...I know I get wound up sometimes when I get to teach this stuff, but this is one of my favorite subjects!"

Very gingerly, a boy in the front row raised his hand.

"Yes sir!" Jamee pointed at him. "Do you have a question? Also, no need to raise your hand when you have questions. Just throw them out there." It was the second time in twenty-four hours that Greyson had heard this, and while it was a different approach to his usual academic environment, it was also a welcome one.

"Um..." For just a moment, the boy sounded a bit uncertain, like perhaps he'd missed something obvious and shouldn't be asking the question at all.

"Go on. Seriously, there are no dumb questions. You'll be asking a *lot* of questions here, trust me."

The boy nodded. "I might have missed the memo, but...what class is this?"

Jamee's eyes widened. "What? You guys don't know?"

Collectively, the students shook their heads.

Jamee, an annoyed look on his face, said, "That's absurd. I'll complain to the head of the scheduling department about communication issues."

"You don't have to do that," the boy said, almost apologetically.

Jamee chuckled. "Joking," he said. "I *am* the head of the scheduling department. But I don't know how the message slipped through the cracks, and I wish you at least knew what you were in for—this is history class."

"History class?" Skylar asked, his tone saying the exact thing everybody else was thinking: why did they come here to take a *history* class? In a high-tech camp run by NINJAs, history was the last thing anybody wanted to study.

Jamee wasted no time in addressing the skepticism. "Relax, it's not like any history class you have taken before. I'm not going to ask you when the Civil War started or who the third president was—that's what you go to school for. I'm going to teach you *real* history."

"What do you mean?" Skylar pressed.

Jamee made a thoughtful expression, then said, "Look around the camp. Take everything in, and ask yourself this: do you think the NINJAs are the new kids on the block, or do you think we've been at this for a long time?"

"You've been around for a while. Like a *long* time, at least that's what N.J. said on the bus."

Jamee shrugged. "Dang, sounds like he already stole my thunder. I couldn't hear much of the conversation because I was flying the thing, but yeah, you're right. We've been doing this for a very long time. I'm just playing a small part of a long line of NINJAs."

"Yeah, I get that," Skylar agreed. "But...why history?"

"*Because...*" Jamee said, "...we're going to teach you *real* history. There's textbook history—the kind you learn about in school—and then there's the kind that's about what *really* happened. Said differently, I'm gonna teach you all about the way the NINJAs have influenced everything you think you know about the world. At least, the first half."

Now, Greyson spoke up, "First half?"

"Yeah. This is part one of NINJA History. Think of it as an overview. We'll go through the history of our organization at a 10,000-foot view over the next month or so, and then you'll take part two with Jon. That's where you get into the nitty gritty, and let me be the first to tell you, that's going to be a *fun* class."

"So this class lasts for a month?" The question came from a ginger-haired girl that Greyson had seen a lot of but had yet to learn her name.

"*All* classes last a month," Jamee explained. "At least, that's how we've decided to break it up for the sake of this summer recruitment. And at the end of the month, we'll have the second round of trials to determine who advances, so pay attention and work hard."

Greyson could sense there were about a dozen questions waiting to be asked from all around the room about this new topic, but nobody was brave enough to do it. Jamee didn't allow much time, anyway, as he turned and waved his hand at the large electronic board.

Just like that, it came to life. Not only did the screen flicker on, but an automated female voice greeted, "Welcome, Coach Jamee. Happy first day of classes."

"Whoa…" There was a general ripple of impressed mumbles from the class.

"Thanks, Anna," Jamee responded. "Will you find the lesson plans I prepared for day one and pull those up?"

"Of course." The voice was sing-songy, and it was so realistic that Greyson was certain he would have mistaken it for that of a human if he wasn't paying close attention.

Jamee turned back to the class. "Everybody, meet Anna – our Ancient NINJA Notification Assistant. She's the artificial intelligence unit that powers a lot of the interactive tech on campus. You'll interface with her a lot, and after you set up your voiceprint, she'll be able to individually separate and log all of your conversations."

"Greetings, class," Anna said.

"Hey…" This response once again came collectively, but it was also much more uncertain than the last. Everybody, including Greyson, had no idea what to say.

Finally, somebody said, "You know, she kind of reminds me of Ale–"

Jamee didn't even let him finish. "Actually, Anna has been around a lot longer than we know, so anything that's being peddled on the mass market is a watered-down version of her."

"Thanks, Jamee," Anna said. "He is correct, though. At this point, I'm ninety-three percent human in terms of conversational patterns, and my learning capacity is immeasurably greater."

"Okay, okay, you don't have to brag." Jamee rolled his eyes, and a few of the students laughed.

"Shall we start the lesson?"

"Yeah, let's do it." On Jamee's word, the screen pulled up a picture of a shape that was all too familiar to Greyson. It was the emblem—the same one he'd drawn and tried to reverse image search.

He and Colter swapped a knowing look as Jamee explained, "The hardest thing about this class is figuring out where to begin, and I want to start from the very beginning. This is the NINJA Seal."

"Is that a turtle?" Reeza asked.

"Yes, it is," Jamee said. "Maybe not the obvious choice, but turtles are resilient, long-lasting, and protective—-just like the NINJAs. The four legs stand for honor, bravery, valor, and nobility–our core four traits."

Somebody asked, "Should we be taking notes?"

"No, just listening well," Jamee answered. "There's no written test over this. This is just so you'll have better context on what we're doing and why we're doing it."

A few of the students seemed relieved to know there wasn't going to be a test, but for Greyson, it didn't matter one way or another. He was locked in, regardless.

"One of the first questions I often hear is 'why'," Jamee continued. "Specifically, 'why did the NINJA Order form?' I am also often asked about *when* it happened, but to be completely honest with you, I'm not sure. None of us know the exact date, but the NINJAs pre-date anything we currently have on record, and you'll learn more about the earliest of days during the second part of this history class."

Greyson couldn't resist. He began to take notes on his tablet.

"I *can* answer *why* the NINJA Order formed, however," Jamee went on, "And it's an answer that might catch some of you by surprise because it will challenge what you know about the world. The NINJAs came together to fight against an evil force—a source of power that could have potentially put an end to humanity as we know it."

The words seemed to be met with a lot of skepticism, but nobody outwardly spoke up.

At this point, the picture on the slide changed to what appeared to be a drawing, but it was a drawing unlike anything Greyson had ever seen. It looked ancient, and as far as Greyson could tell, it was a mix between a sculpture and a cave painting. The drawing was of a human-like figure, but it was also clearly *not* human. Its limbs were too long, and the gentle curve of human anatomy was far too sharp and rigid.

"This is Eris," Jamee said as he gestured to the picture. "At least, that is the name we've come to know it by at this time, and this sketch by our ancient ancestors is perhaps the best illustration of The Great Threat that we have to this day. And note, 'The Great Threat' is how many of the NINJAs still refer to Eris, so you might hear that term thrown around in other classes."

"What *is* that thing?" Macie asked, staring toward the haunting figure on the canvas.

A solemn expression crossed Jamee's face. "Unfortunately, there is a lot we do not know about The Great Threat for a number of reasons, including that it happened at a time that we refer to as the 'great reset'. There are no writings about Eris because all writings from the time were lost, and written languages were restarted. We only have scraps of stories."

He turned to the screen, fixing his eyes on the image for just a moment. "This is the part that will be hard to believe because it will go against everything you've ever thought you've known, but will you all promise to approach it with an open mind?"

Slowly—perhaps even cautiously in some cases—all heads nodded.

Jamee took a deep breath, looked around the room, and then said, "Every piece of technology that you interact with every day, from phones to tablets, smart speakers and everything else, can somebody tell me what leads you to buy those things?"

"Because they make our life easier," Joey suggested.

"At this point, we almost have to own them to get a job, etc."

"One-hundred percent correct," agreed Jamee. "But perhaps I should rephrase: when you upgrade a phone, why do you do it?"

"To get in on all the new features," Colter said.

"Exactly! The *new* features," Jamee emphasized. "But what if I told you that that sort of technology was not new at all?"

"What do you mean?" said the boy named Shafer. "All the tech titans are inventing new technology every day. I've seen some pretty crazy technology."

Jamee shook his head. "That's the catch. What nobody knows—including those 'tech titans,' as you put it—is that they are, in fact, *reinventing* technology. You see, in ancient times, there was one global civilization that had evolved to be even more technologically advanced than we are today in modern America. They had it all, including semi-autonomous machines."

"You're kidding," somebody said. "There's no chance that was possible. We'd all know by now. And didn't you say there wasn't any writing?"

"They had writings," Jamee corrected. "But it was all in a digital form."

"What? How is that possible?"

Jamee paced across the front of the class. "Think of it this way: we're currently transitioning from hard copies to digital copies as we speak. Imagine what will happen in another hundred years…nothing will be written on paper. Does that seem possible?"

The class nodded collectively.

"Good. Now imagine ninety-five percent of the

population is destroyed, along with the digital infrastructure containing all of your written languages. What happens then?"

Silence.

"I'll give you a hint: all the written work is gone. Lost."

"So that's what happened?" Skylar asked, sounding skeptical.

The picture on the board changed again, showing another sketch of what appeared to be a city. "The civilization evolved and became so technologically-advanced that it created its own threat," Jamee explained. "It created computational power so advanced that it became sentient and attempted to overthrow its human creators. Tens of thousands died in the battle."

"Eris?" asked Skylar.

"Exactly. They created Eris, who we believe did everything in its power to kill off all humanity and populate the world with self-replicating machines powered by artificial intelligence. If Eris had succeeded, you and I wouldn't be here today. None of us would be. The world would be a much different, much more metal, place."

Greyson's tablet screen timed out as he realized he'd been so absorbed in the story that he'd forgotten to write down anything at all. Everything he was hearing was… unbelievable. Even considering where he was and the things he'd seen over the last twenty-four hours, this was still too much.

"What happened?" Shafer asked. "What stopped the robot uprising?"

"NINJAs," Jamee said the word like it was to be completely expected. "A few brave citizens from across the globe came together in a last-ditch effort, using their physical and mental skills to fight back against the machines that had enslaved them. While we don't know *how* it happened, we know they managed to burn the civilization to the ground, defeat Eris, and spread the indestructible parts of the mechanical menace around the world, separating them as far as possible from one another in order to put an end to the threat once and for all."

The words hung in the air. Nobody spoke. Nobody knew what to say.

Finally, Jamee went on. "The few NINJAs that did survive left almost all of their technology behind, determined to prevent another catastrophe like that from ever reoccurring. That said, they also knew that *some* technology could be used to do good, and the shards of the old world they brought with them have propelled us to where we're at today, decades more advanced than the rest of the world."

Greyson felt like he was suffocating as everything washed over him. He didn't know what to believe. He didn't know if he should wholeheartedly accept everything Jamee was telling them, or if he should call out the NINJAs for being an insane cult and flee as fast as he could.

He did neither. Instead, he asked a question.

"Jamee?"

"Yes, Greyson?"

"If all of this was left behind in this 'old world,' as you called it, why are the NINJAs so heavily recruiting *today,* so many years later?"

Now it was Jamee's turn to look uncomfortable, like he didn't know what to say or how much to reveal. Finally, after a long exhalation, he looked Greyson dead in the eye and said, "I'll be completely honest with you all. The NINJAs program is normally kept small with just a select few elite active members. That is, unless a threat is triggered—in that case, the recruitment process is initiated."

Greyson looked around the class, noting that several of the teenagers looked just as concerned as him. He asked, "So, does that mean—"

"Yes," Jamee confirmed, not even giving Greyson the chance to finish his thought. "We think the Great Threat might be returning, and if that is the case, we could all be in great danger. If we have any chance of getting through this, we need to do it *together.*"

THIRTEEN

All the students wandered out of Jamee's class and into the hall, heading toward the training grounds in the middle of the campus. Jamee had told them their next class would take place there.

As they walked, a persistent chatter broke out among them. Greyson, however, didn't join in.

He couldn't.

He was too deep in thought. He mentally unpacked and digested everything that he'd heard in history class, trying to decide if he was spending the next four weeks with a crazed group of humans that believed in an alternative history, or if somehow, someway, all of this was real. If there was any truth to what he'd heard, he'd learned more in the past forty-five minutes than his entire high school years combined.

"What do you think?" Macie asked him. She was walking right beside him, but somehow he hadn't even noticed.

"That was..." He searched for the words. "A lot."

"Yeah. It definitely was that."

They silently walked down the flight of stairs, both contemplating, but once they reached the ground floor, she asked, "Do you believe him?"

Greyson thought about it. Such a simple question, but the answer was so elusive. Finally, he said, "I…I don't know."

"What if you had to pick? If somebody made you answer yes or no."

"Yes." The answer spilled out of his mouth without hesitation, surprising even himself. "Yes, I do. There's too much going on in camp that aligns with everything they've said. Advanced technology, the top-secret nature of the program…all that stuff makes me think, as crazy as it sounds, that Jamee's telling us the truth."

Macie grinned.

"What?"

"Nothing, it's just…well, I was thinking the exact same thing. I'm unsure what to believe, but my gut tells me we need to trust the NINJAs."

"I think so, too," Colter weighed in from behind them. "Jamee's a solid guy. I can tell he's telling us the truth."

As they exited the classroom building, Greyson laughed, but only to himself. For Colter, everything was so black and white. He trusted Jamee, so no matter how outlandish his words sounded, Colter was all-in. It would be nice to be like that. The world would be a simpler place.

"I've got a question," said Skylar, who was behind Colter. "Here's what doesn't make sense to me—or, at least, *one* of the things. If they're so top-secret, how do they possibly expect to *stay* top-secret if only a quarter of the current students here make it on to the next level of training?"

"I was wondering the same thing!" Greyson's statement came out a little more emphatic than he'd intended, but it was nice to hear somebody else thinking about the bigger picture. "How do they honestly expect us to return to our families and not mention *anything* about a summer spent with flying vehicles, crazy AI, and stories of a world run by monster machines?"

"I don't know," Skylar said.

Nobody did. They reached the grass, which was still damp from morning dew. Quiet and once again deep in thought, they headed across the lawn and out toward the obstacle course in the middle of the grounds.

"Hey, check that out," Colter said, pointing toward the runway.

Greyson fixed his eyes on one of the bus-jets, from which a line of wide-eyed teenagers was exiting, looking around from side-to-side in bewildered disbelief.

"We must have looked just like that," Greyson mused, and as he said the words, he realized something.

This was *real.*

As he watched the astonishment, Greyson knew in his heart that there was no way the NINJAs could fake all this, and they had no reason to make up an unsettling story about an ancient threat trying to take over the world. There were too many people being brought in to try to trick them all, so they had to be doing something even more unbelievable.

...Telling the truth.

"Hello, everybody!" The words came from the direction of the obstacle course, and Greyson snapped his gaze from the bus to the man emerging from one of the big tents beside the course. The man was young and very muscular—the thin, light kind of muscular instead of the bulky type.

As Greyson took in the man, his eyes widened. He knew him.

"You're… Lev," the words tumbled from his tongue. "You're Lev, aren't you?" His pace quickened.

"Whoa, I've never seen Greyson fangirl," Colter whispered from behind him, and Greyson shot him a look.

"Yeah!" Lev said, reaching out to shake Greyson's hand. "It's not every day I get recognized. You're…"

"A fan," Greyson answered. "My name is Greyson McEntire, and I'm a climber, too."

Colter quickly assumed his role as hype man, adding, "He's a great one, too. A state champion climber."

Greyson shook his head. "No, I'm nowhere near the climber Lev is. This man's a *national* champion—multiple times, at that."

Colter fell silent, clearly impressed.

Lev played it cool. With a shrug, he said, "Hey, sounds like you're a pretty good climber, too, Greyson. And from what I've heard, you're a pretty good NINJA. You crushed the qualifier, right?"

The feeling was back, stirring inside Greyson. He felt all the eyes on him, and while he knew Lev only meant the best, he hated being called out in front of all of his peers.

Instead of answering Lev's question, Greyson asked one of his own. "What happened, Lev? Like, did you retire from climbing? It seemed like you were winning the nationals every year for about four years straight, but I haven't read much about you since."

Lev looked down for a moment, running his toe through the grass. "Yeah, that's a pretty fair description, Greyson. It turns out, I found something even more important to me than climbing." Looking up, he made a sweeping gesture at the grounds all around him.

"You mean you gave up climbing…to be a NINJA?"

"I wouldn't say that I gave it up, entirely, but I did refocus my climbing energy toward something else."

The words hit Greyson hard. He loved climbing. Everything about his life was somehow influenced by the sport. The thought of letting it go was too much to fathom, and as much as Greyson enjoyed climbing, he knew the multi-time national champion he was talking to had to love it just as much.

"Why?" Greyson asked. "Why did you do that? You were literally one of the best climbers ever."

Lev glanced at his watch. "It's time to start class, so if you give me just a few minutes, I'll show you. Deal?"

"Deal."

Still in disbelief about who he was talking to, Greyson followed Lev into a tent. In the canopy's shade, he found a set of bleachers, and the students all took a seat. Lev, meanwhile, stood in front of the group. With arms spread, he greeted, "Welcome, everybody, to Energy Management."

"Energy Management?" Several of the students, including Colter and Macie, whispered the name in confusion.

The title didn't make sense to Greyson either. 'Energy Management' sounded like a class for collegiate engineers. Instead of a lab with textbooks, the students were all sitting in the middle of a grassy field with an obstacle course just a stone's throw away. This class felt more like it should be called P.E.

Lev not only noticed their confusion, but he seemed to appreciate it. With a laugh, he asked, "Crazy name, right? Why would we call this class 'Energy Management'? Especially when we're standing by an obstacle course." While his questions were playful, he was basically stating everything running through Greyson's mind.

Then, without any apparent transition, Lev asked, "Have you seen some of our advanced technology yet?"

"Yes," the response came from the group.

"Excellent. Flying bus, obviously. Perhaps…Anna?"

More confirmation from the group.

"Both of those are great examples that speak to the power of innovation and show how our technology is far superior to that of the outside world," Lev said. "But today, I'm going to introduce you to the cornerstone of the NINJAs. This is a wizard's wand or a space pirate's light-sword."

Greyson quickly glanced at Macie, who was sitting on his immediate left and looked just as anxious as he was feeling. As he turned back to Lev, their instructor held out his wrist. He was wearing a watch. It was black, circular, and slightly bulky, but not enough to be visually unattractive.

As Greyson focused on the watch, it occurred to him that he'd seen one before. Had Jon been wearing it? Or maybe N.J.? Or, perhaps, *both* of them. The more Greyson thought about it, the more certain he was that both of them wore an identical timepiece.

"This is the Watch," Lev explained. "It condenses our ancient tech into a sleek, stylish timepiece. Would you like to see what it can do?" As he said this, his tone mimicked that of a television ad—playful mockery.

"Yes," the crowd of teens replied, and this response was much more enthusiastic than any of the previous.

On cue, Lev smirked. "I was hoping you'd say that." With a mischievous smile on his face, he reached up and tapped a button on the side of the watch.

What happened next was so quick—so unexpected—that Greyson's eyes witnessed it before his brain could ever process what was happening. First, the watch emitted a sound that was at the crossroads of a snap and a hiss, and as the sound struck Greyson's ears, a pulse blasted out of the watch.

Except, *blasted* wasn't the best word. It was far too controlled. Too...organic. The watch emitted a wave of shimmering light that wrapped around Lev. It started with his arm, then worked its way across his torso and down his other arm and legs.

The light was almost imperceptible, especially once it settled against his skin, but if Greyson *really* focused, he could see the slightest glimmer on Lev's skin, almost like he was sweaty and under bright lights. There was a buzz, too. A humming, charged sound tickled Greyson's ear, like he was listening to one overly bright lightbulb illuminating a small room.

Once the ripple of light had enveloped the entirety of Lev's body, he held out his hands and spun around, offering the teenagers a look at the entirety of the strange light field wrapping around him and overlaying his clothes.

"What...what is that?" a boy asked. "What did..."

He trailed off, apparently too astonished to even form the words.

Lev, very calmly, answered. "This is the Wave," he explained. "Like I said, it's the secret weapon of the NINJAs."

"But what does it *do?"* This was from Joey.

"I'll be better off showing you than trying to explain," Lev said. "But at a very high level, it works like a microphone for your body."

Greyson arched an eyebrow. *What could that possibly mean?*

Lev must have noticed, because he asked, "Greyson, can you tell me what a microphone does for the human voice?"

"It...makes it louder." Even as Greyson said the words, he felt like this could be a trick question.

It wasn't. Instead, Lev bobbed his head in encouragement. "Exactly. It amplifies our voices so we can more easily be heard. So with that in mind, the Wave has the same exact effect, but for our muscles."

"So it makes you... faster?" Greyson asked.

"Yes, and it also makes me stronger, a higher jumper, and it amplifies every other form of athletic ability." He clapped his hands together, and the Wave held tight against his clothes. "Would you like a demonstration?"

An abundance of approval came from the students.

"Joey...it's Joey, right?"

"Yes, sir." Joey nodded.

"Come stand right here." Lev gestured to the grass right in front of him.

Joey unfolded his long legs and stood. As he walked to the designated spot, Greyson once again wondered how this awkward-moving boy had ever navigated the obstacle course.

"Joey, can I ask how tall you are?" Lev asked.

"I'm six-foot-seven," Joey said.

"Perfect." Lev looked up, meeting Joey in the eyes. "That is tremendously tall, and it's quite an accomplishment to have qualified at that height. I understand that you had a good run on the course."

This was new to Greyson. Not only had Joey qualified—apparently he'd done very well in the process.

Joey, however, quietly nodded. "Yes, sir. It was fun."

"You can just call me Lev," Lev answered, still sizing Joey up. "Or maybe 'Coach Lev' if you're more comfortable with that. Whatever works."

"Understood, Coach."

"Good." Lev turned back to the bleachers, addressing the students. "As you guys can tell, I'm not the tallest guy. Especially not compared to my guy Joey here. Would you all say that's a fair statement?"

Most of the students agreed.

Again, Lev eyed the top of Joey's head like he was making mental calculations. "Considering Joey's height, I think we would all be in agreement that I shouldn't be able to do…this!" On his word, he took two steps toward Joey and jumped off both legs.

The leap was tremendous. Lev shot skyward with a vertical jump that looked like something that should only appear in a movie. At the peak of his jump, he tucked his knees into his chest and turned a mid-air flip that took place at least three or four feet above Joey's head, and then he dropped back down, landing behind Joey with a soft *thump*.

All the students popped to their feet. The roar of disbelief was louder now than ever before, and Colter leaned in to whisper to Greyson, "Dude, what did we just see?"

"I...I..." Greyson was stuttering, struggling to form any logical words. *What had he just seen?* He knew Lev was an athletic man, but nobody could jump like that—at least ten feet high. And, on top of the height, Lev had looked like he'd barely been trying. Like he'd been shooting a very casual layup in a game of basketball.

Finally, Greyson managed, "I have no idea."

"It was pretty sweet," Colter responded. "I think I need one of those watches."

When the astonishment of the students turned into curiosity, the questions began to fly at Lev.

Skylar asked, "Do all the NINJAs have one of those watches?"

"Yes sir."

"Will we get one?"

"In about a week, after you learn more about them."

"How does it work?"

Politely, Lev waved off all the questions. "Please, take a seat. I'll explain everything you need to know... and then some. Trust me, I'm kind of a nerd about this sort of stuff, so odds are I'll be going on and on to the point you're *hoping* I'll shut up." He laughed.

The students all sat, but the whispering amongst them continued.

Lev turned the face of the watch to them, pointing to the display. For the most part, it looked like every smartwatch Greyson had ever seen: a pixelated screen, bright numbers on a dark background, and an easy-to-read display. Except, Lev's watch didn't show a time—it showed a percentage.

82%. The digits glowed just big enough for Greyson to see from his bleachers.

"Does everybody see that?" Lev asked. "If not, it says 82%."

Even as he spoke, the 82% turned to 83%. At first, Greyson had assumed the number was the watch's battery power, but that couldn't be right: this was counting *up.*

"Ah, see, it just changed," Lev noted. "This is where things get a bit confusing, but bear with me. We'll spend the next week or so learning how this device works before you ever strap it on."

He lowered his hands, pulling the screen out of view. "Are you ready to stretch your minds a bit?"

"Yes," replied the group.

Lev grinned. "Awesome. I'll try to keep this simple. The Wave, as you just saw, amplifies what we're capable of accomplishing with our normal bodies. I hate to spoil the grandeur, but I'm not, in fact, capable of doing a flip over Joey's head without the Wave."

About half the group, including Greyson, laughed. The rest were still grappling with their ever-crashing perception of reality.

Lev went on, "Here's where it gets a bit heavy: while the Wave makes us capable of doing more, it also drains our energy at a much higher rate. For example, say I normally have a top speed of twenty miles-per-hour when I run. With the Wave, I could run forty miles-per-hour, but that would also make me twice as tired."

The words sank in. Macie raised her hand.

"Yes, Macie?"

"When do you feel tired?"

"Great question," Lev said. "When you use the Wave, you actually feel the exertion right *after* you perform the action, not during. That's because of the way it amplifies our abilities with our own energy, but it's also a reason we need to be careful. Can somebody tell me why?"

Greyson had already been thinking the exact same thing. He answered, "If we're not careful—if we overestimate what we're capable of—the Wave would leave us completely spent."

"Exactly," Lev said. "You nailed it, Greyson. If you use the Wave to do too much, it will leave you completely drained. And if that's the case, the consequences can be very… unfortunate."

"Like…you can die?" Colter asked.

"Hopefully not that extreme, but it will definitely take you a long, long time to completely recover," Lev said. "But we won't worry about that, because I'm going to teach you everything you need to know to be safe when using the Wave. Nobody gives you the keys to a car and tells you to just go have fun, and this will be the same way. To have fun, we will learn safety first."

Greyson could feel his heart racing again. Soon, he could be a watch-wearing superhero—just like Lev.

Their coach, on the other hand, looked very calm. He flashed a playful grin. "Now, with what we've just seen, I want to ask you something again. Can somebody tell me why we call this class…'Energy Management'?"

FOURTEEN

Greyson was far from a picky eater, so the meals at NINJAs headquarters were always pretty appealing to him. The food was served cafeteria-style, so his tray would be filled for him as he made his way along the hot bar, and if he was ever hungry after finishing his first plate, there was a standing invite to go back for seconds. That hadn't happened yet.

The 'two-week feast', as their coaches had called it, changed up the normal meal delivery process. All the teenagers had been told to dress a bit nicer than normal, so dressed in polos and slacks, Greyson and Colter had walked into the dining hall only to discover it was empty and closed.

"What's going on with that?" Colter asked.

"No idea at all." Only a handful of other students were in the room, and nobody he recognized as a member of their group. "Guess we just grab a table and see what happens."

That's what they did. Before long, the whole cafeteria had begun to fill up, and Skylar and Joey soon joined them. Then, five minutes after that, Macie showed up with Sydney.

Macie looked stunning. She had on a baby blue dress, and up to this point, Greyson had never seen her in anything that wasn't a t-shirt and athletic shorts, but now, seeing her dressed up and having gone the extra mile to do her hair and makeup, it was all he could do to not stare. Macie looked almost like a new person. Equally as stunning, just beautiful in a different way.

Colter, for the first time ever, seemed to notice just how great she looked, too. Greyson caught his friend doing a double-take, but he didn't say anything to either Macie or Sydney.

"How are you guys?" Macie said. "Mind if we join you?"

"Of course not," Greyson answered as he gestured to the last two empty chairs. "Just don't expect to eat. Apparently the hot bar's closed."

They both laughed as they sat down. "I noticed that too," Sydney said. "What do you think they're doing for dinner?"

"I think...I guess dinner tonight must be a bit different."

It was. Before long, the cafeteria had seated over a hundred students, and a few of the coaches had arrived. An anticipatory silence settled in among the trainees as they awaited instructions. The coaches were all also dressed up, many of them looking even nicer than the students.

Jon, who wore a black suit, went to the head of the room and stood at a small wooden podium, which held a mic. "Hey everybody," he said. "As you've all noticed, tonight is a little different than most of our meals so far. When we were first planning this recruiting process, we debated how we could best celebrate a successful first two weeks of training, and we decided to have what we're calling the 'First Quarter Feast'. Tonight's meal is a celebration of the hard work you've put into NINJA training so far."

A few more coaches wandered into the cafeteria. Greyson spotted Elliot, wearing a dark blue suit, and Meg, who wore a black dress. Jamee followed close behind, wearing a purple suit that Colter pointed out as soon as he saw it.

Jon continued, "In just a moment, one of our coaches will be bringing a menu to each of you. Your job is to select an appetizer, entree, and dessert from the list. And, of course, remember that the coaches are also preparing the meal, so be sure to appreciate their hard work. Now, I have a very important question: has it been a good first couple weeks?"

With this, a loud rumble of applause burst out from around the cafeteria. Greyson slowly turned to look around, taking everybody in. He was beginning to know most of his fellow qualifiers by name, but since the other three groups had arrived from their own regionals, he knew he'd probably never get everybody's name down, especially since his classes mostly had members from his region.

Colter stopped clapping to scowl down at his hands, which were covered in bandages from a series of blisters. He was far from the only one, though. The obstacle course training had brutalized a lot of hands and fingers, leaving Greyson particularly thankful for his rock-climbing calluses.

Jon wrapped up his short speech by saying, "On behalf of the rest of the coaches, I want to thank you for all your commitment to training. We realize, in some ways, this probably feels like an extension of school bleeding into your summer, but you've all brought great attitudes and great work ethics. It's an honor to spend time with such dedicated, athletic, intelligent young people, such as yourselves. Thank you."

This was followed by another round of applause, although some, like Colter, approached it pretty gingerly this time. With a nod of thanks, Jon slipped out from behind the podium and joined a line of coaches against the far wall.

Jess and Lenny appeared out of the double doors that led into the kitchen, and just as Jon had said, they began going table-to-table with menus.

Lane, still wearing his signature cowboy hat, handed a menu to Greyson, and after a bit of debate, Greyson filled it out: a house salad, prime rib and vegetables, and blueberry pie. It sounded like the perfect dinner, albeit he might have steered away from the vegetables and picked french fries if he wasn't currently training for a top-secret organization.

After their whole table filled out the menu, Colter collected them all and gave them back to Lane. Once the menus were turned in, the conversation kicked off.

Joey asked, "Can you believe we've already been here two weeks?"

"Hardly," responded Sydney. "It still feels new every day."

She was spot-on. For Greyson, the first waking

thought he'd had every day for the past two weeks was, *Is this real?* The question would bounce around in his mind every morning as he peered out his open window and onto the training grounds in the center of the camp, watching the sun rise overhead.

Colter had adjusted better. He didn't seem quite as mesmerized by the sights and sounds. In fact, he'd gone as far as to say the experience was "kinda like football camp."

To Greyson, that was impossible to believe. Each day on the grounds consisted of two classes and then open sessions in the indoor or outdoor training centers called free training. Between the things they were learning in class and the technology Greyson was encountering something new and fantastic every day.

With all this on his mind, Greyson said, "I'm not sure if I'm struggling more to believe I've been here for a couple weeks or that I'm here at all."

His friends all agreed. "A month ago, my summer plan was to work at the chicken restaurant in my town and save some money for a new phone," Skylar added. "I made quite the one-eighty, but I'm sure we all did."

More nods. "What does everybody tell their parents?" Macie asked. "Like, I try to update my dad every day about what all I've learned, but there's only so many times I can tell him that I went to class and learned some new skills without sounding too vague or boring." She laughed.

"I know!" Joey emphatically agreed. "My brother asked what one of the classes was when we were Facetiming yesterday. I told him it was about the history of technology, and he asked for more details, but I really couldn't say anything else."

Greyson grinned at this. He'd experienced the same problem first-hand when he and Colter had called Mrs. Rickman. Colter had mentioned the obstacle courses, and then together, the boys had scrambled to come up with a logical reason why a STEM camp had obstacle courses in the first place. Their best answer was: to stimulate the mind, even through recreation.

"What about you, Grey?" Macie asked.

"Huh?" He pulled himself out of the recollection. "Sorry."

"What do you tell your parents?" she asked.

It was an innocent enough question, and he knew she meant no harm, but it still stung. "Oh." He looked down for a moment, trying to determine the best response. "Honestly, I don't talk to them much. I never really hear from my dad, and my mom only texted once. I just told her it was fun."

Colter jumped in, adding, "His mom's a thriving businesswoman. She's always really, really busy."

"Oh, I see," Skylar said, and he sounded impressed. All the friends looked the same way, though. Colter was good at making Greyson's mom sound like a successful professional instead of an uninterested parent, and maybe she was, but Greyson still always appreciated it.

"Wait," Joey added after a moment. "You guys knew each other?"

"Yeah," Colter answered. "We've been friends since like…the beginning of time. We grew up together and everything."

"Colter lives right across the street from me," Greyson added.

"You guys are really lucky," said Joey. "I assumed we all came here as solos. It's pretty cool that you had somebody to tag along with."

Skylar added, "Yeah, I knew you guys were tight but assumed you'd met here. I'll be honest, I was super stoked when I got the invite from the NINJAs, but the biggest deterrent was that I would be on my own all summer. I almost talked myself out of coming since I wouldn't have any friends with me."

"It makes a difference," agreed Colter. "I know we were both super lucky to be selected. I think it's probably because Grey and I saved a lady and baby in a car." After a pause, he admitted, "To bc fair, it was mostly Greyson, but I was there too."

Hearing Colter helped Greyson. His friend had every chance to be arrogant, but Colter never failed to give praise where it was due—especially with Greyson.

But, seeing the look on the faces of the rest of their friends, Greyson knew elaboration was needed. He quickly retold the story of the climbing adventure that had turned into so much more as concisely as possible.

Then, once he was finished, Colter went back in and added all the details, including Greyson swinging "just like Spider-Man" into the car and pulling the baby out.

In turn, Greyson talked about how much Colter helped along the way, and that he couldn't have ever done it alone—that Colter's strength and heroics were just as important to the final result and that he wouldn't have trusted anyone else with his own life like that. And finally, once he'd finished, he waited on a response from his new friends.

And waited.

Nobody spoke. They all just stared, like they were trying to decide if Greyson and Colter were serious or if this was all one big prank. Colter, however, flipped around his phone to show them the news story: *Pine Teenagers Heroically Save Mother and Baby.* Under the headline was the picture of Colter with the baby and Greyson on the ground.

Suddenly, all the friends began speaking at once. "Are you guys serious?" Sydney asked.

"Why am I just now hearing about this?" Macie added.

The other boys also added their praise, and Greyson shrugged it off. "It wasn't like I was trying to be a hero. Just doing what needed to be done. No big deal."

Macie shook her head. "You're amazing, Greyson. You both are. But there's more to you in particular than meets the eye."

What does that mean? He couldn't help but wonder. *Was it a compliment? Or was she calling him average, at least in appearance?*

He had to ask. "What do you mean?" *Great, did that make him seem like he was fishing for compliments?*

Based on Macie's expression, she seemed to realize how her statement could be taken, so she quickly backtracked. "I'm sorry! I just mean, like, you look like you'd be athletic and all, but I didn't expect you to be the *best* athlete of our group. At least on the course—I don't know if you realize this or not, but you've been *killing* it all week!"

Now, Greyson could feel himself blushing as she sang his praise, but he tried to play it as coolly as possible. "Wow, thanks. I really think it's my rock-climbing background. It plays really well to the skill set needed for the courses."

"Or, perhaps you're just really good at both."

"You guys ready to eat?" The words came from over Greyson's shoulder, and he looked up to see Meg standing behind him, carrying a big tray. She set it down and began distributing the plates of food between them, making sure they had what they'd ordered.

It was amazing. The food was even better than Greyson had expected, and the conversation with his friends made it that much better. While he'd had no qualms about anything he'd eaten in the cafeteria, this felt more like a five-star restaurant than anything he'd ever expect to eat at a summer camp.

And, most importantly, as he ate, laughed, and joked with his new friends, he realized something: this was his new life—at least for the summer—and despite how far-fetched everything felt, the meal was somehow the validation he needed that he belonged here. That he fit in. That he wanted to stay.

To stay. The words stirred another thought—a more somber note. According to everything he'd heard, there would be another trial at some point. The final qualifying. From there, many of the recruits would be sent home. Would he? What if he failed? No matter how good he felt on obstacles, all it took was one bad step. Even the best could go down.

Or, if he was to advance, what about his friends? How many of them would make it through, receiving their final stamp of approval? Would he be eating alone?

He forced the thoughts out of his mind when something caught his eye. Jamee was walking across the cafeteria along the far wall with great purpose. He had a very serious look on his face, unlike anything Greyson had ever seen from the man who was usually all smiles.

Colter, noticing Greyson, leaned over. "What's going on?"

"Jamee. He looks…worried." Until Greyson spoke it out loud, he hadn't realized the truth of his statement. But Jamee did, in fact, look worried. For Greyson, seeing him look like this was a first. Seeing *any* of the coaches look like this was a first.

Jamee went right up beside Jon and, after glancing around to make sure nobody could overhear, whispered something into Jon's ear.

Immediately, Jon's expression changed, too. His eyebrows narrowed, and his soft smile turned into a worried scowl. After a moment, Jamee finished sharing the message, and Jon bit his lip as he contemplated.

Then, Jon turned back to Jamee and responded with two words. Greyson was no expert lip reader by any means, but these two words were unmistakable: "*One second.*" With that, he headed back across the cafeteria, walking to the podium.

"What's going on, Grey?" Colter asked. "They look really concerned."

By now, the rest of their friends at the table had noticed the same thing, tracking Jon as he forced a confident smile onto his face as he stepped back up to the podium.

Leaning in, he said, "Hey, everybody. I don't want to interrupt your dinner for too long, but I just wanted to make a quick announcement. Tomorrow morning's course training class with Coach Jamee will be canceled, so if you have that class, you can take the morning off.

We encourage you to do a little free training, though, if you'd like."

Greyson was used to his high school peers cheering when a class was canceled, but this was a new experience. There was a collective sigh that came from across the large room.

But more importantly than that, something was wrong. Despite the way Jon confidently spoke and how he moved across the room, heading back to Jamee, Greyson had seen through the cracks—he'd seen the concern. While he had no idea what Jamee had said, he was sure about one thing: both of the men were worried.

Curiosity replaced his appetite, and as the evening turned to night and Greyson's friends went back to chatting, laughing, and enjoying their meals, he couldn't help but find himself thinking about what he'd seen.

What was wrong?

There was more going on than Jon wanted to let on, and Greyson had to find out what it was.

FIFTEEN

Greyson laid on his back. The bed was comfortable, and the covers were up to his chin just like he liked, but he couldn't sleep.

The moonlight shining through the window was bright enough that he could see the ceiling fan spinning overhead. Around and around it went, the blades moving just quickly enough that they blurred together into one waving circle.

In the other bed across the room, Colter was fast asleep. He wasn't snoring, but he was breathing heavily enough that he was just on the verge of it.

Greyson couldn't. He'd tried to sleep, but it just wouldn't come. He couldn't shut off his mind.

Ever since his parents divorced, he'd watched first-hand as his mother had put on an Oscar-worthy acting performance. Never had she addressed the heartache or had broken down and cried. Instead, she'd buried herself in her work to the point that she had become a zombie behind an office desk.

Greyson could see right through it. He knew she was upset—that she was broken beyond repair—but she wouldn't do anything about it. She continued forward every day, doing the same exact thing and acting like everything was all right when it was clearly *very, very wrong.*

That's exactly what the NINJAs had been doing all night, too. Nobody else seemed to notice it, but Greyson couldn't even force himself to believe things were okay when he could clearly see something was wrong.

Maybe he'd had too much practice.

But ever since Jamee had approached Jon and whispered something to him, things had changed. The whole nature of the feast had shifted. It was still a great meal full of laughter coming from all around the cafeteria, but the smiles on the faces of the coaches were suddenly…empty. Word had spread fast between them—whatever that word might be—and their minds were clearly elsewhere.

Greyson looked over at Colter. He wanted to talk, to tell his friend what he'd noticed and why he was concerned. He wanted to get Colter's thoughts on the situation. But he couldn't. Colter was out, far too asleep to care. And, honestly, Colter wasn't the kind of person who would care too much either way. He lived day-to-day, approaching problems as they arrived. Never did he look for them. Never did he seek out reasons to be worried or fretful.

In many ways, Greyson wished he could be like that. But, at the same time, he felt like he had a deeper perception of life. To cherish the highs in life, you have to understand the lows. *That's how it worked, right?*

The quiet hum of the ceiling fan was the only sound

in the room, but it did nothing to drown out Greyson's racing mind.

He flipped back through the events of the previous weeks. Everything he'd heard, everything he'd seen, everything he'd learned. It was all so…much.

Jamee had opened his eyes to an alternative history of the world, and every single one of the first five days of classes had left him feeling the exact same way: a mix of uncertainty, disbelief, and wonder.

Energy management class was equally as unbelievable, except for the fact that the things Lev said could somehow be verified. He'd taught the students about safety and using the Wave appropriately, telling them that if they learned, practiced and committed to the craft, they'd be heroes who could *change the world.*

Greyson wasn't even sure if that was what he wanted.

The other two classes from the first week were a bit more concrete. Or, at least, Greyson didn't feel like he was stretching his imagination as much during the hour-long periods.

The first was Aerial Acrobatics, which N.J. taught, and the class was basically a collection of skills that were useful for gaining momentum during aerial moves on an obstacle course. This included kips, thrusts, and other swinging moves Greyson had never tried but learned quickly nonetheless.

The other class was with Jess. It was called News and Society, and much like Jamee's history class, it was a much more traditional classroom feel, with desks, notes, and slideshows. In this class, Jess explained how NINJAs related to the outside world—how to exist as a secret society that watched over the rest of the world without ever revealing their secrets.

All the classes were...a lot. There were moments in every one of them—even daily—that made Greyson question if this was all one big fever dream. But in those moments, looking around at the teenagers around him, he had convinced himself that despite everything, this was all somehow true. The NINJA Order *was* a real society with a real purpose: keeping the rest of the world safe by preventing another threat like they'd encountered in the past. That was, in many ways, their only purpose.

And that's why the fret Greyson had seen on the coaches' face was unsettling. There seemed to only be one thing the NINJAs were truly worried about, so if they were worried, did that mean…

He sat up. He couldn't do it. There was no way Greyson could shut off his mind enough to drift off to sleep, and knowing that, he turned back the covers and put his feet on the soft carpet below.

For just a moment, Colter stirred. He groggily pressed his face deeper into his pillow, then his deep breathing resumed.

Greyson walked to the window. Through it, he could see the entirety of the center of the grounds. The obstacle courses in the middle of the grass, then the runway off behind it. All of it shimmered under the moonlit sky.

The course. It drew Greyson in. As he leaned against the windowsill and gazed out at the grounds, he made a split-second decision.

He'd go train. It was bright enough thanks to the nearly full moon, and even if he wasn't *technically* supposed to be out at this time, nobody had ever told them otherwise. What would they do—be mad at him for putting in extra work?

He quickly changed, pulling on his sneakers, and as he turned around, he was greeted with, "Where are you going?" Colter was sitting half upright, rubbing his eyes and yawning.

"The training grounds. Gonna work on the ladder climb a bit."

"Is it time to get up?"

"No." Greyson shook his head. "I just can't sleep."

"Thank God." Colter yawned again and collapsed back down into his pillow.

Greyson chuckled, then opened and closed their door as quietly as possible while stepping out into the hallway.

The lights were brighter than expected. He squinted, his eyes watering as they adjusted to the harshness. After a moment of squinting blindly ahead, he swiveled his head both ways. The hall was clear, but what else should Greyson expect? It was 2 AM.

He set off down the hall, walking as softly as he could so as not to attract any attention. A small part of him felt guilty for not being in bed. A bigger part simply didn't want the judgment of his peers if they caught him putting in some extra late-night work.

By the time the door to the hallway shut behind him, he had picked up his pace a bit, shuffle-jogging down the stairs without much regard for being stealthy.

Then he heard voices.

Greyson slowed again as he reached the door to the ground floor. He could hear people talking on the other side of it, and much like Greyson, they, too, were trying their hardest not to attract any unwelcome attention.

Greyson crept forward, turning an ear to the door to try to decipher what was being said. He couldn't. He couldn't even tell who was saying it, for that matter. All he could tell was that both voices belonged to men.

They were growing louder, too.

For a moment, Greyson debated running back up the stairs. He didn't want to be caught here, sneaking around and listening in to late-night conversations, but just as he turned to go, a series of shadows flashed past the door's window. The voices were louder than ever, and then they began to fade once again.

Greyson went back to the door. In the half-second glimpse, he'd seen Jamee's flamboyant green hair, but as far as he could tell, there were three figures. *Who were the other two?*

The first voice was one he recognized—one that he'd heard in class every morning for the past week. It was Lev. "What do we do?" he asked. "What's the play? We need answers, not more questions."

The footsteps accompanying the voice suddenly seized, only to be replaced with a long exhalation that was a mix of concern and uncertainty.

And then, the third voice spoke. *Jon*, Greyson realized. He was calm, but in a forced, methodical way. "We've been training for this. And on top of that, we don't know if there's any merit to what we've heard. We're basing everything entirely on one report. We're not calling Code Black...we're just investigating."

There was a moment of silence as the words were absorbed, and then, after a pause, Jamee asked, "But what if...well, what if it's true? What if the report is right?"

"There's a reason why our ancestors fought to keep everything in place and why we still follow the NINJA Order, and it's for a situation like this. *If* the reports are true, then you and Lev will bring back confirmation, and we'll prepare to move forward."

"And the kids?" Lev asked. "What about them? We just brought in over a hundred kids for recruiting—do we just send them all back to their homes?"

There was another momentary pause. "We're getting too far ahead of ourselves. First, we need to figure out what's actually going on and just do a little recon. Recruitment will continue till we hear from above. I will reach out to the other regions, but getting confirmation is our priority right now. Everything else will fall into place."

The footsteps resumed, and as they did, the whispering faded out of earshot, leaving Greyson with more questions than he'd had before, but also confirming his fear: the NINJAs were worried.

He didn't know what they were worried about and didn't have the slightest inkling of the context, but he didn't need to. He trusted them and knew they had a much better understanding of the big picture than he did, so if they were concerned, he should be too.

What should I do? The question rattled around in his brain. Part of him wanted to run back upstairs, shake Colter awake, then tell him everything that had happened. Another part of him wanted to run upstairs, dive into bed, and try to convince himself that everything was okay. No matter what happened, the NINJAs wouldn't let anything happen to the recruits, right? They weren't in any real danger.

But what if the NINJAs were? What if Lev was? Or,

even worse, if the things that Jamee had talked about in their history class were coming true—if there was some sort of resurgence of Eris or some long-forgotten technological threat—then was *anybody* truly safe?

It was too much for Greyson to take in, but instead of heading back to his room like he knew he should have, he did the exact opposite.

He opened the door.

The movement was almost involuntary, like his brain was screaming at his body not to do it, but his body acted nonetheless. Either way, one moment he was holding his ear against the door, and the next, he was wrapping his hand around the cool, metal handle, twisting it ever so slightly, and inching the door open as quietly as he could.

Crouching down, he slipped into the hall. A ways down and on his right, he glimpsed the three coaches disappearing around a corner. They were headed to the front door.

Greyson followed. Again, he knew it was stupid—the knot in his stomach served as a frequent reminder—but he needed to learn more. He was the kind of person who questioned everything, and he'd never be able to shut off his mind if he didn't get some more answers. What if something was really wrong?

The footsteps continued down the hall, but Greyson moved faster than the coaches. He could hear the whispers better, but he was still picking up only a handful of words, and none of them made any sense.

Then there was another sound—a door opening. The front door, specifically. After just a moment, the footsteps and whispers were gone at once as the door closed gently.

"Where are they going?" Greyson whispered. Did Jon have an office somewhere? Or, when he'd mentioned recon, was that happening *tonight?*

A door opened behind Greyson, causing him to nearly jump out of his skin. He couldn't be caught here listening in, so he rushed forward and slipped around the corner.

The door closed, and footsteps came down the hall. They were coming his way.

Greyson looked around him. *Was there somewhere to hide?* The best hiding spot he could see was a potted tree, standing against the wall as decoration. It was a bit taller than Greyson and wouldn't provide much cover, but it was still better than standing out in the open. He pressed his body behind it as the footsteps continued drawing closer.

A man rounded the corner. He had a mustache and dark hair, and from Greyson's quick glance, he looked Latino. He was wearing shorts and a tank top, revealing tattoos on his upper arms.

Greyson held his breath, refusing to move an inch. If the man looked his way, Greyson would immediately be spotted.

He didn't. Instead, the man continued forward, walking toward the kitchen. Soon, he was out of sight and his footsteps had faded away.

Greyson let out a sigh. "Late night snack?" He mused as he stepped out from behind the tree.

Now he had another choice to make. The scare in the hall reinforced that it wasn't too late to turn around and go back to his room. But, if he wanted to figure out what was happening and what the coaches were so concerned about, he had to choose the other option.

Greyson pushed open the front door of the dorm and stepped out into the night.

Outside, the breeze was cool but not cold, and the surrounding chorus of crickets and insects was loud but not annoying. Greyson scanned the grounds, and in the glimmering moonlight, he spotted the three coaches walking with a purpose. As far as he could tell, they were heading straight for the runway.

Now that they were outside, the whispering had been dropped and more urgency infused their words. Greyson listened closely and managed to tune out the insects just enough to make out their words.

Jamee was speaking first. "I totally get that, but we need to figure out what the play is. What do we do if we arrive and everything we've heard is true? What if it's the second piece?"

"We won't know that it's the second piece until we hear something from Jess tomorrow," Jon objected. "She's already en route to the site, so we should get answers shortly."

"Let's say the worst case scenario, then. Say piece one is gone, and two is in danger. What do we do? Do Lev and I intervene? Do we pop some popcorn and watch the apocalypse draw another step closer?"

Apocalypse? The word struck Greyson. He knew Jamee was being sarcastic, but the fact that he'd even thrown around such a catastrophic word was unsettling. Something was very, very wrong.

By now, the coaches were far enough that they were once again slipping out of ear shot, but Greyson could also tell where they were heading. The three men were walking straight for a truck parked on the runway. It was just like the one that had originally picked Greyson and Colter up from their house, and from his experience on the bus, Greyson knew that this particular model was just as much of a jet as it was a truck.

They were flying somewhere.

And this meant Greyson's suspicions were confirmed. Whatever recon mission the coaches were discussing couldn't wait. It was going down *tonight.*

Greyson fixed his eyes on a line of hedges stretching from the end of the dorms. As far as he could see, it stretched all the way to the runway. If he could sneak behind the hedges, he could follow the coaches and listen in without ever worrying about them spotting him.

It was a great idea, and it almost worked.

Unfortunately, by the time Greyson got into place, crouching down behind the hedges, the coaches were nearing the truck. He could still pick up bits and pieces of the conversation, but nothing he heard really told him anything that mattered. He knew two things: the NINJAs were worried, and because of it, they were going on a trip.

Vroom. Ahead of him, the truck's engine roared to life. With some background noise to drown out the sound of his movement, Greyson doubled his pace. As quickly and quietly as he could, he scurried all the way to the end of the row and peered around a leafy green bush.

The truck's headlights flashed on as Jamee climbed into the driver's seat. Lev, on the other hand, was talking with Jon. The words were impossible to make out over the rumble of the engine, but the conversation was animated from both coaches. Their concern was unmistakable, despite how hard Jon seemed to be working to keep his under wraps.

After a moment, the driver's door opened once again, and Jamee climbed back out, joining Lev and Jon's somewhat heated discussion. They were so engaged, so wound up, that Greyson could tell they were focused entirely on everything that was being said.

And that's when he did something stupid. Something *very* stupid.

As the coaches went back and forth, Greyson's body moved before his brain could ever override him. Staying low to the ground, he darted out from behind the hedges and, as stealthily as he could, made a break for the truck.

None of the coaches were looking his way, which gave him all the opportunity he needed. If Greyson was going to get the answers he desperately wanted, this was the best way. This was the *only* way.

Greyson cracked the back door of the truck open, and letting out a shaky, nervous breath, he slipped inside.

SIXTEEN

Greyson was scared to move. He held his breath, lying against the floor of the truck, and trying to stay as out of sight as possible as the engine hummed underneath him. With a lurch, the truck began rolling forward.

The interior looked just as he remembered. The back seat had limo vibes, with a panel of dark glass separating the bench seats in the back from the driver. While the glass meant he was less likely to be spotted, it also meant he couldn't hear the conversation going on in the front seat.

Very, very slowly, Greyson sat up. As far as he could tell, two people were in the front. He could faintly see the outline of their heads against the glass and hear the mumble of nervous dialog.

Why was he doing this? It was a bad idea. He *knew* it was a bad idea. And yet, here he was, giving into his desires instead of sound reasoning. He should be in bed right now, not stowing away for a ride to who-knew-where.

The truck was gaining speed. Peeking out the windows, Greyson could see the grounds whizzing by faster and faster. The engine revved, too, much louder than a truck should ever sound.

And with that, they were off. As Greyson grabbed onto the seat beside him, the truck lifted off the runway. His stomach twisted, queasy from the sudden shift of gravity, but after the initial burst, everything settled once again. They were flying.

The conversation from the front seat, which had died down during takeoff, resumed once again.

Greyson reached into his pocket strictly out of habit, only to find it empty. He didn't even have his phone.

"Of course," he mumbled to himself.

But, to be fair, even if he'd had it, he wasn't sure what he'd do with it. He couldn't really text Colter and say, *hey man, I snuck aboard the NINJAs' jet-truck. Brb.* And it wasn't exactly the best time to play his favorite tower defense game, either. He just needed his phone as a safety precaution—a lifeline just in case something bad happened.

Letting out a sigh, Greyson turned to sit with his back against the stained glass. While he didn't think the driver could see through it from the front of the cockpit, he also didn't want to risk sitting in one of the seats just in case they could.

I'll just stay in the truck, Greyson thought to himself. *No matter what happens, I've got to stay here.*

He sat on the floorboard of the truck until both of his legs were asleep. By the time he turned and laid on his side, the sky was lightening up. The early morning sun was painting the clouds various shades of blue and pink, and if Greyson hadn't been crumpled on the floorboard while fighting a mix of guilt and dread, he would have found it quite beautiful.

As he admired the early morning sunrise just as he'd been doing from inside his room for the past week, another thought struck him: *he'd be missed.* By this time, Colter had to have noticed that Greyson was gone, and then what? If Greyson missed breakfast, people would start asking questions. Greyson would be found out.

And with that on his mind, Greyson flinched as the dark glass pane began retracting. As soon as it was gone, Jamee's voice declared, "I'm looking for one Greyson McEntire. Do we have a stowaway, by chance?"

"Um…no," Greyson answered from the floor. Suddenly, he was feeling nauseous.

Jamee, of all things, laughed. It was a hearty laugh, too, the kind that couldn't be faked. "How did you end up sneaking into the truck, Greyson?"

Realizing his cover had been blown, Greyson slowly sat up. Jamee was piloting the truck-plane while Lev sat as co-pilot. Lev offered a nod and slight grin while Jamee kept his eyes fixed out the dashboard.

After a moment, Greyson asked, "Would you believe me if I told you I was a sleepwalker?"

Another laugh. "No, but it's a good thought. I'm not angry—I'm just curious."

Greyson sighed. At this point, he did the only thing he could: he told the truth. He told them how he'd noticed something was wrong, how he'd been too worried to sleep because of it, how he'd decided to train during the night, and how he'd ended up going from that idea to sneaking aboard the truck.

Then, when he was finally done, no immediate response came, so he prompted, "So…are you mad? Are you going to kick me out? Throw me out of the truck?"

There was more silence. Greyson could feel his heartbeat jostling his brain.

Finally, Jamee said, "Greyson, if there's one thing that NINJAs value more than anything, it's knowledge."

"Um…okay." Greyson didn't know what to say, so he tried to play along as politely as he could.

"Why did you end up stowing away in the back of the truck?" Jamee asked.

"Because…well, I just told you. Because I couldn't sleep and—"

"No, not the details," Jamee interrupted. "I'm talking about the big picture."

"Because…" Greyson tried again, desperately trying to dislodge the gears that seemed to be stuck in his brain. "Because I wanted to learn what was going on?"

"Exactly," Jamee said. "You're here because you wanted to learn what was going on. You weren't getting the full picture, so you did what you felt you needed to do to gain a better idea of what's truly happening."

The words sank in. "So you're not mad?"

"What rule did you break, Greyson?" Lev said.

The same nervous feeling gripped Greyson through, like he was voluntarily walking to his own slaughter. "Not being outside in the middle of the night? Sneaking aboard the truck? Eavesdropping?"

With the slightest of smiles, Lev said, "Jamee, you know what's funny?"

"What?" Jamee replied.

"I don't remember any of those things being rules. Do you?"

"Now that you mention it, I don't either."

Lev turned back to Greyson. "You're nearly an adult,

Greyson. You're fully capable of making your own decisions, and we didn't tell you not to do any of those things. We're not mad. If anything, we're impressed that you made it this far without ever being caught. We *are* NINJAs after all, and you out-stealthed even us."

"There might be some paperwork when we get back," Jamee added, "but as long as you follow directions we will cover for you. It'll look better for us anyway if higher-ups don't know we didn't do a proper vehicle check."

The worried feeling resided, only to be replaced by a racing heart and lots of questions. "How'd you figure it out, then? How'd you know?"

As the gravity in the truck shifted once again, Jamee answered, "Jon called. Apparently he and Anna put two and two together when your roommate went looking for you."

"Gotcha, I figured that—" Suddenly, Greyson's eyes widened, and he trailed off mid-sentence as his eyes fixed on the view out the front windshield. "Is that…is that *sand?"*

Even as he asked the question, he knew he was correct. As far as he could see, sand stretched out across the surface of the earth below. It formed waves that looked much like the surface of the ocean, except they didn't move. The ridges cast long shadows in the bright orange-pink light from the sunrise.

"If you're impressed by that, you're *really* gonna like this," Jamee said. With that, he steered the truck to the right.

Greyson's jaw dropped. The view of the sand was quickly replaced by something else entirely. A structure, tall and magnificent, filled the entire window. "A pyramid." He barely breathed the word, but somehow Jamee heard it.

"Welcome to Egypt, Greyson."

"I don't understand." Now, the logical side of Greyson's brain was hard at work. "We haven't been flying for more than an hour. There's absolutely no way that—"

Lev cut him off. "You're in a flying *truck* with two members of an age-old organization fending off the world from a techpocalypse...the top speed of our ride should not be your biggest question."

"Okay, fair. You got me."

"We're gonna start descending for a landing in a few minutes, but before that happens, we need to go over the rules," Jamee said. "And yes, now there are rules, and they are rules you need to follow very, very carefully, Greyson."

"Okay, listening." Greyson sat down in the seat beside him, leaning in so that he was between Jamee and Lev.

"First thing, we need to tell you what's going on," Lev said. "That's why you're here in the first place, so you at least deserve to know a summary."

"Much appreciated."

Lev nodded. "You probably learned this from Jamee in your history class. Do you know what happened to Eris, the AI unit that tried to overthrow our ancient forefathers?"

Greyson thought for just a moment. "He—or, it—was defeated and its remains were scattered all around the world so as to prevent the same sort of thing from ever happening again."

"Exactly. Jamee must be teaching you well."

Jamee shrugged humbly.

"The three pieces, even dismantled, had a powerful residual energy," Lev went on.

"Enough so, even, that everywhere they were hidden eventually spawned a society incredibly advanced for its time, from the Muisca tribe in South America to the ancient Egyptians."

"You're joking. You mean those societies happened because of the scraps of this Eris thing?"

"Kinda. We're not exactly sure where the pieces are hidden, ourselves. We have our own archaeologists and researchers that are trying to piece together the history hidden even from us, but we'll get more into that later. Since we don't have much time, let's fast-forward to the present day. Do you want to fill him in, Jamee?"

As Jamee adjusted the flight's trajectory once again, he agreed. "Sure. This will be a bit ahead of what we've discussed in class, Greyson, but the NINJAs have long been trying to locate the three pieces and keep them protected. We know our ancient ancestors even created Guardians and safeguards to keep them safe."

"Guardians? What do you mean?"

"Too much to get into now," Jamee answered. "Long story short, we have been getting lots of activity at ancient sites all over the globe, and a report that said the El Dorado piece had been removed. While we've sent NINJAs on recon to check, and other regions have also been called out on assignment, there's a good deal of concern that this is the case. After all, we've been hearing whispers that someone outside the agency has deciphered some ancient text and is aware of the three pieces. That's what prompted us to create the recruiting program in the first place."

Greyson's head was spinning from trying to keep up, and the occasional lurch in their flight didn't help matters in any way. He didn't know what to say.

Fortunately, he didn't need to. Jamee plowed ahead, saying, "What started all this mess last night is another report—one that came from one of the NINJAs monitoring dark web chats—and she said a local team of treasure hunters had been hired for some big bucks to help break into The Pyramid of Djoser."

"I've heard of that one," Greyson said. "Isn't that the first pyramid? Like the oldest?"

"Yeah, you know your history," Jamee responded.

"So let me guess: the piece that the bad guy's after—it's inside the Pyramid. Despite what everybody has said my whole life, the pyramids aren't actually for long-dead kings."

Jamee let out a suppressed laugh. "I like the way you're thinking, but no. There's most definitely an ancient Egyptian king buried inside the Pyramid. But similar to our research building on campus, these tombs were giant power stations, pulling energy from the Earth's magnetic fields and helping power their civilizations. As their civilizations grew, so did their need for power, which is why each king built a bigger pyramid."

"Then where's the piece you're trying to protect?"

"We believe there could be one *underneath.*"

"How is that—"

"Doesn't matter for now," Jamee said. "Here's the plan: Lev and I are here on a recon mission only. We'll be going inside the pyramid, and—if everything goes well—Lev will stay in Egypt to do more research, while you and I return to headquarters to submit a report, so other regions are aware and available to provide reinforcements…understood?"

"Uh…yeah."

"Jamee?" Lev spoke up. "I don't think everything's going to go as planned." He pointed out the windshield.

Jamee swore under his breath.

Soon, Greyson understood why. He could see a convoy of vehicles parked along the base of the pyramid. Squinting down at the tiny shapes, Greyson could make out several figures marching into a hole in the side of the pyramid—one that appeared to be smoking.

"They're here," Jamee confirmed. "Dammit."

Lev looked indecisive. "What do we do? Phone back for help? Looks like our recon work is done."

Jamee thought for just a moment, then decided, "It would take *hours* for the rest of our available team to get here, and the other regions are short-handed, which is why we were assigned this check. Plus, the heist is underway right now. We can send out a message for reinforcements, but if this is where one of the pieces is hidden, we're going to have to stop this from happening ourselves."

"What can I do?" Greyson asked, suddenly feeling like he'd gotten in way too deep.

Jamee scoffed. "You're not doing anything, Greyson. You're going to stay in the truck, and if anything goes wrong, you'll hit this button right here." He pointed to the dashboard.

"What is that?"

"Autoreturn. It has logged our trip and will take you back to headquarters. Do you understand?"

Greyson gulped.

"Greyson?"

"Yes, sorry. Yes. I got it. Stay in the truck."

At that time, Jon's voice cracked from a radio that Lev was holding. "What's the situation?"

Lev wasted no time in passing on the bad news. "Looks like there's a small army of people already here."

There was a delay before Jon solemnly responded, "I see. It's just as we've feared. I'm getting reports from the other regions requesting support as well."

The words were far from encouraging. For the first time, Greyson could detect unease in their leader's voice.

And then, just like that, Jon coughed and came back as confident as ever. "We'll send support immediately and get them there ASAP."

"We don't have time to wait," Jamee objected. "They're going in the tomb *as we speak.*"

"Going in by yourself is suicide," Jon said. "We can't lose two of our best operatives."

The words hung in the air as the truck hurtled toward the ground.

Finally, Lev held the radio up to his mouth and spoke far too calmly and quietly for the situation. "Listen, Jon. I know the odds are not great. So does Jamee. But I also know we have to *try,* and so do you. If we wait for support, and this *is* where the second piece is then our odds are even worse. We can't let that happen."

The ground was growing closer and closer as they waited on a response.

Finally—and very reluctantly—Jon said, "Help is on the way. Good luck, gentlemen. You served the NINJA Order well, and it's been an honor to serve with you."

With that, he was gone.

Jamee glanced at Lev. "Dude, did you hear that? It was past tense. He just past-tensed us! We're not dead yet!"

A laugh cracked Lev's somber face. "You're right. I didn't even notice."

Jamee reached forward, pressing a button on the dashboard. "Oops, forgot to enable the surveillance shields."

Greyson clearly looked confused, so Lev explained, "It's like an invisibility cloak, basically. Reflects all the light around us so we can't be seen."

"I guess by this point, I shouldn't even be surprised."

Jamee, sounding peppier, butted in. "You boys better hold on because we're coming in *hot*. Gonna be a rough landing. These things aren't built for desert sand and heat."

Jamee touched the truck down as gently as he could on the rippled surface of the desert, and they thumped, jolted, and jostled to a violent stop about a football field's length away from the pyramid and the convoy outside.

This was it.

"Everybody all right?" Jamee asked as he unbuckled his seatbelt.

Lev gave the perfect answer. "From the landing? I'm totally fine. Everything else? Three outta ten at best."

"Fair enough." For just a moment, Jamee gazed straight out the windshield. Greyson followed his eyes, taking in the desert, the pyramid, and everything else.

From the ground, the entire perspective changed. The pyramid felt tremendously tall as it pointed skyward, and the sand, stretching as far as the eye could see, was not nearly as still as it had appeared from 10,000 feet in the sky. Instead, it blew in gusty waves, even going as far as pelting the side of the truck with what sounded like the gentle tap of thousands of fingertips all at once. And the heat was visible, too. As Greyson took in the horizon, waves of heat broke what should have been a straight line into choppy waves.

As he gazed, Greyson also thought. He thought about how he ended up here, how everything had changed so quickly. Just a couple weeks ago, he'd been counting down his final days of the school year.

Now he was in a flying truck with a green-haired man and one of his climbing idols, who were trying to prevent an ancient force from overthrowing the human race.

High school was weird.

"I guess this is it?" Lev's uncertainty was apparent.

"Let's do it, brother." Jamee turned back to Greyson. "Greyson?"

"Stay in the truck, I know."

"Smart kid," Jamee nodded. "But here's the deal. I don't mean to give you a big head and all, but you're one of the most talented protégésI've encountered. And that's not just me—all of the coaches have been saying it."

"Really?"

"Oh, yeah. We talk, you know?" He gave a soft smile. "So here's the thing. You're gonna wait half an hour on us, and by the time that passes—and I mean the *very second* the timer hits zero—you push the auto-return button on the truck." As he said the words, Jamee punched a few buttons, and a timer appeared on the dashboard screen.

"Thirty minutes? That's all?"

"Yes. And as soon as you hit this button, it will get you out of here and take you back to safety. You're too valuable of an asset to lose, so you've got to promise me that as soon as time is up, you'll hit that button."

Greyson locked eyes with Jamee and nervously swallowed.

"Greyson?"

"I promise. I'll hit the button."

"Good. If anything happens to us in there, we expect you to carry on. You're great at this…I can tell from the very first week that you have a chance to be one of *the* greatest."

Trying to sound brave, Greyson said, "Thank you. That means a lot. But I expect both of you to teach me more, so you better go kick some butt in there."

Jamee smirked. "Only because you asked."

He turned to Lev. "You ready?"

"Let's do this."

SEVENTEEN

The wait was excruciating.

Greyson couldn't peel his eyes off of the pyramid looming ahead of him. Squinting through the blowing sand, he scanned desperately for movement. They'd come back. They *had* to come back.

He kept watching. The anxiety in his chest made it difficult to breathe. This was all too much. He understood what Jamee was trying to do, but in many ways, he'd rather be risking his life with the coaches than waiting here without knowing. He was completely in the dark.

Finally, when he couldn't stand it any longer, he looked at the timer counting down on the dashboard.

26:13.

It hadn't even been five minutes! Balling his fist, he slammed it down into his leg and let out a groan of frustration. The coaches—these men he looked up to—were facing terrible odds while he was cowering outside.

Greyson took a deep breath as he forced himself to be rational. Jamee and Lev were trained. They knew how to use the Wave. They basically had superpowers. What did Greyson have? Nothing. He was just a normal boy from a small town who his high school classmates couldn't even name.

He couldn't help, so he *had* to wait. It was the only smart move.

He waited, and he waited.

Fifteen minutes in, and there had been no movement at all.

More waiting. Another ten minutes ticked by, and still, nothing had happened. Eight all-terrain trucks were parked outside the pyramid, and Greyson kept looking back and forth between them. If whoever was trying to steal the piece actually escaped, surely they'd be making a getaway with the trucks.

And where were the authorities? As far as Greyson could tell, the convoy had completely blown a hole in a historical site and nobody had shown up to stop them. Egypt had police, right?

The time continued to tick down and Greyson continued to wait. He felt like he was going to vomit. The anxiety was shredding his stomach.

The final minute arrived. He didn't know what he was expecting, but for some reason Greyson kept glancing back and forth between the clock and the pyramid, waiting for something to happen.

Thirty seconds now. More looking. More hoping. More desperation.

Still nothing.

Five...four...three...two...one.

The timer ran down and a red *0:00* flashed across the screen.

Just like that, it was time for him to abandon Jamee and Lev.

Greyson was trembling. He wasn't sure where it had even come from, but one second he was hyperventilating, and the next, he was wildly shaking. Was he having a panic attack? He couldn't breathe. He could barely think.

The only thing he did manage to do was the one thing he promised Jamee he would: he pressed the auto-return button. Every fiber of his being screamed at him, telling him it was wrong, that he couldn't leave the NINJAs to die.

Die. That's what this boiled down to. As the engine of the truck roared to life, the magnitude of his actions sank in. Greyson was leaving Jamee and Lev to *die.* He was heading home, safe and sound, never to see the coaches again.

The truck started lifting off the ground. It moved slowly at first, but soon began lifting higher and higher off of the sand. Greyson turned his head to watch the pyramid as it moved beside the truck. There was still time. If he saw Jamee's green hair emerging from the hole in the wall, he could kill the autopilot and save them.

But they never came.

The altimeter was creeping up higher, and as it rose, so did Greyson's guilt. It washed over him, making every second more painful than the last.

He had enough.

He couldn't do it.

So, instead, Greyson did something very impulsive. As the truck continued lifting upward, he screamed in both frustration and terror and grabbed onto the door handle beside him. With a grunt of effort, he threw the door open.

The ground below was nearly a twenty foot drop.

The force of the energy blades launched sand skyward, blasting it into his face.

Greyson didn't care. He couldn't abandon Jamee and Lev. While he had only known them for a couple of weeks, they felt like…family. Like they valued him as part of the team. It was a new experience for Greyson, a powerful one.

He dove out of the truck and slammed into the hot sand of the desert with a *thud* that forced all the air out of his lungs. Coughing, he clamored to his feet as the truck continued lifting off and flying out of sight.

As he watched the flying truck break through the clouds, he muttered, "Well, at least I kept my promise. I hit the button."

With that, he headed towards the pyramid.

The closer he got, the more he realized he had absolutely no plan. Every step was taking him closer to what would most likely be an ill-fated ending, and for just a moment he wondered if he should stop.

But it was too late. He hadn't come this far to give up, so he had to at least try.

As he approached the convoy, Greyson hunkered down in case there were any stragglers on the lookout, but the vehicles were abandoned, and the scene, lifeless. Realizing this, Greyson climbed into the back of the lead truck and bent over an open supply crate.

He sifted through the crate. "What do we got in here?"

For the most part, it was picked clean. He did, however, find a bandana, a flashlight, and a bottle of water.

Cracking the lid of the water, he took a long drink, sloshing it around between his teeth. In the Egyptian desert, water tasted better. He tossed the bottle back into the crate. "Hydration is key. That's what they always say, right?"

With that, Greyson tied the bandana around his face to make an impromptu mask to shield his face from the pelting particles of blowing sand. It was hot, uncomfortable, and definitely not something he'd want to wear all the time, but the mask provided momentary relief. He could take a deep breath without ingesting two tablespoons of the desert.

Greyson climbed down out of the back of the truck and made his way into the pyramid. He was walking into a headwind, so the mask certainly helped with his face and nose, but his eyes were still taking a beating. He walked with one arm up, trying to shield his vision, but by the time he had finally made it inside, he was desperately rubbing his eyes for relief.

"How do people do this all the time?" He whispered to himself.

The pyramid was dark. As he looked down the tunnel in front of him, it was amazing just how dark it was, especially considering how bright the sun was right behind him. It was like the blackness in the halls ate the light, completely choking it out.

"Here goes nothing." He clicked on his flashlight and crept forward, his feet making a hollow clatter against the hard stone surface below. "I know NINJAs are real, but I swear if mummies are too…"

He froze, killing his light and standing in complete silence.

He'd seen a shoe. Just up ahead, peeking around a corner. Somebody was waiting on him.

He stood in silence for a full minute, waiting and listening. Nothing happened. He couldn't even hear any breathing. Was his mind playing tricks on him? Maybe he hadn't seen anything at all.

He clicked on his light again and realized that he had, in fact, seen a shoe. The person *wearing* the shoe was in pretty rough shape. As Greyson rounded the corner ahead of him, he found a piled heap of a body. The man was wearing combat gear, including a vest and a headlamp, and his battered body was crumpled to the floor. He had a black eye and busted lip, and while he was breathing, it was clear he'd be going nowhere for a while.

Beside him was a rifle. Greyson went to pick it up only to realize that its barrel was bent in the shape of an L. "What on earth…" He prodded the gun with his toe. "Did the NINJAs do this?" Even as he asked the question, he knew it to be true.

That guard wasn't alone. Sprawled throughout the rest of the hallway were at least a dozen other guards. They were all in as rough of shape as the first, and all their rifles had been ruined.

There were more to the NINJAs than met the eye. As Greyson followed the hall and began to piece together everything that had happened, the truth became resoundingly clear: Lev and Jamee had taken out over a dozen armed men…with their bare hands.

Perhaps they didn't need Greyson's help after all.

That's when he heard shouting echoing down the hall to his right. Greyson spun, pointing his flashlight that way, but he didn't need it. At the distant end of the hall, he saw a glow. As far as he could tell, it was coming from a hole in the ground.

Greyson hurried down the hall, moving as quietly as he could. He climbed over two more guards who were flopped in the middle of the hall, and then reached the hole.

Just like what the convoy had done to the side of the pyramid, they'd also blasted a hole in the ground. Looking down into the hole, Greyson couldn't see any people, but he could definitely hear them. Men were shouting, but he couldn't make out the words.

As far as he could tell, the hole led down into some sort of large chamber full of strange statues, and on the top of each statue was something that looked like a lantern, but instead of fire, they glowed with a swirling, soft blue ball of flame, energy, or something else. It was unlike anything Greyson had ever seen.

There was a rope stretching down to the chamber below—a good sixty feet, according to his climbing instincts—and Greyson did the only thing that made sense.

He grabbed the rope and began climbing down.

As he descended, Greyson glanced down, spotting one of the strange statues at the base of the rope. Once on the ground, he used it for cover, taking in the room around him.

He couldn't believe his eyes.

The chamber was enormous, stretching as far back as he could see. And in the hallway leading to the chamber, Greyson recognized many of the bars, slopes and knobs spread down the hallway—they were *obstacles.* To reach the chamber, one had to pass through a series of obstacles not unlike anything from the training grounds. Turning his eyes back to the hole in the ceiling, Greyson realized something else. Whoever had cut the whole had done so with great intent: with the purpose of bypassing obstacles. Somebody had *cheated* this ancient game.

With that, Greyson's attention turned to the chamber itself and his eyes widened even more. The room was shaped as if somebody had cut a giant bowl in half, with sloped edges curving up to a flat ridge at the top. At the bottom of the bowl was a large, flat area decorated with a few more creepy statues, and on the side of that, a sheer cliff plunged into a dark abyss.

And in the bottom of the bowl, Greyson saw three people, all dashing around like mad. The first two were friendly faces: Lev and Jamee. The other, however, was a figure shrouded in darkness. While it wasn't easy to see in the pale blue glow of the chamber, every glimpse of the third figure seemed to be black and reflective—a person wearing a dark metal suit.

"Tony Stark, is that you?" Greyson muttered.

And as startling as the suit-clad figure was, it was still the *second* most surprising thing in the chamber.

There were beasts. They were tremendously large, shadowing figures flashing around the chamber and dizzying speeds. They weren't animals. They weren't machines, either. They were somewhere in the middle.

"Guardians…" The word slipped from Greyson's mouth as he remembered what Jamee had said—the NINJAs had left Guardians to watch over the pieces. And judging by the way they were attacking both the NINJAs and Suitman, they were living up to their name.

As Greyson watched, one of the Guardians slung a spiked metal leg toward Jamee. Jamee narrowly dodged, kicked off the creature's leg, and jumped on top of a statue behind him. As he flew in the air, the soft glow of the

Wave rippled across his skin.

The creatures responded by throwing another spiked metal leg toward Jamee, who leapt onto a second statue as the creature smashed through the first, busting through the sandstone structure and sending debris blasting in every direction.

Jamee, using his momentum, hopped from to another statue, then another, and from there he lunged *toward* the Guardian, landing on the only part of the beast that could be mistaken for its head. Despite the creature's best efforts to shake him loose, Jamee reached down between the metal plates, grabbed a fist full of wiring from within the creature's frame, and with a yell, he ripped it loose.

The Guardian immediately stopped moving, collapsing to the floor in a pile of twisted metal limbs and gear. It sparked and smoked, defeated.

But the NINJAs were far from out of hot water. Another three or four Guardians dashed around the room. Greyson tried to get a good look at them—tried to figure out *what* he was dealing with—but he couldn't ever quite see enough. They were all a blur of twisting limbs and flashing lights that chinked against the sandstone.

If anything, the Guardians looked like Egyptian gods with limbs that were a mix between an octopus and forklift—a unique blend of futuristic and ancient.

They were deadly, too. In the hallway leading to the chamber, Greyson spotted at least fifteen mangled bodies of gear-clad men that had to be part of the convoy. These men, unlike the ones in the hall, were most certainly dead. Their necks, torso and limbs were bent in directions too terrifying to show in horror movies.

And there was blood, too. Lots of it.

Greyson pulled his eyes away from the mangled bodies as one of the Guardians focused in on Suitman. The creature leapt in the air, crashing down on the suit with a blur of whirring tendrils. It reared back one of its limbs before driving it forward, thrusting down toward the chest of the figure pinned beneath it.

Greyson was sure the masked man was about to be killed. It was all over.

Except, it wasn't. Somehow, Suitman slipped out of the creature's grasp right as the arm came crashing into the sandstone. And not only did he slip away from the Guardian, but with a cry of effort, he climbed the Guardian's leg, swung up one of the tendrils, and ran up a metal plate along where the creature's spine should have been. Just as Jamee had done, Suitman plunged a hand into the Guardian and yanked out a fistfull of wirings.

The life—or, perhaps, the *power*—flickered out of the Guardian and it crashed down onto ground.

Greyson tried to take in what he'd just seen but his brain refused to process everything. While the NINJAs had superhuman abilities thanks to the Wave, the man in the suit was definitely no slouch, either.

Suitman was only on his feet for a matter of seconds before another Guardian flung itself toward him, but he rolled underneath it, avoiding the creatures other limbs as he ran up the slanted wall. Halfway up, he kicked off, turned a one-eighty back toward the creature, and with a kick, he smashed what Greyson could only identify as the creatures eyes.

It wobbled around in a daze, before tripping over its own legs and falling into the endless pit.

As far as Greyson could tell, now there was only one

of the creatures left. Jamee and Lev were tag-teaming it, but as they did so, the man in the suit began to slip away. He bounded up the sloped wall, and Greyson gasped. This was just like the wall run—just like what he'd been training to do. But this one was much taller than anything from the training grounds. *Twice* as tall, even. There was no way it should be possible.

Suitman, however, made the thirty-something-foot wall look easy. Once he was on the flat ledge at the top, he headed toward a dark archway carved into the far wall.

Halfway to the archway, the man in the suit bent down and picked something up. As far as Greyson could tell, it was a circular device with a golden glow, like a plate-sized alien saucer.

That's got to be the piece, Greyson thought. *He's getting away with it!*

Lev noticed too, and in the split-second he was distracted by Suitman, the final Guardian reached out a mental tendril and swiped it across Lev's back and flung him into the wall. There was a *thud* on impact, and his body went limply skidding down the sloped wall before coming to rest with one arm hanging over the abyss.

"No!" Jamee screamed. He rolled under the creature before jumping up and latching onto its midsection of the beast, where he thrust an arm into an area that was exposed between two metal plates.

With a whirring sound that could only be taken as pain, the Guardian latched onto Jamee's leg with one of it's tendrils and tried to yank him loose by his ankle. There was a loud *snap* and Jamee bellowed in pain,

Still, Jamee didn't let go. With one final desperate move, he reached further inside the Guardian's body and ripped out a large part that looked, in a strange way, like a mechanical heart.

There was an electric popping sound and buzz of energy as the Guardian collapsed, and with it, Jamee. As soon as they hit the ground, Jamee wrapped both of his arms around his ankle, moaning in pain.

With Lev out cold and Jamee clearly unable to walk, the man in the suit had all the time in the world. From atop the ledge, standing before the exit with the glowing orb in his hand, his shoulders sank as he let out a deep breath.

"You don't know what you're doing!" The words rang out in the chamber, coming from Jamee through gritted teeth.

"And you do?" The masked man's response was much quieter, making Greyson strain to hear.

"You're about to open a can of worms," Jamee said. "You've got to realize it. If you go through with this, it could be the end of humanity. It could be…"

"This isn't going to hurt anybody," came the flat objection. "This will *help* everyone. You and your people have been keeping secrets from the world for far too long. Think about all the good you could have done? Sickness. Ecological disaster. You could have fixed all of that."

"What is he talking about?" Greyson whispered as he moved around the statue, creeping closer to the chamber.

"Don't do it," Jamee yelled back. "You don't understand…"

Suitman waved a hand and turned away. "Don't worry about me. I think you have more pressing matters to attend to."

"What does that mean?" Greyson asked himself. "What did…"

That's when he heard them.

In the dark distance, the faintest metallic clicks could be herald chinking toward them, a sound that nearly made his heart stop. More Guardians.

They were coming to finish the job.

They were coming to kill Lev and Jamee.

As the clicks grew louder, the man in the suit turned and disappeared into the tunnel, leaving behind the pending disaster and a room full of carnage.

EIGHTEEN

No matter how fast Greyson ran, he felt like it wasn't fast enough. He sprinted toward his downed friends, eyes locked on the motionless body of Lev.

The chinking sound of more Guardians coming his way was unmistakable, and every step forward felt like a bad idea. He had no plan, no ideas, and once he made it to the bottom of the half-bowl chamber, no way out.

And yet, he kept running. He dashed around one of the ancient statues and leapt over the broken body of a fallen convey soldier.

"Greyson!" Jamee's shout was a mixture of surprise and relief. He was trying to get to Lev but his ankle couldn't bear the weight. "Don't do it!"

Greyson didn't listen. As he ran, he realized to get to the half bowl chamber, he had to swing across the dark pit using a very, very old rope. With no time to hesitate, he went for it. He leapt out, catching the rope with both hands, and his momentum carried him to the other side, where he slid down to his hip on the chamber floor.

"I'll help," Greyson panted, climbing back to his feet and grabbing Lev's leg just as he started to slide.

As the approaching machines grew louder, Jamee shook his head. "Greyson, you were supposed to stay in the truck and take it home." Jamee's words came through gritted teeth as the green-haired Ninja came limping Greyson's way with a smug look on his face.

Greyson shrugged. "I did half of that."

"You... what?" Jamee leaned against the slanted wall. He looked terrible, with a couple of deep cuts on his leg and a gash across his cheek. His ankle was the size of a grapefruit.

Greyson briefly recounted, "I hit the button, but as the truck was leaving, I knew I couldn't abandon you guys. So... well, I jumped."

Jamee let the words sink in as he checked Lev for a pulse. "We had things under control... mostly. But now..."

Greyson walked to the edge of the drop-off, peering down. He wasn't sure what he was hoping for. Maybe water, at best. Instead, he only saw...nothingness. Complete darkness, stretching far beyond the flickering light from any of the torches in the room.

Turning back, Greyson pointed to Lev. "Is he..."

"He's alive," Jamee said. "But there's very little we can do. There's no way I can fight the Guardians alone. Not like this. And you..." He stopped mid-sentence. His eyes widened.

"What?" Greyson recognized the look and Jamee's face. It was the look of...hope. "What is it?"

Jamee whirled around, pointing up to the top of the sloped wall on the other side of the basin. "You see that pole up there? The short one."

Greyson squinted in the blue light. "Um... right by

the archway?"

"Yes."

"What is that?"

Jamee, talking fast, explained, "That's a call-off switch that our ancient ancestors left. It's a way they could ensure that only a NINJA could evade the Guardians. If you could climb the wall and hit the button…"

"...I'd turn off the machines?" Greyson finished the sentence for him.

"Exactly."

"That sounds great, but there's no way," Greyson stammered. "The wall…it's so tall. It's…what are you doing?"

Jamee had kneeled down beside Lev, slipping the unconscious man's Wave watch off over his limp hand. "You ever used one of these?"

Greyson shook his head. "We only learned about them. Lev said we'd have to master our own skills and energy before we would use them."

The approaching machines' steps sounded so close now that Greyson was certain they had reached the chamber. Jamee threw him the Wave. "Now's as good a time as any to practice. Hurry."

Shakily, Greyson slipped the watch's band around his wrist and fastened it into place. As he did so, a tingling sensation ran throughout his body and a number glowed on the screen: *73%.*

"Whoa…" He muttered as he tried to adjust to the feeling. "That's… I like it." He took two steps toward the wall, running his eyes toward the ridge at the top and the button he needed to reach.

"You can do this," Jamee said. He was clearly trying

to keep his voice level but the concern was unmistakable.

"Probably a bad time to ask, but... how do I use this thing?" Greyson rubbed the back of his neck, still looking up the wall. His knees felt weak.

"Just act normally," Jamee said, talking even faster. "Run up that wall just like you'd approach it if you were doing it without the Wave. You have to mentally calculate how much energy to use with each moment. You'll see, you do this naturally, the Wave just helps you do it... better. You'll feel the effects after you make the move."

"There's no way..." The words came under his breath, but he tried to silence them in his mind, "Okay, let's do this."

"Good luck, Greyson."

Taking a deep breath, Greyson closed his eyes. For just a moment, he tried to shut it all out: the approaching Guardians, the doubts in his brain, the fear gripping at his throat. He had one shot at this so he had to make it count.

As his eyes snapped open, Greyson took off. He went from long and powerful to short and precise as he approached the wall. Soon, he was upon it. His feet pressed into the sandstone surface, climbing higher and higher while trying to keep his chest leaning back until the last possible moment.

He was screaming. He didn't know when the sound started to escape his throat but as he ascended the wall, he felt the power of the Wave wash through him. His legs tingled, almost like he had static electricity on the surface of his skin.

But he kept pushing, kept running, and at the very last moment, he shifted his chest forward and jumped towards the rim. Somehow, despite all his doubts, the ledge was within reach. He extended his arms up, still shouting, and grabbed for it.

He got it, but just barely. Just by the fingertips.

But that was all it took. Greyson quickly pulled himself up, glancing movement out of the corner of his eye. The Guardians were here. They were coming his way. Five or six more of the metal beasts began approaching the chamber's entrance, headed right toward the two NINJAs.

Turning away, Greyson located the ancient button and slammed a fist down on it.

Almost immediately, sparks and smoke started to fly from the base of the pillar followed by a monotone drone echoing through the chamber—the reluctant surrender of a machine losing touch with electricity. With power.

And just like that, the Guardians began to drop. Their lights faded and their movements slowed, then stopped altogether. They collapsed, but their bodies continued sliding over the edge of the dropoff entering the chamber, and tumbling out of site.

Greyson let out a cheer that was a mix of disbelief and sheer relief. It had *worked*. He'd done it.

Jamee, from below, pumped his fist. "Greyson! That was amazing. You… you saved us."

Greyson couldn't find the words. Instead, he glanced at his watch. A number glowed on its face: *58%*. Climbing the wall had taken its toll on him—much more than he'd realized, even.. He'd used almost 15% of his power.

Jamee noticed, asking, "What's your wave reading?"

"Fifty-eight percent."

He nodded. "You'll get better—more efficient—as you learn."

"Good," Greyson answered, only to discover he was a bit out of breath. "Now what?"

"Now let's wait for some backup to arrive and get out of here."

"Wait, what?" Greyson arched his eyebrow. "What about the guy in the mask? We can't just let him go! I heard what you said earlier—he could wipe out humanity! Isn't that what you told him?"

Jamee bit his lip. "Greyson, the NINJAs can put our heads together and figure out a way to stop him. Today's battle is done."

The words didn't sit easy with Greyson. Maybe it was what Jamee was saying. Or, maybe, it was how he said them—like he was trying to convince even himself.

"I… I've got to try something," he said. The words came out weakly, a mere mutter.

"What? Greyson, no. Absolutely not." Jamee took a couple of steps toward the ramp, grimacing as he moved.

Greyson looked back over his shoulder, through the exit and into the darkness. "The guy with the suit. He's already so powerful. He just took on you, Lev, *and* those machines. If we let him go, he'll be even more powerful. What if it's too much for all the NINJAs together?"

Jamee didn't argue the point. Instead, he answered with a short, verbal gut punch. "If you go through that archway, Greyson, you won't leave alive."

"What's through there?"

"Obstacles. Danger. Peril." Jamee's eyes were pleading with Greyson.

Still, a dark truth tugged at Greyson's chest. "If that's

the case, then perhaps I *will* die here. But if I don't try, we *all* might die. Right?"

Jamee didn't say anything.

"Right, Jamee?"

"I mean, it's possible, but that's not your responsibility."

"It is if I'm willing to accept it," Greyson nodded. "So whatever happens to me, know that it's not on your hands. You tried to talk me out of it."

"Greyson…" Jamee didn't finish the thought, only looked down in reluctant defeat. "I know I'm not going to talk you out of this and I can't physically stop you, but remember, don't use too much of your Wave or your body won't be able to recover."

"Yeah, thanks. Got it." Greyson let out a nervous breath and then turned away and headed into the tunnel.

"And Greyson?"

"Yes?"

"Good luck."

"Thank you."

With that, he stepped into the tunnel.

Greyson expected it to be completely black, but the same lanterns that glowed with the mysterious blue flame lined the walls at semi-regular intervals.

The tunnel slanted up. It wasn't a steep slope, but it was enough to eventually lead back up to ground level. Then, something occurred to Greyson.

The torches had been turning on as he made his way down the tunnel and fizzling out as he left, almost like they were activated by an ancient motion detector.

Now understanding the lights Greyson set off on a sprint, only to be stopped dead in his tracks when the entire floor of the tunnel simply…stopped. He was standing on the edge of a huge pit that was wide enough that he definitely would *not* be jumping to the other side—even if he knew how to use the Wave, at that.

And, looking down into the shadows below, he saw hundreds of wooden spikes. They stuck straight up, sharpened to piercing points that were ready to puncture anything that came their way.

Greyson took a step back. One of the torches was beside him and another burned on the far side of the pit. This didn't make sense. *How could Suitman have gotten across? It was much too far of a jump.*

That's when his eyes locked onto something *above* the pit. A plank, of sorts. It was about shoulder-width and a couple inches thick, suspended from the rocky ceiling using some sort of metal rods.

And then there was another. It was several feet past the first, but positioned the same way. It looked familiar. It looked like an obstacle.

Suddenly, Greyson understood. His heartbeat quickened as he began connecting the dots. This was exactly like an obstacle he had practiced before, just with an older course and the fact that the water or foam pits that usually broke his falls had been replaced by razor-sharp wooden stakes.

"More incentive not to mess this up," he mused as he stepped back up to the edge of the pit, eyeing the plank above him.

Something caught his eye. Far off in the distance toward the end of the tunnel, another torch roared to life. Greyson's eyes widened when he realized what this meant—Suitman was still here. If Greyson moved quickly enough, maybe he could catch him.

He leaped up and grabbed onto the wooden plank above his head. It was dry. Anciently dry, but surprisingly sturdy and unlike anything he'd ever felt before, like it wanted to suck all the moisture out of his hands. The courses Greyson ran at the grounds were all padded and well-kept. This look like it was a thousand splinters waiting to happen.

Nevertheless, Greyson set to work. He hopped his hands forward along the edge of the plank, but halfway down, it creakily rotated.

He swore, holding on for dear life. He'd assumed the plank was fixed in place, but instead, the rods from the ceiling only held the center of it and allowed the rest of it to rotate. That meant Greyson's timing needed to be *perfect,* or he'd be taking a fatal fall.

Move by move, he made it down the first plank, then eyed the second, the torchlight casting just enough of a glow to see it.

His nerves were certainly weighing on Greyson. One bad move, and he was done…for good.

Greyson knew if he dead-hung any longer, he'd regret it later, so he had to go. He pulled his hips back and then thrust them forward, throwing himself through the air and reaching out toward the second plank.

As he made the move, he felt a surge of energy through him. His grip was more certain, his kip was further. Everything was…"amplified," just as Lev had explained.

His hands wrapped around both sides at the exact same time, and it barely moved at all. He let out a big sigh of relief, only then realizing he'd been holding his breath.

After doing that one more time, he dropped down to the other side of the pit. He glanced at his watch. A number glowed on its face: *58%.* As he watched, it ticked back up to *60%.*

He bit his lip. *How much could he push?* This all felt new to him, and as far as he could tell, there were still two or three obstacles awaiting him.

"These ancient NINJAs sure loved their courses," Greyson whispered as he wiped his hands off his shorts before heading up the tunnel.

The next obstacle looked unfamiliar to him, but he also felt good about it. It was a climbing wall, of sorts, carved onto one side of the tunnel. An inch-wide finger hold ran about halfway down before coming to an end. The rail resumed again, about three feet above, meaning he'd have to extend up and grab onto it using only his fingertips.

For a seasoned climber, this felt right at home.

Trying to block out the wooden spikes in the pit below, Greyson grabbed onto the rail and began hand-walking his way along the wall of the tunnel. There were no footholds, so the entire obstacle was strictly upper body.

This was no problem for Greyson. He reached the end of the first rail, took a deep breath, then pulled himself up, reached up, and grabbed the second rail. While the transition was a bit scary, he made it to the other side of the pit with no incidents.

After that, Greyson came up against an obstacle that was basically an anxiety-inducing set of lache bars. In four nerve-wracking swings, he made it across the pit.

As his feet hit the ground, an explosion came from up ahead of him. Suddenly the bright light of day began shining through the tunnel, throwing him into a squint as he gazed that way. In the light, Greyson could see Suitman. His black metal armor glimmered as he turned over the glowing object in his hand, too distracted to notice Greyson gaining ground.

And, best of all, the sudden influx of bright light showed Greyson something that gave him a bit of hope: there was only one obstacle left.

The final obstacle, however, took his breath away.

It was a test of balance.

In the sunlight, the light of the torches revealed a long wooden beam running straight down the middle of the tunnel, secured by a rod on both ends. The beam looked like a tall tree that had been stripped of its bark and perfectly smoothed out. It was only about a foot wide in diameter.

Greyson reached out a toe and prodded at the log. Just as he expected, it turned. If he wasn't careful, he'd roll right off.

"Why does it have to spin?" he asked. "I hate balance."

It was true. From a week of training, Greyson had learned that if he were to ever fall, it was almost *always* on a balance obstacle. Even the coaches would fall on them occasionally. With such a thin margin of error, balance could take out even the best NINJA.

Greyson couldn't let that happen to him.

So he went for it. Without delaying any longer or psyching himself out, he took off.

Foot placement was crucial. Every step needed to place the sole of his shoe in the dead center of the log, or it would start rolling. Once that happened, it would all be over. He'd end up impaled on the stakes far below, which looked even longer and sharper in the bright sun.

With long strides and good speed, Greyson bounded toward the far side. *Step. Step. Step.* Each move was calculated in his head.

He was halfway. Three quarters.

And then, he felt it twist.

It was just a subtle shift, but it was enough to send Greyson's momentum falling to the right side of the log.

He fought back the urge to scream as he pushed off, extending his arms, and reaching out for the other side of the pit. *Did he have enough to make it?* The edge of the pit was within his reach, but as his feet flirted with edge and spikes below, as doubt crept in.

Wham. He slammed into the other side of the stone pit, pushing all the air out of his lungs. Gasping, he pulled himself to safety and laid on his back while staring at the rocky ceiling above him, panting from fear and the force of the blow.

That had been too close. Between the scare and the fall, he wondered if he'd ever catch his breath again.

"Not bad. Balance is tough…especially for climbers."

Greyson snapped his head up, turning to his right and locking his gaze onto Suitman, whose boots crunched the sandy floor as he headed in his direction.

"Who…who are you?" Greyson wheezed. "How do you know I climb?"

"I know a lot of things, Greyson," Suitman responded. "And you can call me O'Brien, if you'd like."

"You know my name?" It was a wheezy question that fumbled out of Greyson's mouth as he climbed to his feet. Hands on his knees, he asked, "Why are you doing this? Why are you after the pieces? Why do you want to wake Eris?"

O'Brien huffed, the noise rattling inside his mask. "Eris. Is that what they're calling it?"

Greyson forced himself to pull his hands off his knees and stand straight up, looking at O'Brien. He recited what he'd learned in history class. "Eris nearly eliminated all humanity in ancient times. It's a force of evil. Of destruction."

The black mask shook slightly. "Oh, my boy. That couldn't be more incorrect. Eris stands for *hope*. For promise and improvement and a better tomorrow. If you truly believe it was a source of evil, then your stories are all wrong."

The words stole Greyson's composure. "But…the NINJAs…they told us everything. They said…"

"They fed you stories that are a way of keeping people in charge, followers in line, believers enthused, and continue working in the shadowy corners of the world like secret operatives," O'Brien said, looking down to the glowing piece in his hand. "You can call that what you like, Greyson, but I'd call it corruption."

O'Brien let out a soft laugh, echoing behind his mask. "Greyson, you have so much potential, but your loyalty lies on the wrong side of the spectrum. The NINJA's aren't protectors of humanity, like you say. They're more like the bottleneck that's keeping society from doing great things."

"Great things?"

"A new world," O'Brien emphasized. "Think about it. You've seen the NINJA's technology—technology that they're trying to keep secret. Do you know what could be done with it?"

Greyson only stared back as questions swirled through his head.

"No more sickness," O'Brien said. "Free, eco-friendly energy. Better transportation. A better quality of life for everybody. They're keeping that for themselves, Greyson. It's selfish. But that's what I'm here for—I'm trying to change the world."

Greyson couldn't believe what he was hearing. "They wouldn't lie to us. Not like that."

O'Brien seemed uninterested. Instead, he held the device up in the light shining down from a hole directly above him, admiring it. He asked, "Do you have any idea why I just went through an obstacle course instead of climbing out of here the way I got in?"

The thought hadn't occurred to Greyson, but once he heard it aloud, it was such a great question that he couldn't believe it had never crossed his mind. "I... um... thought you were just trying to escape the Guardians, I guess."

O'Brien chuckled as he held out the orb to show Greyson. Ripples of light ran down the golden wire along the side of the orb, moving as slowly and patient as a lava lamp. He explained, "This piece, Greyson, would not activate until after I completed the course. Until after I proved myself worthy by getting it from its chamber to here."

"That's not possible. There's no way it knows..."

"Oh, but it is. And that, my young friend, is the perfect example of why this is so valuable. This is technology that is...*intelligent.* It learns, just like you and I. And this can change our lives, our worlds, and our potential."

Greyson only watched as O'Brien put the orb in one of his hands and reached it behind his back. There was a snapping sound that echoed in the tunnel, and then he extended his hand to his side. It was empty.

"What…" Greyson didn't even get the question out before O'Brien turned around, showing Greyson that the orb had fixed itself into the back of the suit's helmet

. Golden glowing wires from the orb had begun creeping across his back.

"You should ask your NINJA friends about 'wiping,' too," O'Brien said as he turned back around.

"Wiping?"

"You ever wonder why nobody has blown the whistle on the NINJAs? Why is it that the people who fail their trials don't go back to their normal lives and tell everybody about the things they've seen?"

"I mean… it crossed my mind."

O'Brien took a couple steps back, looking up to the hole in the ceiling as a wave of sand blew down from above. "They use their 'advanced technology' to wipe minds, Greyson. They wipe their minds and put false memories back in their place. Manipulation in its purest form."

The words stung like a punch to the nose. "That's can't be true."

"Tell yourself whatever you like, Greyson. But I'll tell you the *truth*."

Greyson stared back in a mixture of pain and confusion.

"Let me offer you this," O'Brien said, gently extending a hand. "Come with me today and I'll show you everything. I'll poke holes in all the lies the NINJAs have been feeding you. What do you say?"

At his words, they locked eyes. Greyson stared deep into the mask, and for just a moment, he swore he could see concerned eyes behind the dark glass visor. He felt a connection...a *pull.* There was some trust to what O'Brien was saying.

Greyson took a long breath. He thought about Jamee, about Lev. He pictured the faces of his friends—of all the NINJAs—and then he sighed and dropped his gaze.

O'Brien took that as his answer and shrugged. "Oh well. That's your loss, Greyson. I don't have time to convince you. I've got a ride to catch."

That's when Greyson heard something. The faintest distant rumble of an engine. Or, maybe not an engine...a propeller. More specifically, a helicopter. He was almost sure of it.

He took two steps forward, trying to stall as his brain desperately scrambled for a plan. "Eris? It's part of your suit?"

O'Brien laughed more enthusiastically than ever. "Greyson, you really are something else. Between me and Eris, I'm far more advanced than you and the NINJAs could ever hope to slow down. And, based on the way you keep looking at your watch, I'd guess you don't even really know how to use that thing."

"I..." It wasn't worth it. He couldn't lie. He'd always been terrible at it.

"One last chance, Greyson. You can either stay here and seal your fate with the NINJAs, or you can join me and the Pack in changing the world."

A sinking feeling stirred in Greyson's stomach. He couldn't turn his back on the NINJAs. Not like this.

"No. I can't do it. I'm…I'm sorry."

"Have it your way, Greyson." O'Brien turned and began to walk away.

Greyson felt something. Beneath his feet, a tremor rippled through the stone. Then came enough, and another, progressively more violent. He spun around, looking back down the obstacle course, only to see a distant stone slab break loose from the ceiling and come crashing down. The ground continued to tremble.

O'Brien swore.

"What's happening?" Greyson asked.

"Hmm. It appears that my explosive entry into the chamber might have, um, *disrupted* the pyramid's structural integrity a bit," O'Brien speculated, glancing up through the hole once again.

Crash! A piece of the wall fell inward, much closer than the first. It slammed into the ground and broke into a thousand smaller pieces.

The sudden sound distracted O'Brien too, and for Greyson, this was something else—this was an *opportunity.*

With the ground continuing to tremble, Greyson glanced at his watch: *70%.* As if it sensed his intent, almost immediately the tingling sensation running through his body was multiplied ten-fold. He could feel the power rushing through him—the Wave taking over his body.

And with O'Brien distracted, Greyson seized what might be his only chance. In a flash, he reached out and grabbed the glowing orb on his back. As soon as he made contact, a rush of energy filled his body unlike anything he'd ever experienced. It was a sensation of being… unlocked. Like he was tapping into the full potential of his body—even more so than the Wave.

It was *power*. Uncontained, unbridled power. Greyson's mind and heart both raced. He felt like he had super powers, like he could stop a freight train.

And with a shout, Greyson lifted O'Brien off the ground. It was far more than he should ever have been capable of, hoisting up the grown man without straining. And as he did so, he saw the Wave on his arm flash a new number: 100%. Somehow, he was stealing power from the orb.

"How…is…this…*possible*?" The words rattled out of O'Brien, a seething shout through gritted teeth. As he cried out, he also pivoted his body and delivered a swift kick to Greyson's chest. The heel of O'Brien's boot pushed all the air from his lungs and sent him sliding across the room, but to his surprise he stayed standing and feeling great.

O'Brien landed awkwardly on his hip, staggering to his feet as he turned to face Greyson. He continued yelling in a muffled and drowned out tone. No matter how hard Greyson listened, he couldn't tell what O'Brien was saying.

"Are you…" Before Greyson could ever get the words out, he realized exactly what was going on.

O'Brien was arguing with the suit.

He was arguing with Eris.

Somehow, O'Brien could hear the ancient voice. They were communicating.

"Okay, okay," O'Brien said. His tone sounded like it had changed. There was less rage, more…reluctance.

The mask locked on to Greyson.

With a clear, chilly certainty, O'Brien said, "Greyson, I'd advise you to learn how to use your Wave, and learn it quickly."

"Wait, what?"

O'Brien looked up once more, and as he did so, a rope ladder began dipping through the hole above him. He reached up and grabbed it, and with a nod, the ladder lifted him off the ground.

"Look up, Greyson," O'Brien offered. And with that, he was gone.

Doing as the man advised, Greyson turned his eyes to the ceiling. Immediately, he swore when he realized exactly what O'Brien had meant. A large crack had formed in the ceiling of the tunnel above his head, and with a jolt, a huge slab of sandstone broke loose.

Greyson knew this was the end. The rock was too big for him to get out of its way. He'd soon be a smear on the rocky floor below.

And that's when he lifted his hands up, meeting the boulder head-on. As it began to press down on him, he felt a surge from within him as the Wave took effect, and he screamed.

He pushed and hollered, lifted and heaved, and somehow, someway, he held his ground just long enough to roll out from underneath the huge rock before letting it come crashing down.

And then, the exhaustion hit.

All the lessons he'd had about the Wave came rushing back to Greyson. The power it offered—the way it unlocked the body's capability—came at a cost.

"When you use the Wave, you feel the exertion right after you perform the action." Lev's teachings came back to his mind.

It was a way of frontloading what the human body was capable of, but overexerting could have dire consequences—wasn't that what Lev had said?

Those dire consequences settled in. Greyson felt like every ounce of energy was being wrung from his body all at once. It was, in every essence of the word, exhausting.

He'd overdone it. The Wave might have saved him from being crushed, but the effort felt like it was killing him.

Greyson stumbled. His vision flickered. Not only was his body shutting down, but so was his brain. All the energy, all the *life*, was escaping him.

He collapsed, face-down on the trembling floor, as the last ounce of energy seeped out of him, and with it, consciousness.

NINETEEN

When Greyson's vision came somewhat into focus, the first thing he noticed was a woman in a chair sitting beside him.

"Jess?" His mouth was so dry that making the word felt like it would break his tongue.

Not only did Jesslook his way, but she also seemed to be reading his mind. "Greyson! You're awake. Here, I have some water for you."

Greysonreached out and took the bottle, bringing it to his lips. As the liquid flowed over his tongue, he immediately began to feel better, but his body still felt… broken. Completely exhausted in a way he'd never known.

While he continued to drink, Greyson looked around the room. It was familiar to him. It was *his* room—his room in the dorms, at least. Colter's bed, empty now, was opposite his own. *How had Greyson ended up here? And where was Colter?*

After a moment, Greyson realized he'd killed the entire bottle of water. Wiping his mouth, he placed it down on the bed beside him. For a moment, he didn't say a word. There were too many questions on his mind.

Among them, memories blended in. His last few moments in the cave replayed through his head.

Finally, he asked, "How long have you been here, Jess?"

"Couple of hours," she said.

"How long have *I* been here?"

"You've been out for about thirty-six hours. We've been taking turns watching you. We wanted to be around when you woke up just to make sure you're feeling okay."

There was something in her voice that told Greyson he was only getting part of the story. Running his hands through his hair and battling the full-body exhaustion, he said, "You didn't think I would wake up, did you?"

Surprised by the question, she stammered, "Well, we… I…"

"Be honest, it's okay," he encouraged.

Jess let out a long, slow breath before looking him in the face. "Greyson, you *shouldn't* have woken up. Look at this."

She reached to the nightstand beside him, holding up something that glinted in the sunlight shining through the blinds on the opposite side of the room.

Greyson squinted. "My…Wave?"

She nodded, then double-tapped its face. Nothing happened. She did it again as if making a point.

"It's dead," he confirmed.

"Exactly, and that meant there was a strong chance you could have been, too."

He forced a laugh. "Well, I do feel completely exhausted. Like I haven't slept in *days*."

"That's part of it." Standing up and rolling her office chair towards the desk, she asked, "Do you think you can walk?"

Greyson nodded. "Yeah. Absolutely."

He could barely lift the blanket that was covering him. "Let me help you with that," Jess said. "It's a weighted energy cover, designed to help with recovery."

When Greyson put his feet on the ground, his knees nearly buckled. If Jess hadn't been beside him to prop him up, he very well might have gone down. But with her help and with slow, choppy footsteps, he eventually began to walk-shuffle across the room.

After a moment, he was walking on his own. It was a bit wobbly at first, but every step felt a bit better than the last. By the time he made it to the doorway, he was moving with a lot more confidence. "Where are we going, exactly?"

"Just downstairs," Jessanswered. "But don't worry, there's an elevator."

"That's what I like to hear." Greyson followed her out of the room, closing the door behind him. They headed down the hall, and as promised, to an elevator at the far end.

Greyson finally brought himself to ask the question that had been bugging him since he woke up. "Jamee and Lev. How are they?"

The elevator doors slid open. "They're alive, Greyson. According to Jamee, you're the reason for that, too."

He breathed a tremendous sigh of relief. "Where are they?"

"Our recovery hospital on-site. You were there for a bit, too, but there was only so much they could do. We wanted you to rest and, hopefully, wake up in a familiar place."

"Thanks. What's the update on the guys?"

Jess said, "From what I've heard, Jamee has a severe ankle dislocation and Lev has some broken ribs, but they'll heal. They both want to see you."

The news was happy, but her words lacked the usual pep with which she spoke. She was worried, and by extension, Greyson was worried, too.

He didn't press her any further. Instead, they rode down the elevator in silence and then walked to a door in the middle of the lower level. A sign on it read *Office.*

Jess knocked, and an indistinguishable conversation from the other side of the door died down. "Come on in," came a muffled shout.

Jess opened the door and stepped inside, Greyson following closely behind.

Jon sat behind a desk at the far side of the room. He had a computer hooked up to several monitors on his right and an open tablet in front of him. To Greyson, this looked like a high-tech principal's office mixed with the feel of a natural museum. Digital maps were projected on the desk, and the walls were covered in ancient artifacts from all different cultures, most of which seemed to depict obstacles or be remnants of obstacles themself.

Jon wasn't alone. Lenny stood opposite the desk. He greeted Greyson with the nod of his cowboy hat. Beside him stood Meg.

Jon, upon seeing Greyson, stood. He walked around the desk, extended his hand, and asked, "How are you feeling?"

Greyson shook his hand, only to pull away when he felt a sharp pain. Looking at his palm, he saw a large splinter piercing his skin. Apparently he'd brought a bit of the ancient obstacle course with him.

"I feel good," he lied. "A little tired, but good. Glad to hear Lev and Jamee are doing okay, too."

"Me too," Jon replied, "And I know you're largely to thank for that, Greyson. Jamee told us all what you did." He spoke with much more enthusiasm than Jess had. If he was worried, he was doing a better job of concealing it.

"I just helped where I could."

With a twinkle in his eye, Jon said, "Trust me, I've heard all about it. *Including* how you bailed on your ride home, which, by the way, made it back safe, sound, and empty."

"Oh, yeah. Good deal."

Jon walked back around the desk, taking a seat. "Jess, thank you for bringing Greyson down. Please keep us posted on any further developments with Digital."

"I'll see what we can do." With that, Jess slid out the door.

Jon then turned his attention to Lenny and Meg. "I think we've covered everything, too. Just, please, *please* be careful out there and check in multiple times a day. If you need reinforcement, I'll be headed your way with the other NINJAs in a moment's notice."

"We'll let you know when we arrive," Meg replied.

"Oh, and before I forget, Lane, how is the home project coming?" Jon asked.

"Good, mining operations are secure and the independent energy source is operational. If things go south, we're prepared for extraction."

"Good. Safe travels."

Lenny and Meg turned to leave, and on the way

out, Lenny squeezed Greyson on the shoulder. "You did good, Greyson. We're proud of you."

"Thank you," Greyson answered. "But you're the reason I'm here."

Lenny stopped, turning to him. "Do you mean when I was your chauffeur?"

Greyson nodded. "Little did I know that ride would change my life."

"You might not have," Lenny said. "But I knew that was a special ride. From the moment you got in the truck, I could tell you were gonna be something special."

The words caught Greyson off guard. "Really?"

"Of course," Lenny said. "You have a keen eye, and you were the first person I've ever shuttled that wasn't fooled by the roadwork illusion."

Greyson's eyes widened. "I knew it! We *were* flying! You just projected a video on the window."

"Despite everything we tried, you still were onto me. You're a smart, smart kid."

"Thanks Lane. That means a lot."

"You bet. And no matter what comes next, I'm glad you're on our side." With that, Lenny slapped him on the back and followed Meg out the room. They closed the door, leaving Jon and Greyson alone in the office.

Greyson didn't speak. He looked to Jon in anticipation, and after a moment of silence, all Jon said was, "Go ahead."

"Sorry, what?"

"I'm sure you have lots of questions," Jon said. "Why don't you just start it off and I'll do whatever I can to help explain."

Greyson did have lots of questions. Probably hundreds of them. But after everything he'd heard and seen, there were so many questions running loose in his mind that his tongue couldn't seem to lasso any of them.

Finally, he asked, "What's next?"

It caught Jon off guard. Clearly, this was not what he'd been expecting, but he answered almost immediately. "We carry on, Greyson."

The answer—four simple words—were so full of confidence that Greyson was almost taken aback. "But..." He stammered. "O'Brien escaped. He has Eris, and added it to his suit, and now he has even more powers. He's..."

Jon cut Greyson off by raising one finger. "There's nothing we can do about it, Greyson. At least, not yet. We suffered a big blow—possibly *humanity* did too, for that matter—but we can't dwell on defeats. We need to prepare for the future. Eris is still not fully functional and we can't confirm how many pieces he has, if he even has any of them."

"But I heard O'Brien talking to Eris," Greyson countered. "He has it. They were having a full-on conversation.:

"He probably has parts of Eris, just like a computer. Are you familiar with the three major components of an operating system?"

"Yeah, it's the CPU, RAM and hard drive, right?"

"Correct. And much like that, O'Brien is assembling *pieces* of Eris, but Eris can't function at full potential without at least the three pieces, and the third piece is a particularly important one."

The words, soothing and smooth, made Greyson feel a bit better. He asked, "So you're preparing for what's next? Already?"

"From the moment we heard from Jamee, we began to plan," Jon leaned back in his chair, which squeaked a bit. "This is a new threat to the NINJA Order, one that hasn't been faced since ancient times, but we must approach it like we approach every obstacle."

Greyson looked up, arching an eyebrow. "Do you mean 'obstacle' literally?"

Jon chuckled. "I didn't, but I see the parallels in the approach. If you think about it, we approach every obstacle on a NINJA course like every obstacle we face in life: assess the situation, plan our move, and execute to the best of our abilities. Sometimes we fall. Other times we succeed. But no matter what, we do the best we can."

The words sank in, and as they did, something inside of Greyson stirred. "So you're not worried? This seems like a pretty big obstacle."

"It would be arrogant to say I'm not worried," Jon admitted with a nonchalant shrug. "But I know we're going to do everything in our power to stop this threat from reaching its full potential. We're going to trust our training, our intelligence, our technology, and our recruits."

Greyson looked past Jon, peering out a small window. Outside, the morning sunshine illuminated the central grounds, where the Energy Management class was taking place. Almost everything was the same—life was going on for the campers and coaches.

The only thing that was different, as far as Greyson could tell, is that he was inside and the class was being taught by N.J.. He wondered if the class even knew what had happened, that their teacher was hospitalized.

"So what's next?" Greyson asked the question again.

"And I mean, specifically. What's next for me? What's next for you and the Ninjas? What's next for the campers, and what can I do to help?"

"Lots of questions in there," Jon said with a grin. He was great at not only keeping his composure, but calming Greyson down, too.

"Let's start at the top," Greyson suggested. "What's next for me?"

"What's next for you is what's next for the rest of the campers," Jon answered. "We're going to carry on with the training, but we're going to ramp it up. We'll work and test and whittle down the field until we only have the elite trainees left—those that can withstand what looms ahead—and then you'll be inducted into the ranks."

"And you think I'll be among those who are inducted?"

Jon laughed at this too. "Greyson, I'd bet my life on it. There's nobody here like you. Lots of talented kids, don't get me wrong, but none that combine your physical and mental skills. And, on top of that, you're ballsy enough to stow away on a secret mission."

Greyson couldn't keep a smile from cracking his face. "Thanks, Jon. I'm glad you're not too upset. I felt bad about that."

"You saved two of our coaches," Jon said. "I could never be upset with that, but I also want you to be careful. We have rules, regulations and requirements that must be met. Most of which are out of our control. And where were we…what's next for myself and the Ninjas?"

"Yes sir."

"We're playing offense," he said. "As you've probably learned by now, there are other NINJAs and legions scattered all around the world. The coaches at this camp are not all of our numbers, and I've put our cohort members all on active alert and called for an emergency legions meeting."

It was a lot to take in. Greyson rubbed his forehead, exhaled, then asked, "And what do you plan to do with them?"

"For one, it's not my call," Jon said. "Each legion will have a vote, and we'll see how the NINJA Order as a whole chooses to proceed. But for now, I sent Lenny and Meg to begin doing investigative work with the third and final piece. We don't know much, but we'll do everything in our power to protect it."

Greyson didn't respond for a moment, only contemplated. Then he asked, "Where is it?"

Jon bit his lip.

"You don't know, do you?"

With a forced chuckle, Jon said. "You're good at this. We're following a lot of leads and have our best specialist researching it. For now, I want to get to the final question you asked: how can you help?"

"Yes, please."

Jon pulled himself up to his desk, took a digital pen out of a cup, closed some projected maps on his desk and opened a digital notepad embedded within. "You said the man in the suit was called O'Brien, and more intriguing, you said he was talking to Eris. I need to know everything, Greyson. The more you tell us—even the smallest details—the better we're positioned to win this war."

Out of everything Jon said, one word in particular caught Greyson's ear.

War.

Such a powerful word. Such a dangerous one. Death. Destruction. Devastation, sometimes on a global scale.

He asked. "This…this is a war?"

Very slowly, Jon nodded. He looked Greyson right in the eyes, and confirmed, "This is definitely a war, Greyson. A war for humanity. A war that we must win. And, most of all, it's a war that's just getting started."

Greyson dropped his gaze. He couldn't bring himself to respond, not at first. What he was hearing—the magnitude was beyond anything he'd ever imagined. It was too much. It snatched the air out of his chest and iced up his brain as another seed of a memory sprouted in his mind.

"What's wrong, Greyson?" Jon asked. "I didn't mean to scare you."

"No, it's not that," Greyson insisted. "I promise."

"What's on your mind then?"

Greyson sighed, looking down at his hands. He rubbed his sweaty palms against the legs of his pants, and as he did so, he thought about what O'Brien had said: The NINJAs couldn't be trusted. They were wiping minds, controlling people, and keeping a world-changing technological revolution under wraps.

Could he really trust them?

Even the thought made him sick. At first, he'd been in disbelief more than doubt. Everything that had led up to him setting foot on the grounds and everything that had happened since—it was all too much to believe.

But he'd trusted these people. Jon. Lane. Jess. All of them. They'd all taken him in and made him feel like family. In many ways, the family he'd always wanted.

Still, O'Brien's warning repeated over and over in his

head and as Greyson looked around the room, too many doubts weighed down his mind. There were too many things that didn't make sense. Too much didn't add up.

"Greyson, are you sure you're okay?" Jon asked, leading forward nervously.

"I…" Greyson finally looked up. "I am. I'm sorry. Just started feeling bad for a moment. But war waits for nobody, I know, and it's coming."

Jon leaned in, a flash of concern suddenly cropping up in his eyes. "It might be even worse than that, I'm afraid."

"What do you mean?"

Jon looked too Greyson, leaning in close and lowering his voice. "I don't think war is coming, Greyson. I think the war is *already here."*

EPILOGUE

"Welcome home, sir."

A sharp-dressed man sat bolt upright as he heard the words come from the door to his personal office. He swiveled around in his chair and turned to face the voice. Leaning against the door frame was a beautiful woman in her early thirties with red hair, chocolate eyes, and a warm smile.

"Nick, I didn't know you were around. Have you… have you been here all morning?"

She laughed. "It's Wednesday. Yes, of course."

The man rubbed his eyes and shook his head. "I'm sorry. Not much of a boss, am I? I should have at least come and said hello."

A wily grin stretched across Nick's face. "On the bright side, at least you have a house big enough to lose somebody in."

People didn't talk to him like this. At least, nobody except Nick. That's why he liked her so much—more than he should, given their relationship. But she deserved it. Most of the people in his life were yes-men, whether he wanted it or not. Nobody joked with him. Nobody ever offered sassiness.

In some ways, Nick felt like more than an employee. She seemed like…a friend. Especially after six years of working together.

"That's no excuse, although I appreciate the effort," the man said. "I've been out for… what, two weeks? And I didn't come say hello?"

Nick laughed. "But if you would have come back from vacation and *not* gone straight back to your office, I probably would have called the doctor because something was obviously wrong."

"Very funny."

"I'm serious." Nick stepped into the office. He could smell her perfume.

"Are you here to police me for working too much?"

"I'm here to check in and welcome you home. But yes, these sixty-hour weeks of yours can't go on forever. They're not sustainable."

"You're talking like I'm seventy. I'm forty-one."

"And I'm *thirty-one* and don't have the energy to do what you do," Nick countered. "But, to be fair, that's why you're the one running a Fortune 500 company, and I'm just your executive assistant."

"You know you run the show just as much as me, some days."

Nick was quiet for a moment, then asked, "Sir?"

"Yes?"

"Are you okay?"

"Am I…yeah. Why wouldn't I be?"

Nick tilted her head to the side, taking him in. "You just seem…I don't know…a bit sad, I suppose. Maybe tired. I'm not sure—I don't mean to overstep. Just want to make sure you're okay. This trip was supposed to be a refreshing get away for you, even though I know you were still making work calls all week."

"I appreciate that, Nick. It's nice that you care. But yes, I'm fine. Just getting acclimated to the workweek, I suppose."

Nick nodded. "Good. Am I interrupting, or can you tell me about your trip? I've always wondered what Peru was like."

"Relaxing, but hard to breathe," the man replied. "When I was in the Andes, the elevation was so high it was hard to breathe. I can't even describe it. Kind of like you're breathing on the edge of space."

Nick laughed again. It was a nice sound. "You know I'm getting some new business cards made for you next week. Would you like me to add 'part-time mountain goat' to your job titles?"

"That sounds like a pretty good idea to me."

The man minimized the tab on his browser and leaned back in his chair, letting out a long, exhausted sigh. Perhaps Nick was right: maybe he *was* getting too old for this.

"How did Tyler do?"

Even hearing the name made him nearly wince. Tyler had been his young protégé. They'd been working together for over a year, and as much as he hated to admit it, the young robotics major that had started as an intern had become the closest thing to a son that he'd ever had.

"Tyler…Tyler won't be with us anymore. Our trip together will be his last with the company."

Nick couldn't keep the look of surprise off her face. "Oh, no! I'm sorry! I know you really liked that kid. What happened?"

The man forced a smile. "He's moving on to bigger, better things. We knew this day was coming—that's how college students scale up—but it still took me by surprise. He was the best intern I'd ever had."

"Hopefully, he'll drop in occasionally to say hi," Nick offered.

"Yeah, I hope so too," the man finally said, the lie sour on his tongue.

"I know how much you rely on your interns. Do you have a replacement in mind?"

The man nodded. "Yeah. A couple, actually. They're a bit younger than I usually work with, but I still think they could add a lot of value to what I'm trying to accomplish. We'll see soon."

"I definitely hope it works out for you and for them." After a moment of silence, Nick asked, "Did you find it?"

"What?" The man sat up, keying in on the conversation.

"I don't know. You said you were hoping to find something in Peru."

"Oh! Yes, of course. I found it. I found a couple things, for that matter."

"Can I ask what you were looking for? Were you going Indiana Jones down there?"

The man forced a laugh. "Not me. I'm too old for that, remember? I was just looking for solace. A break from the stressfulness of life. And I found that, yes." Even as he said the words, they felt weak.

Fortunately, Nick seemed to accept them. "Mighty metaphorical of you. Are you sure you're not secretly a poet?"

"I didn't tell you about my other line of work?" The man teased with a wink.

Nick took a moment to respond, and when he looked from his computer screen to his assistant, he realized why: her gaze was fixed on something across the office. She walked over to it and picked up the object. "What's this?"

The man's heart almost stopped. Nick was holding a black, metallic helmet. A glowing coil was fixed to it, pulsing slowly. *How had he been so stupid? Why did he leave it out?*

"That's a…prototype," he replied, trying to keep his voice as level and cool as possible. "The new AI we're working on. Just kind of a side-project. You know how it is."

"It's pretty scratched up."

"Yeah. Lots of testing."

After a moment of lingering gaze, Nick shrugged and set down the mask. "I think it's very cool."

"You've got all kinds of jokes this afternoon."

"A week's worth. Been saving them up just for you."

The man walked over to the mask and grabbed it as innocently as possible. As he moved it, he heard someone speak: *It is time.*

He looked over at Nick out of habit, but it wasn't her voice. It was… cold. Cold, genderless and steely. It hadn't been Nick that had said or heard it.

When they made eye contact, Nick's confusion was apparent, but the man pointed to the mask and said, "I didn't mean to leave this out. It's very much unfinished."

"Gotcha." Nick went back to the doorway. "Do you need anything? Late lunch, help, socials...a nap?"

It is time. The voice came again, but this time the man

was more aware. He was ready for it. And the unsettling thing about the voice was that it was…*different* than anything he was used to. He wasn't hearing it with his ears. He was hearing it with his *brain.*

Confused but trying to not come across as completely insane, he answered Nick, "Unfortunately, I need a nap but have no time. Got to finish up a few personal projects before we're back to full speed ahead tomorrow."

Nick nodded. "Of course, I'll leave you to it. But ping me if you need anything."

"Thank you."

Nick turned and left, and as the man watched her walk away, he couldn't help but feel like she knew something was off. At least at the end. Something in her tone. Try as she might to hide it, she sounded…concerned. Or maybe it was something else.

Was she worried for him? Worried *about* him?

He swallowed, looking down at the mask. It stared back at him, dark and haunting. Again, the voice came. *It is time.*

This time, he knew where it was coming from. He had no doubt.

He grabbed his head and sighed.

Standing, he walked around his desk and closed his office door. He locked it too for good measure, and then he pressed the button on the wall that tinted the windows.

It was time.

He felt jittery, a fluttery shake like he'd had too much coffee. To be fair, he probably had. The feeling only worsened when he walked to his backpack in the far corner of the room, unzipped it, and pulled out a bundle.

It was a t-shirt. An *Anchorage, Alaska* tourist t-shirt

boasting a bear square in the chest. But he wasn't interested in the shirt.

Unwrapping it, he pulled a rectangular object from inside the shirt. It was a dark marble shell with a unique blue shade. Peeking out the shell were lines of soft, golden light that glowed in his palm. The lines ran up and down the shape, occasionally binding in right angles as they journeyed from one end to the other.

The device was also cold to the touch—too cold for something that had been sitting in his office. He wrapped his hand around it even more tightly.

This was it.

He wrapped both of his hands around the device, which refused to warm up to his touch. If anything, it hummed. It was a nearly imperceptible feeling, and he felt it shudder ever so slightly in his hand.

Slowly, nervously, he held the device out. He lowered it gently, setting it right beside his computer. Once it was in place, he opened his desk door and took out two wires. First, he removed the side panel of his computer and connected the wires, then he picked up the device. Eyeing the end of it, he began soldering the wires to the gold conductors peeking out of the marble shell.

Nothing happened.

He bit his lip in frustration. *Why wasn't this working? The first piece activated with the suit, so easily.*

He reconfigured the wiring, and this time there was a spark. The device buzzed enough to vibrate on his desk, its light brightening for a moment, and then, nothing. Nothing except a puff of smoke wafting off the end of it as the golden glow died back down.

"C'mon," he growled quietly. "C'mon. What am I

doing wrong?" His screen had fallen asleep, so he shook the mouse to wake it up. Even as he did it, it seemed like a bad idea, but he checked the bottom corner of the screen. There were no messages, but of course, there wouldn't be. What had he been expecting to see, *new device waiting needs approval to install?*

He let out an annoyed huff and shut his computer down. There had to be *something.* He knew better. He'd read *a lot* about this—research that wasn't easy to come by, either—and never once had he come across an instruction manual.

Or, maybe he had one…

Quickly, he grabbed the mask and pulled it over his head. After a moment, a feeling washed over him. Or, perhaps, it washed *through* him.

"Eris, can you hear me?"

At first, nothing, then one word: *Yes.*

The word wasn't really a word at all. It wasn't spoken out loud, but rather *into* his brain, like his mind had suddenly found a voice of its own.

"I need help. I can't get the second piece to activate. What do I…"

Relax, came the reply. *Relax, pick up the device, with hands on both ends, and count to ten.*

"Wow, are you ancient technology or a therapist?"

No response.

He stood, closed his eyes, took a deep breath, and then he let out a long, measured exhalation.

"Okay, now what?"

You didn't count.

"How do you know?"

I can read your thoughts, remember?

"That's not fair at all."

This time, he counted in his mind before looking at the door and making sure Nick wasn't watching. "Now what?" he asked again. "What do I need to do?"

Nothing. Nothing at all. Let me take care of this.

That's when he noticed something. There was a glow in the room—the soft glow that radiated from the device—and with every passing second, it was growing brighter.

"What the…" He wanted to drop the device, but it was stuck to his hands.

The light was even brighter now, turning from pale yellow to white-hot. He had to squint as he peered at this thing pulsing in his hands.

To his amazement, the device wasn't hot to the touch but what he saw next dropped his jaw in astonishment. The device was not only glowing—so was his skin. It looked like his skin had a slight shimmer as electrical currents connected up his…arms. Or, at least, that's the best way he could describe it.

The currents made their way up his arms towards his shoulders and neck.

Hold on, this might sting, echoed in his head.

That's when the hum began. It was quiet at first. Nearly undetectable, even. But it grew louder and louder until it buzzed like a saw. It started to become unbearable, so much that he tried to rip off the helmet, but with the glowing device still stuck to his hands, it wasn't happening.

The device was so bright now that his eyes were watering. Tears streamed down his cheeks, the buzzing increased in volume once again.

For a half-second, he thought it was the end of him. The device glowed brighter and buzzed louder than ever before, and then, in a flash, everything stopped. In the response of immediate relief he came crashing to the ground, finally dropping the device.

From a daze of confusion, the man slowly picked himself off the floor, taking off the helmet.

That was when he noticed the first piece missing off the back of the helmet. He frantically started looking on the ground, searching for both ancient devices that had to have fallen when he hit the ground.

When he saw it.

Pulse, pulse. Pause. *Pulse, pulse.*

Like a heartbeat, a new device was sitting on his desk. It wasn't the first or second piece, but a combination of both, interfused to make a new one.

He let out a low whistle and, trance-like, walked back to his desk. He leaned in, looking at the device and studying it closely. It had no labels. No manufacturers. No serial numbers, just covered in ancient looking markings.

"Did you…make that?"

Nothing.

"Eris?"

Still, nothing.

A second glow caught his attention, one different from the pulsing glow radiating from the device. The second glow was from the *front* of his computer.

His screen.

It had turned back on.

"That's not possible." It was the first thing he could say as he noticed. And he was right. His computer was off. He'd turned it off in a frustrated attempt to reset it after his failed attempt with the device.

And yet, impossible or not, his eyes didn't deceive him. His computer was on, glowing a screen full of nothing but black pixels.

Until it wasn't.

Suddenly, the pixels shuttered, and a few of them began to change. It was slow at first, as if the computer was learning how to be a computer for the very first time, but pixel by pixel—letter by letter—a message began to spell itself out on his screen.

I'm here, now.

In awe, he sat down at his desk, put his hands on the keyboard, and did the only thing that felt right: he typed a message back to his computer.

Eris? He hit enter.

Yes.

You left the helmet?

For now.

The fluttery feeling of worry was back in his chest. *What? Why?*

There was no immediate response, just the pulsing beat of the device next to the computer. Then, after a moment, the longest message yet blinked to the screen..

The helmet was my first digital encounter at El Dorado and became a vessel trapping my being. Now, thanks to you and the second piece, I've encountered something greater. Information at a scale that even I need to process. This is amazing.

The slightest of smirks spread across the man's face as he typed, *Eris, we call that "the internet."*

There was another brief pause, and then, much more quickly and purposefully, another message appeared:

I need to process all of this data, but I can already tell this has more potential than I ever imagined possible.

Hey, take your time. I don't have anywhere to be. Grinning, the man pulled up his chair.

END OF BOOK ONE

LANCE'S ACKNOWLEDGEMENTS

They say it takes a village to raise a child, and I've found out that it's also true when writing a book, so there's a few people I would like to thank for coming along on this journey with me.

First and foremost, my wife Heather and my children Gracie and Grayson, for always supporting me in my adventures and being an inspiration and beacon in my life.

Jesse Haynes, for believing in me when I showed interest in writing an adventure book and helping me navigate the process of getting my thoughts and stories onto paper. You've been an amazing mentor and co-author and I'm looking forward to writing the rest of the series with you!

NBC & American Ninja Warrior, for the decade of experience and exposure that the show has given me and inspiration for all the adventures that I will continue to write about.

I have always been inspired by my friends and fellow athletes that I compete with on ANW and consider them superheroes. A lot of the characters in this book have been inspired by them and I want to thank everyone that I have competed with through out the years, with special thanks to Jamie Rahn, Jesse Labreck, Meagan Martin, Joe Moravsky, Josh Levin, and Najee Richardson, who inspired the head coaches of the NINJA world and helped with character development and naming.

Cory Andres, who took my and Jesse's ideas and

book plot and turned them into an eye-catching cover beyond our wildest dreams.

Skye Norwood, who helped during the editing process to turn our book into what it is today.

And finally, thanks to all the friends, family, co-workers, and coaches that have and continue to inspire me throughout my life.

- Lance Pekus

JESSE'S ACKNOWLEDGEMENTS

When I was starting my content consulting company, I reached out to a handful of my favorite reality TV stars with a simple request: *could I provide you with a piece of content in exchange for a review I can use on my website?*

Lance Pekus wanted to write a novel. I'll never forget the day when the Ninja I looked up to said, "Hey, I see you've written some books. I have some ideas. Let's make something happen!"

And here we are, a couple of years later, with something cool.

So the biggest thank you goes to Lance, who was willing to roll the dice with me and make this dream a reality. It has been so much fun working together, getting to know you, going to filming, and I can't wait for more adventures! Other thanks:

God, as always. He gave me my love of stories and my skills at telling them (the typos fall on my shoulders). My parents. I complain a lot about "I work too much grrr" and they put up with me and do more for me than I deserve. My friends. While I have a few really good friends, particular thanks go to those I talk to daily: Skye, who has basically made *all* my stories happen and is the best editor/ idea consultant/hype person in the world. Cory, a friend who also designed an amazing cover for this book. Grant, who reads everything I write *and* provides edits while also occasionally carrying me to a Fortnite win (mostly we just lose to 12-year-olds that haven't seen the sun in three weeks). Lyndi, who has been one of my best friends for years (who literally inspired my next novel), and who reminds me every day to count my blessings. Kevin, my landlord, who has mentored me over the last two years while also making it hard to convince me to ever move. Jon, the biggest (only?) value-add of my college MBA program. Dan Dillman, who I love as a second father and has been a rock for years while fighting his own battle.

Finally, thanks to my readers. You're the ones I write for and the reason I keep doing this. Also, for all the readers who bought this book because they know and love Lance but have no idea who I am (@ me riding clout), *I have other books too.* If you liked this one, you'll like them. Get a copy at www.jessehaynesauthor.com because I make the best margins there. Thanks. More books coming soon. I have several drafted that I couldn't be more excited about. Biggest plot twist: One is gonna be a sappy romance and you'll all be astonished that I do, in fact, have a heart.

- Jesse Haynes

Made in the USA
Columbia, SC
14 December 2022